PARTY TO MURDER

Recent Titles by Betty Rowlands from Severn House

COPYCAT
DEADLY OBSESSION
DEATH AT DEARLY MANOR
DIRTY WORK
A HIVE OF BEES
AN INCONSIDERATE DEATH
TOUCH ME NOT

PARTY TO MURDER

Betty Rowlands

This first world edition published in Great Britain 2005 by
SEVERN HOUSE PUBLISHERS LTD of
9–15 High Street, Sutton, Surrey SM1 1DF.
This first world edition published in the USA 2006 by
SEVERN HOUSE PUBLISHERS INC of
595 Madison Avenue, New York, N.Y. 10022.

British Library Cataloguing in Publication Data

Rowlands, Betty
    Party to murder
    1.   Reynolds, Sukey (Fictitious character) - Fiction
    2.   Women private investigators - Fiction
    3.   Detective and mystery stories
    I.   Title
    823.9'14 [F]

    ISBN-10 : 0-7278-6304-5

Typeset by Palimpsest Book Production Ltd.,
Polmont, Stirlingshire, Scotland.
Printed and bound in Great Britain by
MPG Books Ltd., Bodmin, Cornwall.

One

'What do we know about Sir Digby Kirtling, Dalia?' asked DI Jim Castle as he and DS Dalia Chen hurried down to the cark park at Gloucester police station.

'Not a lot, sir,' she replied, 'except that he's what they call a captain of industry and he owns a large house and estate in Nether Muckleton. The caller was in a bit of a state, but I gather there had been some kind of party going on. Sir Digby noticed that one of the guests hadn't been seen for a while and sent the others out to look for her. It was some time before they found her sprawled on her back under some rhododendron bushes. They thought at first she'd passed out after too much champagne but when they couldn't rouse her they called an ambulance. The paramedic took one look at her and pronounced her dead. He thought it might be suspicious.'

'Do we know why?'

'That's all the detail we have at the moment, sir.'

'I imagine this will have dampened the party spirit,' Castle commented. 'It could be a slow journey,' he added. 'It's still rush hour; the streets will be busy. By the way, I've sent Tony Hill to the scene; he lives out that way so he should be there ahead of us.' He settled into the passenger seat of her VW Golf and clipped on his seat belt. It did not occur to him to ask if she knew the way; the more he worked with her, the more impressed he became at her quiet efficiency.

'I know a few back doubles once we get out of the city centre,' she replied as she started the engine and pulled out of the yard. He sat back and relaxed as she steered the car through the traffic and headed for the London Road. Observing the confident way she took every opportunity to edge ahead of slower vehicles, he was on the point of commenting that she drove like a man – which he would have considered a

1

compliment – but checked himself in the nick of time from making what Sukey would have condemned as a sexist remark. He thought Dalia, with her oriental background, might have been less touchy, but he decided not to chance it anyway. It wasn't until she slowed down on entering the village that he said, 'Superb drive, Dalia,' and she responded with one of her enigmatic smiles and a slight nod that he took for appreciation.

She slowed down still further as she negotiated the main street. 'We're looking for Crook Lane,' she said. 'The caller said it's a little way past the church. Ah, there it is.' She indicated an old-fashioned finger post pointing to the right. Beside it a newer sign read 'Muckleton Manor'.

'The second "o" has weathered,' he commented as she made the turn. 'It looks like Crock Lane. Maybe they should call it Old Crocks' Lane,' he added facetiously, nodding in the direction of an elderly couple, both leaning on sticks and accompanied by an equally elderly dog, walking slowly along the narrow footpath. Dalia turned her head briefly in his direction, but this time there was no smile at his weak attempt at humour and he realized he had blundered. I should have remembered that in her culture they respect the elderly, he reflected ruefully, mentally adding, ageist, sexist, racist, the world's a linguistic minefield nowadays. Aloud, he said, 'Do we know who made the call?'

'Yes, sir. A Mrs Keene, Sir Digby's housekeeper.'

'His housekeeper was at the party?'

'I don't imagine she was there as a guest. She was probably told the woman was missing and ordered to take part in the search.' A further sign reading 'Private Road to Muckleton Manor' appeared ahead of them and she swung the wheel to the left.

'It seems Kirtling isn't short of a bob or two,' said Castle as they approached a pair of shiny new wrought-iron gates, beyond which an avenue bordered by lime trees led up to the house. A police car was drawn up on the grass verge and a uniformed constable signalled to Dalia to slow down, then recognized Castle and operated a remote control system to open the gates. She drove slowly forward and pulled up.

Castle lowered the window and asked, 'Who else is here apart from uniformed?'

2

'DS Hill's been here for about twenty minutes and Doctor Blake arrived a short time ago, sir.'

'What about CSIs?'

'On their way. And DS Hill asked me to let you know he's arranged a rendezvous point behind the house to the left.'

'Good. Okay, Dalia, let's go and see what our eminent police surgeon can tell us.'

The house, of red brick in the Queen Anne style, was flanked on either side by what appeared to be a newly constructed wing that extended as far as the edge of a semi-circular gravelled forecourt, where ornamental urns full of geraniums were dotted at intervals on the perimeter. Following the officer's directions, Dalia drove behind the building, pulled up alongside several other vehicles, including one that Castle recognized as belonging to Doctor Blake, and switched off the engine. They walked round to the front door and were greeted by another uniformed officer who directed them towards a gate set in a wall on the other side of the building, sealed by a length of blue and white tape.

'The body's through there, Guv,' he told Castle. 'Doctor Blake is examining it at this moment. Sir Digby and his guests are in the house.'

'I understand there's been a party going on. What happened to the guests' cars?' said Castle, observing that the only vehicle parked on the drive was a silver-grey Volvo estate. 'Don't tell me they've been allowed to go home already.'

The officer shook his head. 'It seems that some of them live in the village, so they probably walked here. The Volvo was here when we arrived and I understand it belongs to a Mr Philip Montwell, an artist gentleman. Sergeant Willis is indoors with DS Hill, getting all the details.'

'I see. I think we'll take a look at the victim first and see what Doc Blake has to say.'

'Right, Guv. Constable Kelly will show you which way to go. Susan!' He signalled to the young officer on guard at the gate and she raised the tape to admit them.

'Take the path to the right behind the greenhouse, sir, and follow it till you reach the shrubbery,' she said. 'It . . . that is . . . she's quite a long way down, near the bottom of a steepish slope.'

3

'You've seen the body?'

'Yes, sir.' She gave a little grimace and he noticed that she looked pale.

'New to the force, are you?'

'Fairly new, sir.'

'Not seen many goners, I imagine?'

She coloured slightly and gave an embarrassed grin. 'This is my first, actually,' she admitted sheepishly.

'Well, no use pretending you'll get used to it, but you'll toughen up in time,' he assured her.

'I suppose so, sir, thank you.'

There was the sound of more vehicles approaching and he glanced round to see two small white vans disappearing behind the house. 'Here come the CSIs,' he said. He kept his tone matter of fact, even though he recognized Sukey Reynolds as one of the drivers. It was ridiculous, of course, but he always felt an urge to protect her from some of the more unpleasant aspects of the job. More than once she had confessed to having nightmares about a particularly gruesome corpse she had had to deal with. With an effort, he checked the impulse to go over and have a word with her. It wouldn't do to single her out for special attention.

'Right,' he said briskly, 'let's not hang about. Come on, Dalia.'

They followed the path PC Kelly had indicated. They had not gone far when they encountered another length of blue and white tape stretched across the path, cutting off access to a thicket of rhododendrons. As they approached, Doctor Blake, bag in hand, emerged from among the bushes. He ducked under the tape and greeted them with his customary cheerful grin.

'Nice straightforward one for you this time, Jim,' he said. 'She's the other side of that bush,' he went on with a jerk of the head over his right shoulder. 'Strangled, probably with her own gold neck-chain. The flesh of the throat's badly bruised; it's possible that he used a pen or a stick or something to tighten the chain from behind.'

'He?'

'The killer, of course. Unless it was done by a female,' Blake added. His grey eyes twinkled behind his gold-rimmed glasses. 'Mustn't be sexist, must we?'

'Are you seriously suggesting a woman might have done it?' said Castle. 'Offhand, I can't recall a female strangler.'

'Ah, that's because you're not into pop music,' Blake said knowingly. 'Anyway, she's only a wee slip of a thing, so in theory a heftily built farmer's daughter might have been capable. There's a first time for everything after all.' With a jaunty wave he disappeared along the path leading back to the entrance.

'What on earth was the reference to pop music about?' Castle asked as he and Dalia stepped under the tape.

'Just his little joke, Guv. There used to be a group of punk rockers who called themselves The Stranglers.'

Castle raised an eyebrow. 'A female group?'

Dalia allowed herself a faint smile. 'No, Guv, but one of their numbers was called *European Female*.'

'Really? Fancy Blake knowing that sort of thing.' Privately, he was equally surprised at Dalia's knowledge until he remembered that she had once mentioned a teenage brother. 'Well, let's hope he's right about it being straightforward,' he said with a shrug.

As she followed the directions to the rendezvous point, Sukey Reynolds glanced across at the retreating figures of DI Castle and DS Chen and experienced the familiar pang of jealousy. There was much conjecture back at the station as to whether Dalia fancied Jim. Her manner towards him was never anything other than professional, but the gossips were only too ready to put that down to her inscrutability. Dalia's feelings were of no interest to Sukey, whose only concern was Jim's response to the young sergeant's undoubted charm. Until recently, it was his old friend DS Andy Radcliffe who usually accompanied him on this type of case, but he was away on a course and several times lately it had been DS Chen who had teamed up with him. Somewhat unreasonably, she found herself blaming DCI Lord. He might have sent someone else; he knows how things are between Jim and me, she thought resentfully, then told herself not to be stupid. As if a man with Lord's responsibilities had time for such considerations.

'Something bothering you?' The voice of her fellow Crime

Scene Investigator, Mandy Parfitt, jerked her thoughts back to the job in hand.

'Just wondering whether we should hold back until CID have made their examination,' she replied hastily, annoyed at having allowed her attention to be diverted by personal feelings. There were times when she found Jim's insistence on keeping their affair under wraps a little irksome, especially as, from the odd sly hint from colleagues, she was pretty sure that it was common knowledge.

Mandy's response to her feeble excuse was a sidelong glance and a raised eyebrow. 'That is the usual practice,' she commented.

Sukey gave a self-conscious grin. 'Yes, of course,' she said lamely.

They opened up their vans and put on their protective garments. As they approached the gate where PC Kelly was still standing guard they met Doctor Blake, bag in hand. 'Nothing too grisly about this one,' he commented. 'Just a bit blue round the gills and red round the eyes – nothing to upset old hands like you!'

The three women exchanged glances as the police surgeon disappeared from view. 'Was it my imagination, or did he sound apologetic?' said Mandy.

'Disappointed, more like,' Sukey replied. 'The gorier they are, the more fascinating he finds them. Don't look so shocked, Susan!' she added and the young officer gave a wan smile in response. 'He's not completely without feelings; it's just his way of releasing the tension. We all do it.'

'Here come the Great Detective and his faithful acolyte,' said Mandy under her breath as DI Castle appeared round a bend in the path with DS Chen following him. 'I hope they haven't destroyed evidence by trampling around too much,' she added mischievously.

'They aren't exactly amateurs,' Sukey said sharply.

'Ooh, sorry, no offence intended!' Mandy taunted. They stood to one side as the detectives reached the gate and stopped for a word.

'You can go in now,' said Jim in his brisk, official voice. 'We'll have the usual shots of the body and the immediate location, and then more shots after it's been removed. You'll

6

notice the path itself is tarmac, but the terrain on either side is dampish so you might be able to figure out which way both the victim and the killer took to reach the murder scene. They might have met there by arrangement, or he might have followed her . . . well, you're both experienced so you know what to look for. Come along, Dalia, we must go indoors now and find out what Tony Hill has got for us.'

Two

'It looks as if she put up some sort of a struggle,' Sukey remarked as she stood looking down at the victim. As always at the sight of death, she felt a constriction in her stomach, quickly controlled by a few deep breaths.

'What makes you say that?' Mandy looked up from her task of laying a circle of stepping boards around the body. 'Oh, I see what you mean. The dirt under the nails.'

The woman lay on her back in a small clearing between some rhododendron bushes with her right leg doubled under her and her arms outspread. The fingernails of both hands were stained dark brown, as if in her death throes she had clawed at the soft earth around her in a futile attempt to get to her feet and wrench herself free of her attacker. Her head and shoulders were partially screened by the heavy foliage, so that the two CSIs had to crouch slightly to get a complete view of the body. It was not the first victim of strangulation in Sukey's experience; even without the bruising where the chain had dug into the soft flesh of the throat, the cause of death was evident from the blue tinge of the skin and the red flecks of burst blood vessels round the eyes. She found herself giving a wry smile as she recalled Blake's comment. He was well known for the black humour that so often helped to relieve tension when things were at their grimmest.

Sukey estimated the victim's age at around thirty. She was slightly built, with small delicate features and short dark hair and she wore a long dress of cream-coloured cotton with several tiers of flounces round the hem, three-quarter sleeves and a deep collar trimmed with bands of red. A straw hat with a blue ribbon lay a short distance from the body and on the one visible foot was an old-fashioned buttoned boot with a high heel and pointed toe.

'She's only a slip of a thing,' replied Mandy, unconsciously echoing Doctor Blake's comment. 'She'd have had no chance against a strong assailant.'

'George Barnes said something about a party,' said Sukey. 'Odd sort of outfit for a daytime do. Or an anytime do, come to think of it.'

'Maybe it was fancy dress,' Mandy suggested.

'On a Wednesday afternoon? Funny time to have a fancy dress party.'

Mandy shrugged. 'Funny time to have any sort of party unless it's for kids, but I guess the ways of the upper crust have always been strange.'

'I'm not sure Sir Digby is exactly upper crust,' Sukey commented. 'Isn't he one of those rags to riches tycoons who collect honours in exchange for boosting exports or making fat donations to political parties?'

'Haven't a clue. Let's get on with the job, shall we?'

They began unpacking their equipment. 'Okay,' said Sukey, 'we'd better have a good look at the ground and the surrounding bushes before we move in closer. There's obviously been some disturbance by the search party, and of course Doctor Blake isn't always too fussy about where he puts his feet.'

They worked methodically and in silence for a few minutes, but at first found nothing of any significance. There had been no rain for several days but, as DI Castle had mentioned, the peaty ground beneath the bushes was still slightly damp. Sukey squatted down to take a closer look at an area close to the body where the ground showed more sign of disturbance than elsewhere.

'Come and look at these, Mandy,' she said, pointing at several indentations in the ground where small tufts of grass and weeds had been partially uprooted. 'And look at the heel of that boot; there's quite a bit of earth clinging to it.'

'I'll bet there's some clinging to the other one as well, the one we can't see,' said Mandy. 'She must have made those holes during the struggle.'

'It looks as if he came from that direction.' Sukey pointed to a gap between the bushes. Using the stepping boards, they circled the body to inspect the ground behind the woman's head. The grass had evidently been flattened, but although they examined every inch of the surrounding area they could find nothing that was identifiable as a shoeprint.

It was while she was taking her photographs that something bright, half hidden by the victim's right hand, caught Sukey's eye. Determinedly fighting incipient nausea, she cautiously lifted the lifeless but still warm wrist a fraction, revealing a fragment of broken glass. A further search brought to light the stem and part of the shattered bowl of a wine glass that had been lying hitherto unnoticed beneath a rhododendron bush.

'What do you make of that?' she said.

'It was a party so presumably there were drinks,' Mandy observed. 'I suppose she went wandering off with her glass of wine and dropped it when she was attacked.'

Sukey shook her head. 'It looks to me as if it was broken before she dropped it,' she said reflectively.

'How d'you make that out?'

'The piece of glass under her hand, for a start. It's more than likely—' As she spoke, Sukey once again raised the hand a few inches from the ground and peered at the palm. 'Yes, I thought so. There's a cut here. So she was holding the glass, maybe even drinking from it, when she was attacked. The shock made her involuntarily tighten her grip on it so that it shattered, causing that cut.'

'And at the same time she could have flung her arms outwards so that the rest of the glass went flying and landed where we found it,' said Mandy.

'That's possible, I suppose. Does that mean she didn't hear her attacker coming, I wonder? We've already deduced that he approached from behind. Or did she know him, perhaps?' Sukey's mind went off on another track. 'Maybe she was having a row with him, clenched her fist so hard that she shattered the glass before turning her back on him in a paddy.'

'At which point he decided enough was enough and throttled her?'

'And it's possible he picked up a fragment of glass on one of his shoes in the struggle,' Sukey continued in rising excitement. 'There might be splashes of wine on his clothes as well. Let's think this out a bit further.'

'I've got a better idea,' said Mandy. 'Why don't we get on

10

with our part of the job and let the detectives figure out what happened?'

Sukey burst out laughing. 'Sorry, I got carried away. I keep forgetting I'm not in the CID.' If only, she thought to herself. Then it could be me working alongside Jim instead of Dalia.

Back in the house a group of badly shaken individuals waited to be questioned. As the detectives entered by the front door they could hear sounds of distress; a woman was weeping hysterically and a man was trying to comfort her, although his words were for the most part inaudible.

Sergeant Willis showed them into an empty, luxuriously but tastefully furnished sitting room. 'We – that is, DS Hill and I – thought perhaps you should see this first, Guv,' he said, pointing to a large painting on an easel facing the window, a painting that looked oddly familiar to Castle although, with his limited experience of fine art, he was unable to place it.

'I've a feeling I've seen that somewhere before, Dalia,' he said.

Once again he was aware of a faint twitch of the mouth that could have been a smile. 'You may have seen one like it, sir – or a reproduction. It's based on a painting by Renoir.'

'I've heard of him. Impressionist, wasn't he?'

'That's right, sir. One of his most famous paintings is called *The Luncheon of the Boating Party*. Renoir got a group of his friends to pose for it, and it looks as though Sir Digby has done the same thing and commissioned someone to paint this mock-up of the original. On top of which,' she added, approaching the canvas more closely, 'it looks to me as if that,' she pointed with a slim, olive-skinned, pearly-tipped finger at the figure of a young girl leaning on a wooden rail in the centre of the picture, 'is a portrait of the murder victim. She's even wearing similar clothes.'

'Good Lord, so she is!' Castle exclaimed. 'How weird!'

Behind them, Willis cleared his throat. 'As I was saying, Guv, DS Hill thought you should see that – it's the reason for the party. Sir Digby arranged a sort of unveiling ceremony with lashings of champagne all round. DS Chen is right; all today's guests posed for one of the figures in the painting.

11

All except the artist, of course, a Mr Philip Montwell. He's waiting with the others.'

'Right. I'd better have a word with DS Hill. Ask him to come in here, will you?'

'Yes, Guv.'

DS Tony Hill entered, sat down in the seat Castle indicated and handed him a sheet of paper. Recently promoted to the rank of Detective Sergeant, he was known among his colleagues as 'the charmer' on account of his success in worming vital scraps of evidence from impressionable female witnesses.

'I've had a preliminary word with everyone and taken a few basic details, sir,' he said while Castle ran his eye over the list of names and addresses. 'You'll see that Mr Montwell lives in Cheltenham and George Maggs, one of Sir Digby's high-flying young executives, is from London. Everyone else lives nearby and works on the estate.' Reading from his note-book, Hill continued, 'It seems that after the ceremony they had a light buffet lunch with more drinks and then went wandering off in different directions to relax in the grounds, which are pretty extensive by the way. They were supposed to reassemble on the terrace for tea later on – which they did, all bar the deceased, Ms Una May. After a while, Sir Digby got anxious and he and some of the others went off to look for her.'

'Who found her?'

'A young man called Arnold Ashford, one of the gardeners. He was on his own when he spotted her lying under the bushes. It was a warm afternoon and according to him the girl had been hitting the champagne quite hard, so he assumed she'd simply passed out and ran back to tell Sir Digby.'

'And then what?'

'According to Ashford, Sir D called off the search and told the others to get on with their cucumber sandwiches while he went to see for himself. He came back a few minutes later looking worried and had a word with Mrs Keene, the house-keeper. He said he was afraid Una – the dead girl – had been taken ill and told her to call an ambulance.'

'Why an ambulance, I wonder,' said Castle.

'Good question, sir. Everyone else confirms Ashford's story

so far – except of course they weren't present when he found the body – but no one knows the answer to that one except Sir Digby himself and he wouldn't condescend to be interviewed by a mere sergeant. Insists he'll only speak to the SIO who he assumes will be at least a Superintendent.'

'Well, he'll have to put up with a lowly DI for the time being,' said Castle dryly. 'What's your feeling about the man, Tony?'

'I'd say he could be pretty ruthless in business, and he's certainly full of self-importance,' said Hill. 'He seems to be a demanding but essentially fair employer; his staff speak of him with respect but not exactly affection – except for his housekeeper, Mrs Keene, that is. I have a feeling she might have a soft spot for him. I suspect he's a bit of a womanizer; he's certainly got the looks and the personality. He's naturally pretty upset at what has happened.'

'Right. I'll see him in a minute. What about Montwell, the artist?'

'From his manner, I'd say he doesn't have a very high personal opinion of his client, although he was careful not to say so.'

'Interesting. Perhaps I'll have a word with him before I see Sir Digby. Will you ask him to come in here, Tony?'

Three

Philip Montwell was a tall, spare individual with chiselled features, dark hair flopping over his forehead and brooding, deep-set eyes. He was wearing casual fawn trousers, brown loafers and a cream open-necked shirt; Castle judged him to be in his mid-forties and it crossed his mind that had the man been an actor he would have been ideally cast as an artist.

Castle waved him to a chair and sat down on a window seat opposite with Dalia at his elbow, notebook at the ready. 'This is a very tragic business,' he began. 'I understand you painted this picture, sir, and the dead woman appears to be the model for one of the people in it. Can I begin by asking you how well you knew her?'

Montwell shook his head. 'Hardly at all,' he said. 'In fact, I met her for the first time this morning when we all assembled for the unveiling.' His voice was deep and sonorous and he spoke with a cultured accent that sounded natural, but with what Castle thought was a hint of irony in the final words. 'She was, I believe, employed by Sir Digby,' Montwell went on, 'but otherwise I know nothing about her.'

'You didn't chat to her at all while you were painting her?'

'She never actually sat for me. I was given photographs of her and I worked from those.'

'Why was that?'

'I suppose Sir Digby couldn't spare her from her duties.'

'Do you happen to know what her duties were?'

Montwell shrugged. 'I imagine she was his secretary. You'd better ask him.'

'You're quite certain you never met her before today?'

'Haven't I just said so?'

'Just wanted to make sure, sir. I understand that the picture

14

is the reason for this gathering,' Castle continued. 'Can you tell me how it came to be painted?'

Montwell crossed his legs and clasped thin fingers over one knee. 'I should perhaps begin by explaining that I am frequently commissioned to produce copies of well-known masterpieces,' he began. 'I am known for the very high quality and accuracy of my work; in fact, one of my canvases was actually stolen from my gallery by some ill-informed person who mistook it for the original and had the nerve to demand a ransom for its return.' A slightly self-satisfied smile hovered round his mouth.

'Really, sir? What picture was that?'

'It was a copy of *Nude in the Sunlight*, by Renoir, which of course is still hanging in the Musée d'Orsay in Paris. You may have seen it,' he added. The smile took on a hint of condescension when Castle admitted that he had not. 'Most of the originals are either held in museums and therefore unlikely to come on to the market,' Montwell went on, 'or, were they to be sent to auction from private collections, would command prices beyond the means of any but the most wealthy. In short, if anyone takes a fancy to an old master that is for whatever reason unavailable to them, I can provide something better than a commercial reproduction.'

'I see,' said Castle. 'So do I understand, sir, that this picture was commissioned by Sir Digby, to be in some respects a copy of *The Luncheon of the Boating Party*, also by Renoir, but featuring some of his own friends or employees in place of the original models?'

Montwell nodded. 'Precisely.' His manner became marginally less patronizing on hearing the painting mentioned by name. 'Although,' he added, 'to be strictly accurate, a few of the lesser figures are copied from the original. And the main figure on the left is Sir Digby himself.'

Castle made a mental note to thank Dalia for briefing him so competently. Aloud he said, 'Had you met any of the other people in the picture before receiving this commission?'

Montwell appeared to hesitate for a moment before replying, 'Only one. The model for the lady talking to the young man in the straw hat,' he indicated a woman in the foreground to the right of the picture, 'is Athena Letchworth, the interior

15

designer whom Sir Digby commissioned to decorate and furnish his house. When he told her of his interest in the Impressionists, and in this painting in particular, she put him in touch with me.'

'Is that because she knew you by reputation, or have you some kind of business arrangement with her?'

Montwell appeared faintly irritated by the question. 'My business arrangements are hardly your concern, Inspector.'

'I'm just trying to get an overall impression of the situation, sir,' said Castle. 'This is, after all, a murder enquiry. However, I won't press you on that point, so let's move on. Apart from this commission, had you ever met Sir Digby before?'

'No.' Castle thought he detected a faint edge to Montwell's voice as he uttered the monosyllable and was reminded of DS Hill's comment. The impression was confirmed when the artist added, 'I don't move in the same exalted circles.'

'Er . . . quite. Did he say why he was giving you this slightly unusual commission? Or perhaps it isn't that unusual?' It occurred to Castle as he spoke that some people might like to see their own faces superimposed on famous classical bodies.

'It is fairly unusual. Sir Digby saw the original painting on a visit to Washington DC a year or two ago and took a great fancy to it. At first he wanted a straight copy, but when Athena – Ms Letchworth – mentioned in conversation that all the people in the picture were friends of the artist, he thought it would be a novel idea to do the same sort of thing. As well as his secretary, or whatever her job title is, I believe some if not all of the other models are his employees.'

'I see. Well, thank you Mr Montwell, that's most helpful. Just one other question; did any of the other people in the picture sit for you, or did you work exclusively from photographs?'

'They all sat for me except Ms May – and Ms Letchworth. She declined.'

'What was the reason for that?'

The artist shrugged. 'I suggest you ask her.' He got to his feet. 'Is that all?'

Castle nodded. 'For the moment, sir, yes. No, on second

thoughts, one other question. The dead woman was wearing a dress very similar to the one worn by the girl in the picture. Was she dressed like that in the photograph you were given?'

'Of course not. They were all wearing their own clothes when I painted them. The bodies were straight copies of the figures in the picture; I only needed their faces.'

'So why the fancy dress today?' asked Castle.

The question appeared to amuse Montwell. He gave a sardonic smile as he replied, 'It was a bit of whimsy that for the ceremony they should all wear clothes that matched the originals as closely as possible. I imagine the local theatrical costumiers did very nicely out of it. If that's all, I'd like to go. I have to meet another client shortly.'

'No problem, sir. You've been very helpful, thank you,' said Castle. 'What did you make of that, Dalia?' he asked as the door closed behind Montwell.

She thought for a moment before saying, 'Very self-opinionated and a bit of a snob, especially about art.'

'Wasn't he just? I don't think he has too high an opinion of his client either; did you notice how he reacted when I asked if he'd met Kirtling before? I think I went up a notch or two in his estimation when I identified the painting, though – thanks for putting me wise about that. How did you come to know all that stuff, by the way?'

'I did an Open University course in the history of art while I was a PC, sir,' she replied in her quiet, matter-of-fact manner. 'This is the first time it's come in useful for the job.'

'Well, take a brownie point,' Castle said warmly. 'Apart from his conceit and his snobbery, did you notice anything else significant?'

'Not that I can think of, sir.'

'You don't think that maybe he has a relationship with the lovely Athena outside business hours?'

'It did cross my mind to wonder why he didn't give a straight answer when you asked why she didn't sit for him, but on reflection it seemed more likely he simply isn't interested in what goes on in other people's heads.'

'Yes, that was my first impression, but he was ready enough to talk about the reason why the victim didn't sit for him, wasn't he? Maybe we should pursue that one a little further.

17

Maybe he was trying a little too hard to give the impression he knows nothing about Una May. Supposing I'm right and he is having an affair with Athena?' He went over to the picture and studied the face a little more closely. 'Very beautiful in a dark and sultry sort of way,' he commented thoughtfully. 'Some Mediterranean blood, perhaps? She could be the fiery, passionate type. If she discovered he was playing around with another woman, she might have killed her out of jealousy. Which would mean he was lying when he said he'd never met Una before today,' he went on. 'Make a note to check on that as well, Dalia.'

'Right, sir.'

'That brings us back to the possibility of a female strangler, doesn't it?' Castle chuckled. 'That would amuse Doctor Blake! Not that I think it's likely, but we can't eliminate anything at this stage.'

There was a discreet knock at the door and Sergeant Willis entered. 'Just wondering if you'd like to see the others in a more convenient room, Guv,' he said. 'Sir Digby has offered the use of his private office.'

'That's kind of him.' Castle thought for a minute and then shook his head. 'I think we'll stay in here with the picture. I may want to refer to it.'

'Right, Guv.' Willis lowered his voice discreetly before adding, 'He's getting a bit fidgety, by the way.'

'Well, we won't keep him waiting any longer. Ask him to come in, will you?'

'Powerful' was the word that sprang to Castle's mind when Kirtling entered the room. He was about fifty, six feet tall and heavily built. Like his counterpart in the painting he was wearing a sleeveless white cotton T-shirt that showed off his bronzed, muscular arms and shoulders. Unlike the figure in the original, which Castle recalled sporting a large straw hat and a bushy beard, he was bare-headed and clean-shaven and his thick, iron-grey hair sprang vigorously from his large cranium. But it was not merely the impression of physical strength and energy that struck the detective; there was a hint of determination bordering on ruthlessness in the steely-blue eyes, the jutting chin and the hard set of his mouth. Dalia had

18

referred to him as a captain of industry; it would be interesting to know something of his business career as well as
his private life.

Out of courtesy, Castle stood up when he entered. With a
monosyllabic acknowledgement of the detective's polite word
of greeting and without waiting to be asked he sat down beside
Dalia on the window seat. The effect was the opposite of what
Castle intended; he preferred people to face the light when
being interviewed as it made it easier to read their body
language. However, he sensed that there was little he could
do about it in the present circumstances without antagonizing
his witness, so he sat down on the seat Montwell had just
vacated.

'I hope this isn't going to take long,' Kirtling began before
Castle could speak. His voice matched his physique; it was
strong and resonant and there was a trace of belligerence in
his manner. 'I have important business in London and my
guests want to go home. They're pretty shaken up by what's
happened.'

'I understand that a few of them are your employees.'
Castle referred to DS Hill's notes.

'All of them except Montwell, but this afternoon they are
my guests. I suppose you've heard all about the occasion from
him? He painted that.' He nodded towards the canvas.

'Yes, sir, Mr Montwell has been very helpful. I understand
the dead woman was your secretary?'

The word 'secretary' elicited a disdainful lift of an eyebrow
from Kirtling. 'I have a PA, who is considerably more than
a mere secretary, who runs my London office,' he replied with
a touch of condescension. 'Una was my estate manager, and
I must say she did an excellent job – kept things running like
clockwork.' The last remark came as no surprise to Castle.
He was fairly certain that an inefficient member of staff at
whatever level would not have lasted long in this man's employ.
'Tragic business,' Kirtling went on. 'Poor little Una; whoever
could have done that to her? Such a lovely girl, too.' He gave
a sorrowful shake of his head.

'How long had she been in your employ, sir?' Castle asked.

'Just under a year. She'll be hard to replace; I'll have to
get Fiona to contact an agency first thing in the morning. May

I?' Without waiting for a response from Dalia, he took her ballpoint pen from her hand and made a note on his palm before handing it back.

'Did she ever mention being afraid of anyone?' Castle continued. 'A former boyfriend or partner she had broken off with, for example? Someone who might have killed her out of jealousy?'

'No, nothing like that, although I doubt if she'd have said anything to me. She hardly ever spoke about her private life.'

'But you must have had some conversations with her?' Castle persisted. 'Didn't she ever mention any friends or interests? How she spent her evenings and weekends, for example?'

'I'm a very busy man, Inspector,' said Kirtling impatiently. 'I don't have time for idle chitchat with my staff. As I said, her role here was to handle the administration of the estate and she worked largely on her own initiative. Naturally, we'd discuss things that needed seeing to and I'd give her my instructions at the beginning of the week before leaving for London, usually on a Monday. Most of my time is taken up by my business affairs so I have a flat in town and spend three or four nights there during the week. Sometimes, of course, I have to travel to branches round the country, but if Una had an urgent query she could always get in touch with me, or leave a message if I was unavailable.'

'Could I ask the nature of your business, sir?'

Kirtling sat up straight and thrust out his chest, reminding Castle of a pouter pigeon. 'I own Kirtling Enterprises, a private limited company that controls, among other things, the ServeAll supermarket chain,' he said with unmistakable pride.

'I see, sir. I can understand that must take up a great deal of your time.' Castle deliberately avoided showing any sign of being impressed or over-awed by the statement. 'Going back to Ms May, would you say she was on good terms with the rest of your staff here?'

'Of course. Everyone liked her. That's why this has come as such a terrible shock. No one can understand why anyone would want to kill her.'

'So when was the last time you saw her, before today?'

'Monday morning. I spent Monday and Tuesday night in

town and drove down here this morning for the unveiling. Una and Miranda – Mrs Keene, my housekeeper – looked after all the arrangements. It all went so beautifully, until—' All of a sudden Kirtling's voice cracked; his shoulders sagged and he bowed his head. It was the first time he had betrayed signs of emotion.

'This must be extremely distressing for you,' Castle said kindly, reflecting that the man had a more human side after all. 'Thank you, Sir Digby, I think that's all for now. I may want to ask you a few more questions later. I'm sure you're as anxious as we are to find out who killed Ms May.'

'Of course I am. You can count on me to give you and your colleagues every possible assistance and I'll instruct my staff to do the same.'

'Thank you, sir, I appreciate that,' said Castle.

'I'd be obliged if you'd see George Maggs next, so that we can get back to London if that's all right with you. He's deputy manager of one of my subsidiaries,' he went on in response to a questioning look from Castle. 'We have a breakfast meeting with a supplier tomorrow and we need to make an early start.'

'I'll certainly see Mr Maggs next, and unless there is any reason to detain him it will be all right for you both to return to London, but I may want to speak to either or both of you again so please be sure you keep in touch,' said Castle. Kirtling's only response was a grunt as he left the room.

'What did you make of him, Dalia?' asked Castle as the door closed behind him.

'A typically tough business tycoon,' she replied without hesitation. 'I imagine he could be pretty ruthless with anyone who tried to cross him. Still, he did show what looked like sincere sorrow at the young woman's death.'

'True.' Castle thought for a moment. 'I've just remembered; there was something about ServeAll in the paper recently. One of the bigger supermarket chains has made a bid for it. Kirtling must be worth a packet. Still a bachelor, according to Tony Hill's notes; he'd be quite a catch, especially with the stately home and the knighthood. Anything else?'

Dalia hesitated for a moment before saying, 'It may have been my imagination, sir, but he looked me straight in the

21

face as he sat down beside me. In different circumstances I might have said he was, well, sizing me up. And I had to edge away slightly because his leg actually rested against mine and he made no attempt to move it. It might not have been deliberate, of course, but—'

'I did notice the charming smile when he returned your pen,' Castle remarked. 'You reckon he might be a bit of a womanizer?'

'Just an impression, sir. As I say, I might have imagined it.'

'It's worth bearing in mind. Right, we'd better see this chap Maggs next.' Once more, Castle consulted the list. 'A bright young man by the looks of it; worked for an IT company for a few years before leaving to do a management degree at the London School of Economics. He's been working for Kirtling for about eighteen months. Have him sent in, will you?'

Four

George Maggs was a good-looking thirty-year-old with a jaunty manner. There was a trace of swagger in his walk as he went over to the picture and pointed to the figure of a young man standing behind Athena Letchworth. 'That's me,' he said. 'Good likeness, don't you think? Silly clothes, though.' He ran his hands down the front of his loose linen jacket and rather self-consciously adjusted the floppy black bow at the neck of his white shirt before sitting down. 'The original was a journalist pal of Renoir with a name a bit like mine only Italian. I suppose that's why Sir D chose me as the model. I drew the line at growing a toothbrush, though,' he added with a grin, stroking his smooth upper lip. 'Right, what do you want to know, Inspector? Terrible business, isn't it? Not sure if I can be of much use, but I'll do my best to help.'

'Thank you,' said Castle, a little stiffly. Already he was beginning to dislike this rather cocky young man. He suspected that he adopted a very different attitude when dealing with his employer. 'First of all, Mr Maggs, I'd like to ask how well you knew the victim.'

'Knew her?' Maggs shrugged. 'Hardly at all, really. Met her once or twice when I came down to visit a supplier and stayed at the manor overnight. Pretty little thing; not surprised Sir D fancied her.'

'How do you know he fancied her?'

'Just the way I caught him looking at her now and again, and she at him, come to that. Nothing you could put your finger on; I mean, I never saw or heard anything you might call compromising, but ... well, I can usually spot when something's going on. The chemistry, you know.' He gave a sly wink, which Castle ignored. 'Of course, the old boy's famous for his roving eye,' Maggs went on. 'I remember when

23

the glamorous Athena – you know he commissioned her to decorate and furnish this pile, don't you? – I remember the day she called at head office with an armful of catalogues for him to look at, well, if his hands weren't all over her his eyes certainly were. That's her, sitting in front of me.' He half turned and waved in the direction of the picture behind him. 'The fact that Fiona was wearing a distinctly frosty expression didn't seem to bother him in the least.'

'You were at that meeting?'

'Oh yes, and one or two others as well. It wasn't that he wanted our opinion; he was obviously going to accept Athena's recommendations whatever anyone said. We were there to be impressed with how much he was spending on the place.'

'Fiona's his PA, I understand,' said Castle.

'That's right. It's generally believed they're an item as well, although he's always careful to be very businesslike with her when there's anyone else around, and anyway discretion is Fee's middle name.'

'Going back to Ms May, did you know that she didn't sit for the artist? I understand that in her case he worked from photographs.'

Maggs shook his head and his air of studied nonchalance changed to one of apparently genuine surprise. 'No, I didn't,' he said. 'Why was that?'

'I was hoping you might be able to tell me, or at least have some idea.'

Maggs gave a lubricious grin. 'Perhaps Sir D was afraid the Greek god might make a pass at her.'

'The Greek god?'

'Montwell, the artist. That's what the women call him. He does look rather like a classical statue, don't you think?'

Castle ignored the question. 'Assuming there was some kind of relationship between Sir Digby and Ms May, do you suppose anyone else at today's gathering was aware of it?'

Maggs gave another shrug. 'How would I know? Anyway, I wasn't paying much attention to either of them. I spent most of the time chatting to Miranda Keene, Sir D's housekeeper. She's the one tucked away in the background, on the right.' This time he half rose in his seat and pointed with a manicured forefinger at a woman in the corner of the picture. She was wearing a large fur hat and holding gloved hands to her face as she conversed with two men, one of whom had an arm round her waist.

'Who are the men with her?'

'Oh, I understand they're copied from the original; nothing to do with today's shindig. Anyway, going back to your question about Sir D having it off with Una, Miranda's probably the best one to ask if there's anything in it as she's here all the time. Incidentally, she wasn't in the jolliest of moods, even before this happened.'

'Why was that?'

Maggs shook his head. 'Maybe she was tired after being up at the crack of dawn preparing the food, or possibly she was pissed off with having to keep that dead animal on her head. It's been quite a warm afternoon.'

'Is that the impression she gave you?'

'Not directly. I mean, she'd never complain about anything Sir D asked her to do.'

'Would you say she's one hundred per cent loyal to her employer, then?'

Maggs gave another suggestive grin. 'Loyal? She thinks the sun shines out of his ar—.' He stopped short with an apologetic glance at Dalia. 'Well, you know what I mean. She's worked for him for donkey's years and won't hear a word against him. The poor love is simply devastated at the way the party's turned out. She's been sitting in a corner howling her eyes out. I've been trying to cheer her up, without much success.'

'I understand Sir Digby is anxious to return to London as soon as possible so perhaps we'd better move on,' said Castle. 'I seem to remember seeing a report in the business news about a possible takeover bid for the ServeAll supermarket chain. Do you know anything about it?'

'Only a rumour at present, but knowing Sir D he'll see them off,' said Maggs. 'ServeAll's his baby and he'll never give up control. He built up his empire from a run-down village grocery shop somewhere in the Midlands that he inherited from his father about twenty years ago. A kind of rags to riches saga: from errand boy to tycoon by the sweat of his brow and all that crap. It's entirely down to his business

25

acumen, of course. Never mind the humble origins; when he spots a gap in the market he goes for it bald-headed. Got to admire him for that.'

'And what exactly is your position in the, er, empire, sir?'

Maggs shot Castle a wary glance, as if he suspected the detective was, as he himself might have put it, taking the piss. Receiving a bland look in return, he replied, with an air of self-importance, 'I manage one of the Kirtling Enterprises subsidiaries, Kirtling Markets.'

'And what does Kirtling Markets deal in?'

'We buy all the fresh produce – fruit, vegetables, meat, dairy and so on. Some of our stuff is imported, but Sir D likes to buy as much as he can from British suppliers. Lately he's gone into organics in a big way.'

'Very laudable.' Castle gave an approving nod.

Maggs gave a condescending smile. 'Suppose so, if it's what people want and the price is right.' His tone implied that it was immaterial to him where the goods came from so long as they sold well and made a profit.

'Well, thank you, Mr Maggs,' said Castle. 'I understand you have already given an account of your movements to DS Hill so that will be all for now. We may want to speak to you again, so please keep in touch.' As he spoke there was a discreet tap at the door and Willis entered. 'Yes, what is it, Sergeant?'

'The CSIs think you should see this, Guv.'

Castle scanned the note Willis handed him. He thought for a moment before saying, 'If you'll excuse me for a moment, Mr Maggs, something has come up. If you wouldn't mind waiting here—'

'But I thought you said that was all.' Maggs, who had been on his way to the door when Willis appeared, showed signs of irritation and glanced at his watch. 'I thought Sir Digby made it clear we're in a hurry to get back to London. And what are CSIs for heaven's sake? Another new layer of bureaucracy this bloody government's foisted on us?'

'Crime Scene Investigators – they were formerly known as Scenes of Crime Officers,' Castle explained patiently. 'It seems they have found some evidence that may be crucial to this case, so I'm afraid I must ask you to wait a few moments longer. If you'd like to sit down again, sir, Sergeant Chen will remain here to keep you company.'

'You mean, make sure I don't do a runner,' said Maggs sulkily, but he went back to his seat without raising any further objections.

Castle left the house and went to the pre-arranged rendezvous point, where he found Sukey and Mandy waiting for him, still wearing their protective clothing.

'What have you got there?' he asked, indicating the plastic envelopes they were holding.

'We found these close to the body, sir,' said Sukey. She explained the circumstances. 'We think it's more than likely the killer picked up some fragments on his shoes.'

Castle gave a soft whistle as he examined the remains of the wine glass. 'Too right he could,' he muttered, 'and so could the chap who found her. I'd like to have everyone's footwear for checking. It shouldn't be a problem for the people who live on the estate and of course that includes Sir Digby himself, but it might be awkward for Maggs. I don't suppose he carries a spare pair of shoes around with him. And Montwell lives in Cheltenham; he won't take kindly to being asked to drive home in his socks.'

'Mr Montwell has already left, sir,' said Mandy.

Castle made an impatient gesture. 'Of course, I said he could go. Well, we'll still have to try and get hold of his shoes to make sure we've covered everyone. I'll see about that when I've dealt with the people who are still here. Well done, you two,' he added as an afterthought as he hurried back to the house.

In the hall he met Sir Digby, who was waiting by the front door, briefcase in hand. 'Ah, there you are, Inspector,' he said. 'I take it you've finished with Maggs and we can go now.' It was a statement, not a question.

'Not for the moment, I'm afraid, sir.' Castle opened the door to the room where Maggs and Dalia were waiting and beckoned. As they emerged, he said, 'Certain evidence has come to light. I'd like you both to join the other witnesses, please, Sir Digby.'

'What evidence?' Kirtling demanded.

'I'll explain everything in a moment, sir. If you'd kindly come this way?'

'I suppose you're going to do your Hercule Poirot stuff now,' Kirtling sneered. 'Little grey cells been working overtime, have they?'

Castle ignored the jibe and held open the door of the room where the others were assembled. Kirtling entered with obvious reluctance, followed by Maggs and Dalia Chen. It was a small but comfortable room facing west, simply furnished but nevertheless showing evidence of an expert hand and a generous budget. A few good pictures hung on the walls and light from the evening sun streamed in through wide sash windows, reflected in sparkling highlights on ornaments of silver and glass.

It was the first time Castle had seen the entire party and at his request DS Hill quickly introduced those he had not previously met: Arnold Ashford, one of the under-gardeners, who had discovered the body of Una May; Dick Andrews, the son of the head gardener, Arthur Andrews, and Dick's sister Tricia; Athena Letchworth; and finally, red-eyed but composed, the housekeeper, Miranda Keene.

'I'd like to thank you all for your co-operation,' Castle began. 'I'm afraid I have to put you to one last inconvenience before you leave. As I have explained to Sir Digby, certain evidence has been found near the spot where the body was discovered. It is possible that some of you have picked up traces on your shoes and I should like to take these away for examination. As most of you live either in the house or on the estate, it should not prove too inconvenient. We shall obviously have to make special arrangements for Ms Letchworth and Mr Maggs and I'll have a word with them in a moment. In the meantime, if none of you has any objection—?'

'Okay by me,' said Ashford, whom Castle recognized as the young man in a straw hat on the right of the picture. The others nodded in agreement, but Kirtling broke in with an indignant, 'Just a minute!' He was breathing heavily and his face had turned a dull red. 'I certainly have objections,' he snapped, glaring at Castle. 'I asked you a moment ago the nature of this so-called evidence and you did not even have the courtesy to answer. I have enough knowledge of the law to know that you have no right to force any of us to comply with your request and I for one have no intention of doing

28

so. If any of my employees also refuse they have my full support. To suggest that anyone here could be responsible for that poor girl's death is outrageous,' he went on. 'You, Inspector, should be scouring the surrounding area for evidence of an intruder instead of browbeating her friends. The rest of you can decide for yourselves,' he went on, with a dismissive gesture, 'but Maggs and I have important business in London and we're leaving right away.'

'You are quite correct, sir; compliance with my request is entirely voluntary,' said Castle. 'I shall, of course, make a note of your objections in my report.'

'Do as you damn well please.' Kirtling beckoned to Maggs. 'I consider your handling of this investigation leaves a lot to be desired, Inspector, and I've a good mind to have a word with the Chief Constable about it.'

'Your privilege, sir,' said Castle. As the door slammed behind them, he turned back to the others, who were exchanging bemused glances and whispering among themselves. 'Right, ladies and gentlemen,' he said quietly, 'as your employer has pointed out, I have no authority to force you to hand over your footwear, but if you agree my officers will accompany to your homes those of you who live locally so that you can collect something to change into.' There were nods all round, indicating a willingness to comply. 'What about you, Ms Letchworth?' he added, turning to Athena. 'Do you live near here?'

'No, in Cheltenham. I came with Philip – Mr Montwell – but as he was in a hurry to get back to his gallery to meet a client I said I'd get a taxi home. You are perfectly welcome to take my shoes, Inspector. Tricia – ' she indicated the girl sitting next to her, with whom she had just had a whispered conversation – 'takes the same size as I do and she has very kindly offered to lend me a pair.'

'Excellent. I'm most grateful for everyone's co-operation. My officers will organize the exchange; it shouldn't take long, and then you can all go home. I'll get a lift back to the station from one of Willis's men,' he added in an aside to Dalia. Several interesting points had cropped up during the interviews and he wanted time to make notes of them while they were still fresh in his mind.

Five

O ne advantage of being on the late shift was the fact that
the roads were quiet and the homeward journey reduced
from half an hour – on a good day – to less than twenty
minutes. That, at least, was Sukey's feeling nine times out of
ten when the virtual absence of traffic made driving a pleasure.
Tonight the conditions were perfect: clear, still and moonless,
with the Cotswold Hills rising darkly against the starlit back-
drop of the sky. Yet she found no enjoyment in the drive;
instead she began mulling uneasily over the events of the day.
Dealing with a murder was always distressing, although today's
case had been less so than some she had previously dealt with
and it was always satisfying to find some potentially useful
evidence. Attending at the mortuary to take further shots of
the body was never pleasant, but at least poor Una May had
looked peaceful enough as she lay on the slab. She was thankful
that another police photographer had been assigned to cover
the post-mortem itself. Jim had arrived to attend the grisly
procedure just as she was leaving the building and he had
given her a further word of appreciation for her efforts. This
should have cheered her, but didn't because although he was
on his own he spoke in the same impersonal tone he used
when other people were present.

These thoughts were still running through the back of her
mind as she turned off the A417 at the bottom of Crickley
Hill towards the suburb of Brockworth, where she shared a
modest semi with her nineteen-year-old son Fergus. Yet the
image that overrode all others had nothing to do with the
murder; it was the recollection of seeing Jim with Dalia Chen
disappearing through the gate leading to the shrubbery where
the body was found. His head had been inclined towards her
as she looked up at him, smiling a little in response to what

he was saying. Every sight of them together, every comment that Jim let drop in praise of Dalia's qualities as a detective and her value to the team, caused a stab of jealousy that Sukey found difficult to conceal or control. For the thousandth time she told herself not to be a fool, that Jim was as loving and attentive towards her as ever. Yet Dalia was a dangerously attractive woman and he was a passionate man.

And then, as she turned into Bramble Close and saw his Mondeo parked outside her house, her spirits soared. The next moment Fergus opened the garage door and greeted her with a mock bow as he stepped aside for her to drive in.

'Hi Mum!' he said as she got out of the car. 'Jim turned up a little while ago, completely knackered and hoping you wouldn't be too tired to give him a little TLC.'

'Is that what he said?'

Fergus grinned. 'Not exactly; what he actually said was he looked in your office, found it empty and your desk clear, assumed you'd already left and came here anyway. He was surprised to find you weren't home; in fact, he seemed a little worried. I've been a bit concerned too so it's a relief to see you.'

'Everything had gone quiet so George Barnes said it was okay for Mandy and me to go down to the canteen for something to eat,' said Sukey, privately taking considerable comfort from the word 'worried'. 'If the office was empty George must have popped out for some reason. He can't have been far away.'

'Oh well, you're here now. Jim's been telling me a bit about the murder at the stately home. It sounds pure Agatha Christie. I've given him a beer, by the way, but I think he's hungry.'

'And expects me to feed him, I suppose.'

'Well, actually, I could use something as well.'

'Didn't you eat the shepherd's pie I left?'

'Yes, but that was ages ago.'

She rolled up her eyes in mock resignation and followed him into the kitchen. Jim was there, greeting her with a huge smile, a hug and a kiss. It was only recently that he had begun to show her even that much affection in front of Fergus, although they both knew the young man was aware of how things stood between them. 'I hope you don't mind my barging in unannounced, Sook,' he said. 'It's been quite a day for both of us and I thought maybe we could unwind together.'

'Of course I don't mind, it's lovely to see you.' All the doubts and misgivings had slipped away in his embrace. 'What was the result of the post-mortem?'

'Doc Blake was called away before he got busy with his scalpel so he's going to have to finish it tomorrow. All he'd say was that she was strangled, almost certainly by the gold chain round her neck.'

'No surprises there, I imagine. How did things go after I left Muckleton Manor? Did anyone object to having their footwear checked?'

'Only Sir Digby himself. He made a hell of a fuss, said he had no time to change his shoes, didn't think much of the way I was conducting the investigation and threatened to complain to the Chief Constable. He stalked out, taking his sidekick with him.'

'Gosh!' exclaimed Fergus. 'Why didn't you arrest him?'

'On what grounds? He knew jolly well I had no power to force him to hand over his shoes unless I had some evidence against him, which of course I hadn't. He told the others they were free to refuse as well, although no one else did.'

'It can't look good for him, though. Doesn't it make him a suspect?'

'Not necessarily, and in any case we can't take it for granted that the killer was anyone at today's gathering. Someone might have managed to get into the grounds from outside, although we haven't found any sign of that so far. Just the same, we'll be looking at Kirtling's relationship with the dead girl a little more closely, along with everyone else's of course. One of the witnesses hinted there was something going on between them and possibly between him and his PA in London as well. Which seems to confirm Dalia's impression, by the way. She reckons he's a womanizer.'

'What did he have to say about that?' Fergus asked eagerly.

'She didn't mention it until after I'd spoken to him, but in any case it's not the sort of thing one brings up at a preliminary interview without good reason. All we've done so far is establish what the gathering was about and ask people about their movements from the time the girl was last seen alive until the discovery of her body. DC Page is one of our specialist interviewers – he's done a PEACE training course – and he'll be carrying out the next round of interviews. It may be quite a lengthy process unless we get an early breakthrough.' Jim pulled out a notebook and jotted something down. 'If DCI Lord agrees, I might get Dalia to help out. She's done the course as well.'

'Is there no end to that girl's talents?' said Sukey, then immediately regretted having spoken.

If Jim noticed the sharp edge to her tone he showed no sign, but Fergus, well aware of his mother's sensitivities, hastily changed the subject with a question.

'What's a PEACE training?' he asked.

'It's an acronym for a special course on interviewing techniques,' Jim explained. 'You don't really want to know what it stands for, do you? I can never remember. Sook, is there any chance of a bite for a hungry DI? I haven't had time to breathe since we got back, let alone eat.'

'How about a bacon sandwich? I could do you some chips in the microwave to go with it.'

'Wonderful.'

'And for me too, please, Mum.'

'All right, greedy-guts. By the way, Jim, you do know I'm not in tomorrow, don't you? I've got the day off to help Fergus get settled at uni.'

'No, of course I hadn't forgotten. I do hope you enjoy your course, Fergus. Psychology, isn't it?'

'That's right.'

'I've a feeling he's got ideas about becoming a forensic psychologist,' said Sukey with a grimace as she set a frying pan on the stove and took bacon from the refrigerator.

'Then I look forward to getting extra help with the difficult cases,' said Jim with a smile. 'Thanks,' he added as Fergus offered him another can of beer.

'A glass of something for you, Mum?'

Sukey shook her head. 'Not for the moment, thanks, love. Jim, tell me more about the reason for the party. Mandy and I were wondering if it was some sort of fancy dress event because of the old-fashioned clothes the girl was wearing.'

'In a way, I suppose it was. Sir Digby Kirtling commissioned an artist called Philip Montwell to paint a copy of an Impressionist painting and the unveiling took place this afternoon.' While Sukey prepared the food, Jim explained the history of the commission. When he mentioned the name of the original painting she gave a nod of recognition. 'You know it?' he asked in surprise.

'Of course. It's by Renoir – it often crops up on greeting cards. You must have seen it.'

'Yes, but I didn't know what it was called. Fortunately Dalia did, which meant I didn't appear a complete ignoramus in front of Montwell.'

'That was a bit of luck,' said Sukey. This time there was no rancour behind the remark, only satisfaction that Dalia hadn't outpointed her this time.

'I reckon I'm going to enjoy living in Cheltenham,' said Fergus. 'Anita thinks I'm mad to want to go into student accommodation, but I sort of felt coming home every day would feel a bit like school.' Anita, his girlfriend, was studying modern languages at Oxford. 'You're sure you don't mind, Mum? You'll be okay on your own?'

'Of course I'll be all right. I'm sure you've made the right decision; you'd miss out on all sorts of things if you were commuting every day. Anyway, you can always change your mind if it doesn't work out.'

After completing the formalities and depositing Fergus's luggage in the student flat that he was to share with three others, they set off to explore the surrounding area. They were strolling along a street in the Montpelier district of the town when Sukey stopped, her attention caught by a painting in a shop window.

'Isn't that lovely!' she exclaimed. It was a simple, sunlit scene of fishing boats at anchor, their brightly coloured hulls contrasting with the grey stone of the harbour walls. 'It looks like somewhere in Cornwall.' She moved forward to take a closer look and gave an exclamation as she read the signature. 'It's by Philip Montwell. What a coincidence!'

'Is that the chap who painted the picture for Sir Digby Whatsit? The one whose secretary got topped?'

'I imagine so.' Sukey glanced up at the façade above the

window on which 'The Phimont Gallery' was painted in flowing, gilded letters. 'Phimont – that sounds like a compound of his name. Maybe he owns this place.' She turned her attention back to the picture. 'I wonder how much he's asking for that.'

'If you have to ask the price, you can't afford it,' her son said firmly as he took her by the arm. 'I don't know about you, Mum, but I'm hungry. How about looking for somewhere to have lunch?'

At that moment the door of the gallery opened and a young woman came out. When she saw Fergus she gave an excited squeal of recognition and the next minute the two were exchanging hugs and mutual exclamations of the 'fancy-seeing-you-here' variety. Several moments passed before Fergus remembered to introduce his mother.

'This is Anne-Marie, we were at sixth-form college together,' he explained. He turned back to her and said, 'Do you work here or were you buying a picture? She was brilliant at art,' he informed Sukey.

The girl gave a little shriek of laughter. 'Buying a picture? At his prices? You've got to be joking. No, I'm working here temporarily until I go to art college at the end of the month.'

'In London?'

'No, here in Cheltenham. What about you?'

Realizing that this conversation could go on for some time, Sukey intervened. 'Look,' she said, 'if you two want to chat, how about Anne-Marie joining us for lunch?'

The girl hesitated for a moment, glanced at her watch and said, 'I'd love to, but I have to be back by two because Mr Montwell's expecting a client. He wants me to be there in case there are any visitors to the gallery.'

'Where's the best place to eat round here?'

'There's a café just up the road where they do quite nice toasted snacks.'

'That sounds fine.'

Although it was early October it was still warm and sunny and after placing their orders at the counter they sat at one of the tables on the pavement outside. It soon emerged that Anne-Marie was an enthusiastic admirer of her employer's work; her young face, round and pink as a Botticelli cherub's and

35

topped by a mop of short coppery curls, glowed with enthusiasm as she described his latest commission, a copy of a work by Matisse. 'It's called *La Danza*,' she informed them. 'The client wanted dancing figures and at first he chose Poussin's *Dance to the Music of Time*, but changed his mind when Philip – Mr Montwell – showed him the Matisse. It's so full of energy, I just love it.'

'You must enjoy working for him,' said Sukey when she could get a word in edgeways.

'It's a privilege,' Anne-Marie said earnestly. 'His work is sensational – not that I'd dare tell him so,' she added with a giggle.

'Why not?'

'I once said something complimentary about one of his pictures and he gave me a cold sort of look and said praise from people with no expert knowledge, experience or judgement wasn't worth having. I felt crushed, I can tell you. I nearly cried.'

'That was very unkind,' said Sukey. She recalled something Jim had said about Montwell the previous evening. 'Arrogant' and 'snob' had been two of the words he used.

To her surprise, Anne-Marie rushed to his defence. 'Oh well, he was right of course. I've got everything to learn, really.'

'Do you ever meet any of his clients?'

'Oh yes, I normally show them in and give them tea or coffee while they study the catalogues he leaves for them to browse over.'

'Did you meet Sir Digby Kirtling?'

'Yes, but I already knew he was coming because my Auntie Miranda told me. She's his housekeeper, you see, and when he told her Ms Letchworth – she's done all the furnishing and decoration at Muckleton – had recommended Mr Montwell, she said I worked for him and how good I'd said he is.'

'I suppose he'd been talking to her about wanting pictures for his house.'

'That's right. He talks to her a lot, tells her all his plans. They're . . . you know—' Anne-Marie broke off to take a bite out of her toasted ciabatta.

Sukey had a feeling that she was uncomfortable at having

said something indiscreet. 'You mean they're lovers?' she said, keeping her tone casual.

'Careful what you say or you might incriminate yourself,' Fergus put in jokingly. 'My mum works for the police and she was at the scene of the murder,' he explained.

'Were you?' Anne-Marie's eyes saucered. 'Do they know who killed Una? Auntie M's so upset about it. She's afraid—' The girl broke off and looked embarrassed.

'Afraid of what?' asked Sukey.

Anne-Marie swallowed the last of her ciabatta and stood up. 'I'd better not say. I must go now. Thank you very much for the lunch, Mrs Reynolds. Bye, Gus, see you around.' And she was gone.

'I guess Jim and his team will be interested in that little titbit,' said Fergus.

'I'm sure they will,' his mother replied.

Six

'Any ideas as to who dunnit, Jim?' DCI Philip Lord brushed biscuit crumbs from his black Chaplinesque moustache over the file lying open on his desk and reached for his cup of coffee. 'Early days yet I know, but now and again we have a gut feeling that points us in the right direction.'

DI Castle shook his head. 'Not at the moment, I'm afraid. We've learned nothing about the dead girl so far that might give us a clue as to motive. She seems to have been good at her job, got on well with all the other employees on the estate and lived a blameless life in a cottage on the edge of the village.'

'Alone?'

'Apart from a couple of cats, yes. It seems she was on good – although not particularly intimate – terms with her neighbours; likewise the village shopkeepers. Although according to one of the officers doing house-to-house enquiries, they all commented that she was never one to stop and chat.'

'Kept herself to herself, as the saying goes,' Lord remarked dourly. 'Have you informed the next of kin?'

'Her next-door neighbour told us she had a sister Laura living in London. She – the neighbour – has a key to the cottage and let us in; we found the sister's address and phone number, but when we rang we were told by her flatmate that she's on a package tour to Italy. She gave us details and we've asked the travel company to contact her and ask her to get in touch, but we've heard nothing so far.'

'That'll be a sad homecoming for the poor woman,' commented Lord. He referred back to the report. 'What about boyfriends? I see there's a suggestion here that Kirtling himself might have had an eye on her.'

'That's only hearsay at the moment, although of course

we'll be checking on it along with the other liaisons that George Maggs hinted at. The neighbour hasn't noticed any regular visitors, but she's out quite a bit herself and she doesn't appear to be the nosy sort anyway. I've set up house-to-house enquiries, but I haven't had any feedback so far.'

Lord riffled through the pages in the folder. 'The postmortem result doesn't seem to be here,' he said.

'Doctor Blake was called away to an emergency before he could complete it,' Castle explained. 'He's doing it this morning.'

'Shouldn't you be there?'

'DS Hill is attending. I thought it would be useful experience for him.'

Lord grunted. 'I suppose the lad has to be bloodied some time.' He turned back to the file. 'Is there anyone we can eliminate?'

'Only the artist chap, Philip Montwell, assuming he's telling the truth when he says he'd never met the victim before the day of the party. We're checking on that, naturally, but on the face of it there's no reason to doubt him. Miranda Keene, the housekeeper, says she strolled round the gardens for a while with Maggs, pointing out a few of her favourite bits, and then returned to the house on her own to finish preparations for tea. She was alone in the kitchen from then on. According to Ms Letchworth's statement she found a comfortable lounger in a secluded corner and dropped off to sleep. It seems quite feasible; it was a pleasantly warm afternoon.'

'But no witnesses, I suppose?'

'I'm afraid not – but again, there seems to be a complete absence of motive. The problem is that everyone, including Kirtling himself, scattered after the picture unveiling ceremony and judging from the number of empty bottles some of them must have got through quite a lot of champagne.'

'So no one can be sure where they were at any particular time during that period?'

'That's how it looks at the moment. Obviously we'll be hoping to narrow things down when we have a more accurate idea of the time of death, but it isn't going to be easy.'

Lord took a packet of biscuits from a drawer and offered one to Castle, who declined with a shake of the head. He took one himself and crunched it thoughtfully while continuing to study the report. 'I see the victim was last seen alive around two thirty and failed to reappear with the others an hour and a half or so later. It's hard to believe no one heard or saw anything unusual during the whole of that time. One or more of them must be lying.'

'The grounds are pretty extensive,' Castle pointed out. 'Parts of them have been newly planted, but others – for example, the shrubbery where the body was found, a walled kitchen garden and a rose garden enclosed by hedges – have been restored to their original state and are quite secluded. We're hoping to have a better idea of where everyone went and what they did once they've been interviewed.'

'Good.' Lord closed the folder and handed it back to Castle. 'Keep me posted, Jim. I'd like something definite to tell the Super as soon as possible.'

There was a tap at the door and a young uniformed officer entered and handed an envelope to Castle. 'DS Hill wanted you to have this without delay, sir,' she said.

Castle opened it, scanned the brief message it contained, gave a soft whistle and handed it to Lord.

'It seems we may have a motive,' he said. 'Una May was three months pregnant.'

'Well, that answers one of my questions,' Lord said wryly. 'Our next step is to find out who the special boyfriend is. What do you know about the men at the party?' He ran a stubby finger down the list of names. 'I see there were five, including Kirtling and Maggs. You saw those two yourself – any thoughts?'

Castle sat back in his chair, crossed his legs and clasped his long fingers round his knee. He reflected for a moment before saying, 'Maggs is a rather bumptious young man, very cocksure, but I didn't get the impression that he was particularly interested in Una May – or in any of the other women present, come to that. That could have been a cover-up, of course; we may get a different impression when we start digging a little more deeply. His observations about Kirtling having a reputation as a ladies' man are quite interesting, but I don't think we should attach too much significance to them at this stage. What he observed might have been normal flirtatious behaviour from a compulsive womanizer – which is how DS Chen described him.'

'Ah yes, your lovely oriental lotus flower.' Lord's black eyes twinkled with mischief. 'I hope you're managing to keep your mind on the job while you're working with her, Jim.'

'Of course I am,' Castle replied indignantly, drawing a malicious chuckle from Lord.

'Glad to hear it. Can't have you upsetting Sukey, can we? Okay, tell me about the other men on this list. The chap who found the body, for a start.'

'Arnie Ashford? He's the assistant gardener. There's been nothing so far to suggest that he was interested in Una May, although the head gardener's son, Dick Andrews, did hint he might be sweet on his sister, Tricia. They were both at the party as well.'

'Hmm.' Lord fingered his moustache and frowned. 'Not a lot to go on at the moment, is there? Tell your people to keep digging and let me have details of any feedback as it comes in.'

'Will do.'

An hour or so later, Castle was in his office when DS Hill tapped on his door. 'Got a moment, Guv?' he said.

'Sure, Tony. Come in and sit down. I got your message while I was reporting to DCI Lord.'

'Quite a turn-up for the book, isn't it?' said Hill. Castle observed him closely as he sat down and opened his notebook, but could detect no outward sign of his having been disturbed or distressed by his recent experience in the mortuary. He was generally considered to have a promising future in the CID on account of his cool head and keen, analytical brain. He had a deceptively ingenuous manner and a hint of almost boyish enthusiasm that frequently led people to assume that he was much younger than his thirty years. These qualities were particularly effective during interviews and often enabled him to induce witnesses – particularly females – to lower their guard and on occasions part with information they might have preferred to keep to themselves. 'Any idea who the father might be?' he asked.

Hill hesitated. 'Hmm . . . not sure, but maybe . . . Look, sir, I've just been interviewing Miranda Keene, Sir Digby's housekeeper. I'd like to tell you about that first and get your reactions, if it's all right with you.'

'Sure. Go ahead.'

'Yesterday she was too upset over the girl's death to do more than give a brief account of her movements during the critical time, but she's a lot calmer now and was willing to submit to a more detailed interview. She was quite definite that she could think of no reason why anyone would want to kill Una and went on to confirm everything she had told us yesterday, but in a bit more detail. She also gave me her account of the movements of other people so far as she could remember or was aware of them. It doesn't on the face of it carry us forward, but I'll write that up and let you have it in due course.'

'And then what?'

'She seemed fairly relaxed so I started to chat to her about her job: how long she had worked for Sir Digby, what her duties were, how many staff he employed and what sort of boss he was – you know the kind of stuff. She went out of her way to assure me that he was a very good employer, but I sensed that she wasn't really comfortable with that line of questioning so I let it go for the time being and started talking about the renovation of the house. It was when I asked whether she'd been involved in any of the discussions with the interior designer, Athena Letchworth, that she started to get . . . not uptight, exactly, but noticeably a little more careful with her answers. She never hinted in words that she thought her boss was attracted to the lady, but it was quite obvious that she had, shall we say, reservations about her.'

'Do you think Miranda – Mrs Keene – might have her eye on Kirtling herself?'

'Why not? He'd be quite a catch and she's a very attractive woman.'

'You don't think maybe she perhaps feels her position as housekeeper under threat – in the event that the luscious Athena were to become Lady K, for example.'

'I suppose that's a possibility,' Hill conceded, 'but my gut feeling is that it was more personal than that.'

'I see. Well, you may be right. Anything else you want to talk about?'

42

Before Hill could reply, Castle's phone rang. Sukey was on the line. It was unusual for her to call him at the office other than on matters connected with the job, and knowing that she was not on duty that day he felt a momentary twinge of apprehension that there might be something wrong. The feeling was quickly dispelled by her opening words.

'I'm calling about the Una May case,' she said. 'I've just learned something that may have a direct bearing on it. Would this be a good time to tell you about it?'

'Sure. As a matter of fact, I've got Tony Hill with me and that's what we've been talking about, so fire away.' He listened intently while Sukey told him of the meeting with Anne-Marie and the revelation that Miranda Keene and Kirtling were lovers.

'She actually said that?'

'No, it was more nudge-nudge, wink-wink, but when I said it in so many words she didn't deny it,' said Sukey. 'She went on to say her aunt was afraid of something, but she didn't say what. In fact, it was at that point that she stopped short and made a hasty exit. I had a strong impression that she felt she'd said too much.'

'That is interesting,' said Jim. 'Could I ask you to put it into a written report when you get home?'

'Of course.'

'Do you know where we can contact Anne-Marie if we need to talk to her?'

'No problem. She lives in Cheltenham and she's starting a course at the art college in a week or so. I daresay she and Fergus will keep in touch.'

'That's fine. I take it you'll be in tomorrow?'

'I'm on duty at two. I'll let you have my report then.'

It occurred to Jim after he put the phone down that he had forgotten to mention the fact that Una May had been pregnant. Not that it made any difference; Sukey's part of the investigation was done unless there was any reason to send her back to Muckleton Manor to carry out more tests. In any case, she'd find out tomorrow.

Sukey, likewise, had failed to mention that Anne-Marie was working at the Phimont Gallery. It was merely a coincidence that hardly seemed relevant.

Seven

A fter making her call to DI Castle, Sukey returned with
Fergus to the accommodation block, where they met two
of the students who would be his flatmates for his first year
at the University of Gloucester. They introduced themselves:
Pete from Cinderford in the Forest of Dean, who was a ruddy-
faced, tow-headed young man doing a course in media studies,
and Lester from Cirencester, slight, dark and rather intense-
looking, who was reading English. There were also a couple
of girls from a flat along the corridor who had obviously lost
no time in making contact with their new neighbours. They
sat on stools round the Formica-topped kitchen table or lounged
against any available cupboard or wall space, clutching mugs
of coffee and filling the small room with their cheerful exuber-
ance. They greeted Sukey with friendly nods and smiles,
addressing her by her first name as a matter of course. Pete
offered to make coffee from a tin of supermarket own brand
instant sitting on the table among a clutter of packets of biscuits
and sugar and an open carton of milk. She declined a biscuit
but accepted the coffee, more out of a desire not to appear
standoffish than because she felt in particular need of refreshment. Someone offered her a stool in the angle between the
sink and the cooker; from then on they paid her no further
attention, but picked up their conversation from the point it
had reached when she and Fergus arrived, exchanging details
of places of refreshment and entertainment in the area with
an occasional reference to timetables, tutors and the location
of lecture halls.

Sukey was content to remain in the background, observing
with quiet pleasure the ease with which Fergus was drawn
into the circle. She listened with a blend of amusement and
nostalgia to the animated chatter, recalling her own college

days and comparing the modern accommodation Fergus would enjoy with the rather scruffy bedsits she and her fellow students had occupied. She drank some of the weak coffee, surreptitiously emptied the rest of it into the sink, rinsed the mug and slid off her stool. It was several seconds before she managed to catch her son's eye and signal her intention to leave.

'Don't worry, I can find my own way out,' she said hurriedly as he half rose from his seat. Feeling her throat tighten, she instinctively shied away from the prospect of a formal parting. She told herself not to be a fool; only a short distance would separate them, they would be in constant touch and he could come home on a visit at any time. Yet she knew that today was a watershed. He was starting a new life in a new world, one in which she had no part.

There was no reason to linger in Cheltenham, yet she was reluctant to return home to an empty house. So she drove into the centre of town and parked in Imperial Square, where she lingered for a while admiring the flowers, still bravely blooming in the autumn sunshine. She strolled along the Promenade, beneath tall chestnuts glowing russet and gold above her head as she picked her way among the glossy brown fruits, some still in their spiny cases, scattered here and there on the crisp carpet of fallen leaves. She turned into Clarence Street to avoid the crowds of shoppers and went into the museum, where she spent half an hour browsing among the exhibits before returning to her car and setting off for home.

When she got indoors the light on her answering machine was flashing and she felt a surge of optimism at the possibility that Jim had left a message, but before she had time to play it back, the phone rang. Fergus was on the line. 'Hi Mum,' he said, 'I thought you should know Anne-Marie called me on my mobile about five minutes after you left. She wanted to know what job you did for the police and I said you were in the SOCOs' department in Gloucester and she asked if you were dealing with the murder at Muckleton Manor. I said you were; I hope that's okay, I mean, it's not a secret, is it?'

'No, it's not a problem – except that we're now known as CSIs, but we'll let that pass.'

'Sorry, I keep forgetting.'

'Did she say why she wanted to talk to me?'

'No, but she sounded a bit agitated. I've a feeling she'll try and contact you at work. She asked for your home number, but I didn't give it to her of course.'

'Did she leave hers?'

'We exchanged numbers over lunch, remember? That's how she was able to contact me. Would you like me to give it to you?'

'No, I think I'll leave it for now and see if she tries again. Everything okay your end?'

'Yes, fine. We're all going out for a Chinese in a little while.'

'Good. Have a nice evening. Bye.'

She hung up and pressed the button on the answering machine. It was Mandy's voice on the tape. 'Sukey, a girl called Anne-Marie has been trying to contact you. Said she's a friend of Fergus. She seems very anxious to talk to you but she wouldn't say what it was about. Anyway, I told her I'd pass the message on. She'd like you to call her back.' She dictated a number, and ended with 'See you tomorrow'.

While she prepared her evening meal, Sukey speculated about Anne-Marie's motive for wanting to get in touch with her. To ask her not to pass on to the police the reference to her aunt's relationship with Sir Digby seemed the most likely. Well, it was too late for that; she had already told Jim and had also mentioned the girl's hurried departure after hinting that the aunt was afraid of something. It would, she decided, be better to keep out of it.

An hour later, Mandy called a second time. 'She's been on to me again and she sounds really uptight. I've got a feeling she's going to pester us until she gets a chance to speak to you.'

'I've got a pretty good idea what it's about,' Sukey said. She gave a brief account of her meeting with Anne-Marie.

'Gosh!' said Mandy. 'I wonder if old Sir D has been playing away and Miranda has found out about Una May being in the club.'

'No kidding! When did this come out?'

'At the PM – she was three months gone. How about that for a nice juicy motive for topping her?'

'All that stuff about hell knowing no fury and so on?' Sukey speculated. 'Well, it wouldn't be the first time. Have the press got hold of it yet?'

'It's not in the evening edition of the *Gazette*. The police are still trying to contact her sister, who's away on holiday. It won't be officially released until she's been told.'

'I suppose not. Going back to Anne-Marie, I can see now why she's worried.

She probably wants me to keep quiet about what she told me for fear of her aunt getting involved, but I'm afraid it's too late for that. I've already told DI Castle. I suppose I'd better call her though. Give me the number again, will you?'

As she hung up, Sukey felt a twinge of irritation that Jim hadn't mentioned Una May's pregnancy when she called to tell him about her meeting with Anne-Marie. Maybe he hadn't known at the time, but she sensed that he had. It was the kind of information the pathologist would pass on immediately, even before completing his examination and submitting his detailed report. Well, she reflected with a hint of mischievous glee, she knew something Jim and his team didn't, namely that Anne-Marie worked for Philip Montwell. It wasn't important, but in a way it made them quits.

She cleared away the remnants of her meal, made a cup of coffee and went into the sitting room. Although Anne-Marie's revelations concerning her aunt had immediately roused her professional interest, since passing them on to Jim she had been too absorbed in her own affairs to give them any further thought. This latest development put the girl's anxiety in a new light. Did Miranda Keene know about Una May's pregnancy? After all, they both worked at the manor and it was reasonable to assume there had been plenty of contact between them. If, for example, the girl had shown early symptoms such as morning sickness, the older woman might have guessed, or at least suspected, that Sir Digby was the child's father. Jim had indicated that the man had a reputation as a womanizer. He had also mentioned that of the people attending the party, Miranda Keene had been the one to show the greatest distress. If he had been dallying with Una May and made her pregnant, was it not possible that an uncontrollable surge of jealousy had resulted in an unpremeditated act of murder?

She finished her coffee, picked up the phone and tapped

47

out the number Mandy had given her. It had barely started to ring when Anne-Marie answered.

'Oh, Mrs Reynolds, thank you so much for calling!' she said in a breathless voice. Sukey detected a hint of tears as she went on, 'I've been so worried. It was just after I got back from lunch . . . the police came . . . they wanted his shoes . . . they can't suspect him, surely? He didn't even know her, he only—'

'Hang on a minute,' said Sukey as the girl paused for breath. 'Do I take it that by "he" you mean Philip Montwell?'

'Of course – who else? Why did the police want his shoes? He didn't kill that girl . . . he couldn't . . . he's not—'

'Just calm down. I know what it's about and I can assure you Montwell isn't a suspect.'

'Then why—'

'It's just routine. While my colleague and I were examining the murder scene we found certain evidence. It's possible that the killer picked up traces on his shoes and the police would have asked everyone to hand theirs over for forensic examination. It's for elimination purposes, that's all.'

'What sort of evidence?'

'I can't tell you that. All I can tell you is that because Mr Montwell had already left when it was discovered, it was necessary to send an officer to ask if he would mind having his shoes examined as well. It would have been up to him whether he agreed or not, although it might have looked odd if he'd refused. Do you know what happened? Didn't he tell you why the officer called on him?'

'Of course not. He isn't likely to confide in me.' There was a hint of wistfulness mingled with the anxiety in the girl's voice. 'The policeman spoke to him in his private office and when he left he had his shoes with him.'

'Well, there you are then. Your boss had nothing to hide and he evidently co-operated with the police like a good citizen. Did he seem at all worried after the officer left?'

'No, not at all.'

'So cheer up and forget about it.'

'Thank you so much.' There was a brief pause during which Sukey heard the girl blowing her nose and sniffing. Evidently she had quite a serious crush on her employer and had allowed her imagination to run away with her. When she spoke again she sounded calmer. 'I'm sorry to have bothered you, but I really was worried. I couldn't ask the police directly, but I remembered Gus saying you worked for them and you'd had something to do with the murder, so I thought—'

'It's all right; I'm glad I was able to help. Tell me, how is your aunt? You said she was very upset—'

'Oh, she's feeling much better now, thank you for asking.' It might have been Sukey's imagination, but the response had been a little too pat, even slightly dismissive, as if there had never been any cause for serious concern. Yet only a matter of hours ago Anne-Marie had let slip, obviously without intending to, that Miranda Keene was afraid of something. It would be interesting to know if something had happened to allay those fears, and if so what it was. She was trying to think of a way of probing a little further without appearing overtly inquisitive, but the girl forestalled her by saying 'Thank you' once again and ending the call.

Eight

When DC Derek Page arrived at Muckleton Manor there was a maroon Jaguar already parked on the gravelled forecourt, immediately opposite the heavy oak front door. Evidently Sir Digby Kirtling had returned from London. From what he had been told about the man he guessed that it would be considered an impertinence on his part to park his three-year-old Ford Focus alongside the sleek new limousine, so he drove a discreet distance away, switched off his engine and sat in the car for a couple of minutes, mentally preparing himself for the task ahead. DI Castle had hinted that it might be a tricky interview, a prediction that had been borne out during his conversation with Sir Digby on the telephone the previous day. The man's initial reaction had been so unhelpful that Page had had to bring into play all the techniques he had learned on the PEACE interview training course to persuade him that every scrap of information, every tiny detail that could be dredged from the memory of every person present on the fateful day, or had any connection with the murdered woman, was of potential value in tracking down her killer.

'Oh very well,' he had said at last, 'I'll be back at the manor tomorrow evening as it happens; I suppose I can spare you half an hour then.' His tone made it clear that he begrudged spending time on what he clearly held to be a pointless exercise. 'Seven o'clock, not a minute later or the arrangement's off.'

Page glanced at his watch. It was ten to seven; he might as well go and announce himself although he had no doubt that he would be kept waiting, probably until well after the appointed time. This would, of course, reduce the length of the interview, something he had allowed for when planning it. It was a ploy he had been trained to deal with. Knowing there was a good chance that his arrival had been observed, he took care to move in a relaxed, unhurried way as he got out of the car, locked it, went to the front door and pressed the bell.

A slim, dark-haired woman wearing a simple but beautifully cut mulberry-coloured dress opened the door. He held up his ID and she scrutinized it carefully before saying, 'Good evening, Constable. Please come in.' She smiled politely as she stood aside for him to enter before closing the door behind him. She was, he estimated, in her late forties and still beautiful, with fine bones, perfect teeth, clear skin and bright brown eyes. As he stepped past her into the spacious, lofty entrance hall he caught a hint of expensive perfume. His father was a jeweller and he had learned enough about diamonds to recognize that the pendant at her throat was worth several times his monthly salary. Either she had private means, or Sir Digby paid her exceptionally well, or . . .

She interrupted his train of thought by saying, 'I'm Miranda Keene, Sir Digby's housekeeper. If you wouldn't mind waiting in here?' She ushered him into a room immediately to the right of the front door, which from what he had been told he was able to identify as the one in which the party guests had waited to give their statements after the discovery of Una May's body. 'Sir Digby will be with you in a few minutes,' she added. 'Can I get you anything? Tea? Coffee?'

'No, thank you.' He paused for a moment and glanced round the room. 'This is a lovely old house,' he commented. 'Are those beams in the hall original?'

She smiled again and he felt her warm towards him. He sensed that she had a feeling for the house and was responding to his interest. He had been told of her distress at the tragedy, but she appeared perfectly composed now. 'The beams?' she repeated. 'They are quite old, but they came from another house that was being demolished.'

'I believe this one was in pretty bad shape when Sir Digby acquired it,' he said.

She looked at him in surprise. 'How did you know that?'

'It's no secret. There was quite a lot of publicity in the local press because the people in the village were afraid it was going to be developed as a country club and casino, and attract

51

a lot of what the chairman of the parish council described as "undesirable types".'

She gave a little laugh. It had a husky quality that added to her charm. 'You mean Brigadier Evans? Yes, he stirred up quite a hornet's nest at the time. It was all on account of some imaginative reporter spreading a tale about how Sir Digby was going into the leisure business. He was very angry about it; he even threatened to sue, but the paper admitted there was no truth in the story and it all blew over. All he wanted was a country retreat where he could get away from the pressure of business. He took a great deal of interest – and pleasure – in the restoration. I think he found it quite therapeutic in fact, a complete change from his business commitments. It all went so well and now this dreadful tragedy has spoiled it for him.' The smile faded and the fine eyes misted over.

'I'm sorry, I didn't mean to upset you,' said Page, noting that she appeared to show more concern for her employer than for the victim.

She blinked away the tears. 'It's all right,' she said and added hastily, as if the same thought had occurred to her, 'I haven't really come to terms with Una's death yet. She was such a sweet girl. Have you any idea who might have killed her?'

'Not yet, I'm afraid. We're hoping that when everyone has had time to think, at least someone will remember something to help us.'

'That's what your colleague . . . the Chinese lady . . . said. She came to have a talk with me this afternoon.'

'DS Chen? Yes, she told me she'd seen you. She said you'd been very helpful.'

Mrs Keene gave a wan smile. 'Did she? That was kind. I didn't think I'd said anything particularly useful.'

Page's mind went back to what Dalia had told him after her return from the manor. 'She gave a very good impression of telling us everything she knew about Una May without actually saying anything we didn't know already from independent witnesses. It was, "No, we didn't have a great deal to do with one another really; we each had our job to do and they didn't overlap very much," and "Yes, I had noticed her looking a bit peaky lately, but she never mentioned feeling unwell". And as for her relationship with Sir Digby – well, she made no attempt to conceal the fact that she had been his housekeeper in London for several years before he bought the manor and that she thought very highly of him, but without giving the slightest hint that they were anything but employer and employee. That of course is in direct contradiction to what her niece told Sukey Reynolds.'

That titbit was still hearsay, of course. It would be interesting to see what Sir Digby had to say. Page shot a surreptitious glance at an ormolu clock on the mantelpiece. It was already ten past seven and there was no sign of Kirtling. Mrs Keene must have read his thoughts, for she said with a hint of an apology in her voice, 'I'm sure he'll be with you in a minute. If you'd excuse me—'

'Of course,' said Page politely and she went out, closing the door quietly behind her. It was a further five minutes before it flew open again and Kirtling entered.

Like Castle, Page was immediately impressed with the strength of the man's personality. He seemed to fill the doorway as he stood there for a moment with his hard blue eyes fixed on the young detective, quite evidently sizing him up. He was evidently freshly showered, for he smelled of expensive aftershave and his thick hair was still slightly damp. He was wearing a well-cut grey lounge suit over a snow-white shirt, with a diamond pin in his blue silk tie and diamond cufflinks at his wrists. Page noted the powerful hands and had a momentary vision of them locked round the throat of a helpless girl, then remembered that they were not dealing with a manual strangulation and put the image from his mind.

Kirtling took a couple of steps forward and closed the door behind him without taking his eyes off his visitor. 'Good evening, officer,' he said curtly. 'I don't see the necessity for this interview; I've already told your superiors what I know, but I suppose they have to follow procedure. Keep it short, please. I'm going out soon.'

'I won't take up any more of your time than I can help, sir,' said Page. 'I'd just like to have a bit of a chat about the dead woman and the history of her employment with you. If necessary, we can always arrange a further meeting at a time more convenient to you.'

'Well, I suppose you'd better sit down.' Kirtling indicated an upright chair before settling his big frame on a couch, crossing his legs and leaning back against the cushions. 'What d'you want to know?'

Any thoughts Page might have had about establishing some kind of rapport with him had to be abandoned. Here was a man accustomed to dealing on his own terms with people at all levels; doubtless he was familiar with all the recognized stratagems for dealing with anything from the engagement of a new employee to a top-level business negotiation. Any attempt at dissimulation would be spotted and contemptuously brushed aside; the only hope was the direct approach.

'I understand the dead woman had been in your employ for nearly a year, sir,' he began.

'Correct.'

'Can you tell me how you came to engage her?'

'My PA in London advertised, interviewed all the applicants and prepared a shortlist of three. I interviewed all of them and Una – Ms May – was by far the most suitable. She had all the right qualifications and she lived locally.'

'During her employment with you, was she ever absent on account of ill health?'

'Not that I can remember.'

'Your housekeeper, Mrs Keene, mentioned that she had noticed her looking slightly unwell lately – "a bit peaky" to use her own words. Did you happen to notice anything like that?'

'I can't say I did.'

'She never complained of feeling unwell or mentioned she was thinking of consulting her doctor?'

'Not to me she didn't. She might have said something to Mrs Keene.'

'So as far as you are aware, she was in the best of health?'

'Haven't I just said so?'

'I just want to be sure, sir.' Page sensed that Kirtling was beginning to feel uncomfortable at the direction the conversation was taking, but before he had a chance to probe any further they heard a piercing scream from somewhere nearby, followed by a woman's voice repeatedly crying, 'Oh no!' and rising in pitch until it disintegrated into hysterical sobbing.

'What the hell . . . that's Miranda!' Kirtling leapt from his seat and rushed out of the room. With Page at his heels he flung open a door on the far side of the hall. The housekeeper was standing in front of the elaborately carved stone fireplace. She was shaking from head to foot and clawing at her mouth with both hands as she gazed up in horror at the picture that hung above it. From the description Dalia Chen had given him, Page recognized it immediately as the Philip Montwell version of *The Luncheon of the Boating Party*. Evidently there was one person at least who had not shared in the general admiration. A jagged slash had been carved in the canvas, slicing the main figure in the painting literally in two, while the misspelt word 'Merderer' had been daubed across it in red paint.

Even as his eyes took in the damage, Page's brain registered the fact that distress over the death of one of his employees had not interfered with the arrangements Kirtling had made for displaying his latest acquisition. His eyes turned from the painting to the man and woman standing in front of it. She at least had totally forgotten his existence and was crying on Kirtling's shoulder while he, rather self-consciously it seemed to Page, was patting her on the back in an effort to quieten her. The moment her sobs began to subside, he detached himself from her clinging arms and turned to Page.

'Well, what are you standing there for?' he demanded. 'I expect your lot to find out whoever did this and charge them with criminal damage. Are you going to report it to your superiors or do I have to do it myself?'

'I take it you have no idea who might be responsible, sir?'

'Of course I bloody well don't. It's your job to find out, so get on with it.'

Page had already taken his mobile from his pocket. He went to the door and said, 'If you'll excuse me?'

'I don't see why you have to be so secretive,' Kirtling snapped. 'You can't tell them anything I haven't seen for myself.'

Page glanced at the housekeeper, who was still trembling, and then back at Kirtling. 'It seems to me that the lady should sit down somewhere quiet, sir – and maybe a drop of brandy would help her recover from the shock?'

He was half prepared for an indignant instruction to mind his own business, but to his surprise Kirtling dropped his aggressive manner and mumbled, 'Yes, of course. Come along, Miranda; I'll get you a drink. We'll be in the other room,' he added over his shoulder as he escorted her out.

The moment the door closed behind them, Page called CID and asked for DI Castle. Before he had a chance to speak, Castle said, 'Derek, I was just going to call you. We've contacted the dead woman's sister, and guess what? Her first words on hearing the news were, "So he decided to shut her up to save his precious reputation, the bastard." No prizes for guessing who she was talking about.'

'And she's not the only one with that opinion,' said Page and went on to describe the damage to the picture.

Castle gave a low whistle. 'I think perhaps you'd better bring him in for questioning,' he said.

'You reckon he did it, sir?'

'It's beginning to look like it, wouldn't you say?'

Nine

It had been a tiring, emotionally charged day and Sukey was thankful to relax in a hot bath before settling in bed with a book, but she had read barely half a chapter before her eyelids began to droop. She was jerked awake by the ringing of her bedside phone.

'Sukey, it's Mandy. Sorry to disturb you again, but I thought you'd like to be brought up to date. There have been startling new revelations, as the tabloids would put it. Sir Digby has been brought in for questioning about the murder of Una May.'

'Well, I can't say I'm surprised,' Sukey said sleepily. 'The fact that he wasn't co-operative suggested he had something to hide.'

'And that's not all. I've had another frantic call from Anne-Marie. Someone has damaged the picture and painted the word "Murderer" across a figure in it that's supposed to represent Sir Digby.'

'Good heavens!' Sukey was wide awake now. 'When did this happen?'

'She doesn't know, but the room wasn't part of the crime scene so it wasn't sealed before we all left yesterday. It must have been some time after that.'

'But surely the police are still there guarding the place? I mean, they should have spotted an intruder.'

'Sure they're there, but there was no reason to seal that particular room and, so far as I can make out, the alarm system isn't activated during the day unless the house is left empty for any reason. That's hardly likely in a place that size with all the minions Sir Digby employs. I imagine CID are working on the assumption that it was one of them who slipped into the room and did the deed without being noticed.'

'There's still the possibility that the killer is someone from outside,' Sukey pointed out, recalling a comment Jim had made on the evening of the murder.

'I suppose so, but my money's on Sir Digby at the moment,' said Mandy. 'Anyway, the aunt's having kittens and is screaming that her precious boss is a nice kind man who wouldn't hurt a fly, let alone murder one of his valued employees.'

'I know – tough exterior but a pussy-cat inside.'

'That's more or less it.'

'So what does she expect us to do about it?'

'Not us, dear, you. Anne-Marie has told Auntie about you and she wants you to track down the real killer.'

'You're kidding!'

'Cross my heart. The poor kid was in such a state I promised to pass the message on, but I told her not to hold her breath.'

'Thanks for the warning.' Sukey glanced at her bedside clock. 'It's gone eleven; I'm darned if I'm going to call her now.'

'I know, I'm sorry. I would have called earlier, but I was late leaving and Mum was getting a bit agitated.' Mandy lived in a specially adapted bungalow with her disabled mother; the old lady was surprisingly independent, but she naturally became anxious when her daughter was late home, especially after an evening shift.

'That's okay. I'll give Anne-Marie a call in the morning, but she'll have to accept there's nothing I can do.'

'No?' said Mandy slyly. 'I thought you'd jump at the chance of doing a bit of private sleuthing. Remember while we were working round the body you were having all sorts of ideas and—'

'I know, but this is a bit different. It's pretty obvious the police have got their man—'

'Ah, but have they? How about all the times when a clever amateur unmasks the real criminal at the very moment the heavy hand of PC Plod is falling on the wrong shoulder?'

'You're just winding me up!' Despite the lateness of the hour and the stresses of the day, Sukey could not help chuckling at her friend's teasing.

'Not so; you have quite a reputation for beating Eagle Eyes to the kill.'

'Okay, it has been known to happen and I've taken quite a lot of stick for stepping out of line. I'm not sure I want to make a habit of it.'

'Mustn't scupper someone's chances of being made a DCI, must we?' said Mandy mischievously. 'Well, I'll leave it with you,' she went on as Sukey ignored the taunt. 'Incidentally, what was behind Anne-Marie's earlier call? Did she have some kind of premonition?'

'No, nothing like that. She was afraid Philip Montwell was a suspect and she's got a fearful crush on him.'

'Who's he?'

'The artist who painted the picture. She works for him.' Sukey outlined the visit to the Phimont Gallery by a police officer that had sent the girl into a panic. 'I suppose the fact that I was able to reassure her on that point gave her the idea I might be able to help again.'

'Probably. Well, I'll leave you to your kip. See you tomorrow.'

'Sure. Goodnight.' Sukey put down the phone, turned off the light and snuggled down under her duvet. In the morning, she told herself, she would call Anne-Marie and tell her gently but firmly that she could not possibly accede to her aunt's request; the police enquiry would have to run its course. On the face of it, Sir Digby Kirtling had to be the prime suspect and from the startling fact of the damage to the picture it was clear that at least one other person believed in his guilt. It would be interesting to know who that person was and what had been the motive behind such a theatrical gesture. A disgruntled employee, perhaps? Despite her resolve, Sukey found her thoughts running on. Could one of the men working on the estate have been an admirer of Una May, but been ousted in her affections by her rich employer who had made her pregnant but refused to marry her? In that case, Sir Digby himself would have been the more likely victim. Or could it be that whoever had made the girl pregnant had killed her and then made a deliberate attempt to throw suspicion on him? That might sound far-fetched, but it had been known to happen. It was frustrating that she knew little or nothing about the people who had been present at the party. With luck, she would have an opportunity to get Jim to give her more details and a progress report in the near future.

As she drifted off to sleep, the thought came to her that whoever had damaged the picture must have left evidence at the scene and possibly have traces of paint on their hands or clothing. If it was one of the estate employees it would surely be a simple matter to track them down. No doubt a forensic examination would be ordered first thing in the morning. She felt a pang of disappointment that she was on the late shift, which meant that another member of the team would be given the job.

She was woken a little over eight hours later by another ring of the phone. She was tempted to bury her head under the duvet and ignore it, but the ringing persisted until, reluctantly, she lifted the receiver and muttered a sleepy 'Hullo'.

'Sukey? George Barnes here.' Sergeant George Barnes was the officer in charge of the Crime Scene Investigation department. 'Sorry to disturb you; I know you're on late turn today but I've got a problem – two people down with tummy bugs and a stack of new incidents, including another one at Muckleton Manor. Is there any chance you could do a spot of overtime? I was going to ask Mandy, but she had a heavy day yesterday and I thought, as you'd had a day off—'

Sukey suppressed a yawn and said, 'I suppose I could.' She had been looking forward to a quiet morning, but with Gus at university extra cash would always come in handy even though his father was paying his fees.

'Brilliant!' he said. 'That'll be a great help.'

'That new incident at Muckleton – you mean about the picture being slashed?'

'You heard about that?'

'Mandy told me. Can I take that one?'

'You can have it for starters if you like. There's quite a selection.'

'Yes, keep that one for me. I'll grab a bit of breakfast and be along as soon as I can.'

'Bless you. See you later.'

With a rising sense of excitement, Sukey jumped out of bed, had a hasty wash, hurried into her working clothes, swallowed a glass of fruit juice and a dish of muesli and was at the station a little before nine o'clock. The CSI office was empty except for George Barnes, who greeted her with evident relief.

'It's been like a madhouse this morning,' he grumbled. He handed her a sheaf of printouts. 'That's to be going on with. In no particular order,' he added gloomily. 'They all think they should have top priority.'

She was leafing through the printed sheets as he spoke. As she extracted the one referring to Muckleton Manor and put it at the top she noticed him looking at her with an eyebrow raised.

'Why so keen to take that one?' he asked.

'Put it down to an interest in acts of vandalism against works of art,' she said. It was the first thing she could think of, but she sensed as she spoke that it sounded unconvincing, an impression that was confirmed by his next question.

'It wouldn't have anything to do with a certain young woman who's been making frantic efforts to get in touch with you, by any chance?'

'Oh, her.' Of course, he would know about that; he would have been the one to take Anne-Marie's calls before passing on her messages via Mandy. She made an effort to sound casual. 'She's got a bee in her bonnet about something else. Mandy gave me her number; I'll call her when I've got a moment.' She could tell by his expression that he suspected her of holding something back, but she forestalled further probing by picking up her bag and saying, 'Right, Sarge, I'm on my way,' and leaving.

It was a fine, mild day. The rush hour was over and the roads out of the city were comparatively quiet, which made the half-hour drive through the countryside to Muckleton Manor a sheer delight. The sky had cleared after overnight rain and the Cotswold Hills, their woods and hedgerows a tapestry of the variegated hues of autumn, glowed and sparkled under the October sunshine. In Muckleton village she spotted a small group of women with bags of shopping standing deep in conversation outside the post office. Sukey guessed as she drove past that they were discussing Sir Digby's arrest and the damage to the picture; in her experience, news of such momentous events in a small village would travel faster than a bush fire.

The officer on guard at the manor gates waved her through; she drove slowly up to the house, parked her van and put on her protective clothing before walking up to the front door. Two other officers, one of them her friend PC Trudy Marshall, were standing on the steps drinking coffee from painted china mugs that she guessed had been brought to them by someone inside the house. She barely had time to greet them when the front door flew open and Anne-Marie appeared. She rushed at Sukey and grabbed her by the arm.

'Oh, Mrs Reynolds, thank God you're here! It's so good of you to come.'

'Now just a minute.' Gently but firmly Sukey detached herself from the clinging hands. 'I got your message, but I can't talk to you now, I'm on duty. Someone has committed criminal damage and I'm here to help with the investigation.'

'But this is important!' The girl's eyes were pink and swollen, her face streaked with tears. 'Auntie M is in a terrible state . . . you must talk to her, help her . . . please!'

'Maybe later,' said Sukey impatiently.

Trudy stepped forward and put a gentle hand on the girl's shoulder. 'Just go back indoors and stay with your aunt, love,' she said. 'When Mrs Reynolds has finished examining the scene I'm sure she'll find time for a quick word with her. And thank you very much for the coffee,' she added, holding out the two empty mugs. Anne-Marie took them blindly, shot a reproachful glance at Sukey and disappeared indoors. Trudy turned back to Sukey. 'What was all that about?' she asked.

Once again, Sukey felt herself being scrutinized by curious eyes. 'It's a bit embarrassing, really,' she said. 'She – Anne-Marie – is a friend of my son Fergus and we met up with her yesterday in Cheltenham. He happened to mention that I work for the police and she and her aunt seem to have got it into their heads that I have some sort of influence over the investigation. They're convinced Sir Digby couldn't possibly be a murderer; I think the idea is that I intercede on his behalf. Ridiculous, of course, but—'

She was being economical with the truth, but she had no intention of revealing the actual state of affairs to Trudy at this stage, especially within the hearing of another officer whom she knew only by sight. Later on, there might come a moment when she would need to enlist her friend's help. It wouldn't be the first time. She experienced a flurry of goose pimples at the thought and a feeling – partly uneasy, partly exhilarating – that she was hooked.

'Well, I suppose I'd better get on with it,' she said. 'Who's in charge?'

'DS Hill. He's interviewing witnesses in Sir Digby's study.' Trudy pointed at a door towards the back of the hall. 'He knows you're here and he says you're to go right in.'

'Thanks.'

Sukey had been half expecting a sumptuously furnished room, but although everything was of the highest quality it was all strictly functional: a desk, filing cabinets, bookshelves, a computer and a telephone. DS Hill was seated at the desk with a young plain-clothes officer whom Sukey did not recognize.

'Hi Sukey,' he said.

'Hi Tony. Congratulations on the promotion. Do I have to call you Sarge now?'

'Only in the presence of royalty,' he replied. 'I don't think you've met DC Burgess. Jane, meet Sukey, our top CSI. She occasionally does a bit of off-the-record sleuthing for us when we get stuck on a case,' he added with a grin.

The two women exchanged friendly nods. 'Exactly what happened?' asked Sukey.

'DS Page was interviewing Sir Digby yesterday evening in the small sitting room at the front of the house when they heard screaming from a room the other side of the hall,' said Hill. 'They went to investigate and found the housekeeper, Mrs Keene, having hysterics in front of the picture. You wait till you see it – someone has made a right mess of it.'

'I gather she's still in a bit of a state.'

'To put it mildly. She admits that she has had what she called "a long-standing relationship" with Sir Digby and also, after a little gentle probing, that her boss has a reputation as a flirt, but insists it's just that, he's always been faithful to her and the notion that he might have killed Una May was monstrous. He "didn't have a violent bone in his body" – her

63

words. She can't imagine who might have thought such a thing and is outraged by the attack on the picture.'

'All fairly predictable,' Sukey commented. 'What was she doing in that room, I wonder.'

'She spotted some faint red marks on the floor and went to take a closer look. Then she noticed the paint smears on the door and went in to investigate.'

'Any obvious suspects?'

'It has to be someone who has a particular reason for hating Sir Digby and the obvious explanation is that it was on account of Una May.'

'You're thinking of a man who was in love with her and knew – or thought he knew – that her boss had "done her wrong", as the saying goes?'

'Right. So far we've spoken to Arnie Ashford, the under-gardener who found the body, and Dick Andrews, the head gardener's son, who was also at the party. They haven't been particularly forthcoming; neither will admit to having any particular feeling for the victim although they both describe her as "a very nice lady".'

'Do you think they're telling the truth?'

Hill shrugged. 'I can't be sure at this stage. We reckon whoever did it must have picked up traces of paint on themselves or their clothing, but of course they've had plenty of time to clean up. Either of them could have entered the house during the daytime, but both of them strenuously deny doing so. By the way, when asked to write down the word 'murderer' they both got it right. You'll understand when you see the picture,' he added in response to her puzzled expression.

'If you say so,' she replied. 'Well, I'd better have a look round and see if I can find anything useful. I'll see you later.'

Ten

The police had sealed off an area in the hall around the entrance to the room containing the damaged picture. Sukey ducked under the tape and began her task with an examination of the tiled floor. There were several traces of what looked like red paint, which at a guess had been carried on the culprit's shoes as they left the room. Sukey made careful notes of the position of the marks before photographing them, then pushed open the door and entered the room.

She had been told what to expect, but even so it came as a shock. There was something vicious about the way the knife had been plunged into the canvas, slashing the face and upper body of the principal figure in half and travelling downwards with such force that the blade had made a deep cut in the frame. The red paint trickling from the single misspelled word 'Merderer' daubed across the mutilated features was like blood flowing from a wound. There could, she thought, be no doubt that whoever carried out the attack had been motivated by an overwhelming sense of rage and hatred. Yet neither of the two men DC Hill had interviewed so far had betrayed any such emotion. Either they were all, as they claimed, innocent, or one of them was a good enough actor to deceive the detective, despite his specialized training.

She was familiar with the original version of the painting, since a reproduction of it had hung for many years in the sitting room of her parents' house. After the death of her widowed father she had wanted to keep it, but Paul, her then husband, had sneered at it and refused to have it in the house. She had, for the sake of marital harmony, given in to him in this as in so many other cases where their tastes had differed. Then, after eleven years of marriage, he had abandoned her and their ten-year-old son for the rich and beautiful Myrna.

There had been moments when she had all but given way to anger, bitterness and frustration, and she experienced a certain empathy with whoever had felt driven to attack the painted figure.

Pushing such thoughts to the back of her mind, she continued her examination of the scene. It was obvious that the culprit had taken no trouble to cover his tracks, suggesting that he – her instinct told her it was a man – had been so consumed with fury that he was conscious of nothing but a desire to vent his feelings on a representation of someone he hated, like a practitioner of voodoo sticking pins in a doll. She imagined him plunging the brush into the paint and applying it with a furious energy, heedless of the splashes landing on the carpet. He would surely have paint on his clothes and also on his hands, judging from the smears on both sides of the door. The indications were that he had entered the room from the hall, closed the door behind him while carrying out the attack, and then for some reason taken the trouble to close it behind him on leaving.

The marks on the floor showed clearly that more than one person had trodden in the spilt paint and carried it on their shoes for several strides before the traces petered out. Most of them led straight across the hall and had probably been made by Miranda Keene, Sir Digby and DC Page at the time the damage had been discovered, but one or two others – doubtless the ones that had caught Miranda's attention – led towards the rear of the hall, and were wider apart than the others. They were also slightly smudged, suggesting that whoever left them – almost certainly the culprit – had been in a hurry.

It was possible that an outsider had somehow managed to enter the grounds from outside and slip unobserved into the house, perhaps through an open window or unlocked door, but it seemed more likely that it was a member of the household or one of the estate staff. No doubt the police would have questioned them all about their movements. Sukey found herself wondering whether it had been possible to establish the time when the attack had taken place. Not, she reminded herself, that this was any concern of hers. She was here to gather evidence, not to try and solve the case.

She took samples of the paint and dusted the paint-smeared surfaces for fingerprints. Miranda Keene would probably have left some of them when she entered the room, which meant that she would need to get samples from her for elimination. She was not looking forward to the encounter; no doubt the housekeeper would seize the opportunity to plead for help in clearing her lover of suspicion, but there was no way round it – unless she could persuade Tony Hill to assign the task to Jane Burgess, which was unlikely.

She bagged up her samples and went out into the hall at the same moment as Anne-Marie and a woman whom she guessed was Miranda Keene were leaving Sir Digby's study. She must have been undergoing a further interview with DS Hill and insisted on her niece being present. The girl whispered something to her aunt, who took a step towards Sukey and reached out a hand in a mute gesture of appeal. Her short dark hair, although expertly cut, showed signs of disarray, as if nervous fingers had been repeatedly dragged through it; her face was pale and drawn and there were dark smudges under her eyes that hinted at a lack of sleep.

Without giving either of them a chance to speak, Sukey said briskly, 'Mrs Keene? I'm a Crime Scene Investigator and I've found certain fingerprints in that room, some of which were probably left by the person who damaged the painting, but some may have been left by other people, including you. Would you mind if I took your prints so that we can eliminate them?'

The woman nodded. 'Of course. Perhaps you'd like to come into the kitchen. This way, please.' With Anne-Marie at her side, she led the way through the hall towards the back of the house.

Sukey had been half expecting a traditional, possibly Victorian-style kitchen, but instead found herself in something straight out of a modern showroom, with gleaming surfaces and equipment and fittings of the very latest design. Here, perhaps, it was Miranda Keene rather than Athena Letchworth who had had the last word. She recalled something Jim had said about the woman to whom Sir Digby had entrusted the interior decoration and furnishing of the house. He had described her as 'a very sexy lady' and hinted that it had been suggested by one of the witnesses that Sir Digby had been 'rather smitten' by her charms.

Miranda Keene sat quietly while Sukey took her fingerprints, but the minute the process was finished she said, 'Mrs Reynolds, you know what has happened, don't you? Sir Digby has been arrested for murdering Una May and I know, I just know, he didn't do it.' Her voice rose a pitch and became tremulous as she went on, 'Those detectives won't listen to me; all they do is keep asking me questions. I won't tell them anything; they'll only twist it round to make things worse for him. I know you're not a detective – not officially at least – but Anne-Marie has told me you're good at detective work. Will you please, *please* help me to prove Digby's innocence?' On the last words she flung out her hands in a theatrical gesture of supplication.

Sukey listened with growing astonishment. 'Who says I'm good at detective work?' she asked, but even as she spoke the probable answer came into her head and was confirmed by Anne-Marie's next remark.

'Fergus told me,' she said, 'he's awfully proud of you; he thinks you should be in the CID.'

'Oh, does he?' Sukey made a mental note to reprimand her son at the earliest opportunity. Yet at the same time she was curious to know how Miranda Keene could be so certain of Kirtling's innocence. A dozen questions came flocking into her head, but time was passing and she had other incidents to attend.

'Look,' she said, 'I really can't stay to talk now, but we could have a chat some other time if you really want to.'

Something of the weariness drained from Miranda's face as she replied, 'Oh yes, please. How about this evening?'

'I'm afraid not; I'm working until late. Why don't you give me your phone number and I'll call you when I have a moment, maybe tomorrow or Sunday?'

With luck, she told herself as she headed for her next assignment, she would see Jim tomorrow and have an opportunity to pump him about the progress of the enquiry. She'd have to be very diplomatic, of course. Any suggestion that she was taking too keen an interest in the case would be sure to arouse suspicion and possibly cause friction.

*   *   *

He called her from home early on Saturday morning. 'How's it going?' she asked.

'Not particularly well.' His voice sounded flat and a little weary. 'I gather you were sent to check on the latest incident at Muckleton Manor, and of course you know we arrested Kirtling on Thursday evening?'

'Yes. Has he confessed yet?'

'Are you kidding? He's turning out to be one of the most stubborn suspects we've had to deal with in a long time. Dalia has tried every trick in the book, but he's sticking to his story.'

'Which is?'

'I haven't time to go into details now, but it amounts to total denial. We managed late yesterday to get our hands on the shoes he was wearing on the day of the murder and we're going to try and get them examined this morning for traces of glass; meanwhile we've got permission to detain him for a further thirty-six hours.'

'So I won't be seeing you over the weekend?'

'It doesn't look like it, I'm afraid, but I'll be in touch. Love you. Bye.'

Oh well, Sukey said to herself as she put down the phone, if she was going to have the weekend on her own she might as well find out what Sir Digby Kirtling's housekeeper had to say. It would at least be something to do; she might even learn something helpful to the enquiry.

Miranda Keene was pathetically grateful for Sukey's phone call.

'I managed to get a little sleep last night for the first time since Digby's arrest, thanks to you,' she said. 'Where can we talk? I could come to your house—'

'No, I don't think that's a good idea,' Sukey said hastily. The possibility, however remote, of Jim turning up unexpectedly was enough to make any such arrangement unwise.

'Would you like to come here? Say for coffee at about half past ten?'

Sukey hesitated. 'But aren't the police still at the manor? I wouldn't want them to know I was there.'

'Oh!' Miranda sounded faintly surprised. 'Well, there's a guard on the gate, that's all.'

'There's a good chance I'd be recognized. Is there a pub in the village?'

'Yes, but there might be someone there who knows me. I wouldn't want other people listening.'

'So what do you suggest?'

There was a short silence before Miranda said, 'There's a track leading into a wood that backs on to our . . . that is, Digby's land. The boundary wall is quite low in places and I don't think you'd have any difficulty in climbing over it. If you walk up through the garden to the back door of the house, I'll keep a lookout from the kitchen window.'

'All right. How do I find this track?'

'It's quite easy.' She gave directions and Sukey jotted them down. She set out with some misgivings, torn between curiosity and the risk of incurring Jim's disapproval if he should find out what she was doing.

She found the track into the woods without difficulty. It was evidently in regular use by vehicles and horses as there were wheel and hoof marks in the uneven ground. About fifty yards along, she pulled up at a point where the track widened to form a rough area of hard standing, locked her car and made her way through the trees. She found the wall Miranda had referred to and stood leaning on it for a few minutes to admire the view.

The morning sun shone full on the impressive red brick façade and tiled roof of the manor. It stood at the top of a gentle rise overlooking a sweep of lawns, paths and flowerbeds that had obviously been planned and laid out by experts. An avenue of small ornamental trees led down to a lake with a stone fountain of leaping dolphins in the middle. A pair of rabbits nibbled the grass near the water's edge and a gentle breeze rustled the trees above her head. It was difficult to reconcile the tranquillity of the scene with the violence that had so recently taken place there.

After a few minutes' examination of the wall she found a place where, with the help of a convenient log, she was able to scramble over. It crossed her mind that anyone could obtain access to the grounds in the same way and no doubt the entire boundary had been checked during the police search. The woodland continued for a few yards on the other side of the wall and as she made her way through the trees she caught the scent of wood smoke. A few paces further on she came face to face with an elderly man in working clothes. He was tending a bonfire, using a heavy garden fork to feed it from a wheelbarrow laden with garden refuse.

As soon as he caught sight of her he stopped what he was doing. His features were ruddy and weather-beaten, with bright blue eyes beneath grizzled brows. Her immediate impression was of a typical countryman's face, but without the average countryman's good-humoured expression.

'Who are you? What are you doing here?' he demanded.

'I'm here to see Mrs Keene, Sir Digby's housekeeper,' Sukey explained, a little taken aback by his aggressive manner.

He gave a grunt that clearly indicated disbelief. 'Sneaking in through the back way instead of coming to the front door like an honest citizen? A likely story.'

'I assure you it's true. We ... that is, I ... didn't want anyone to see me.'

She realized as soon as the words were out that it had been the wrong thing to say. He took another step towards her, shifting his grip on the fork and waving it menacingly in her direction. 'Of course you didn't! You're up to no good, that's why. You're from the papers, come to spread your dirt and lies!'

'I assure you, I'm nothing to do with the press, this is just a friendly visit that we—' She was about to say, 'don't want the police to know about,' but thought better of it. At that moment, her eye fell on the hand gripping the handle of the fork. It was callused and grimy, as was to be expected in someone who worked on the land. What drew her attention was not the ingrained dirt but the traces of what looked like red paint embedded under the broken nails. She stood transfixed for a moment, staring with her mouth open at the tell-tale marks. His eyes followed her gaze before lifting to look her straight in the face. His expression was murderous; she had no doubt he had read her thoughts and she backed away in alarm.

'You meddling bitch!' he yelled. 'I'll teach you to come poking your nose in round here!'

71

Pointing the fork straight at her like a jousting knight with a lance, he lowered his head and charged. This was no time for rational discussion; Sukey turned and fled.

Eleven

Being young and fit Sukey outran the old man without difficulty, but she made sure of being well out in the open and in sight of the house before she dared to glance back. There was no sign of him; evidently he had given up the unequal chase and returned to his bonfire. She slowed to a walk, conscious of a shakiness in her legs that had nothing to do with the exertion. As she climbed the flight of stone steps leading to the terrace, Miranda Keene appeared round the corner of the house and beckoned.

'Whatever happened?' she said. 'I was watching from the window and saw you running like a hare with Arthur hobbling after you brandishing a garden fork.'

'I'll tell you in a minute, when I've got my breath back,' said Sukey.

'Come in and have some coffee; it's all ready.' The housekeeper led the way through a door at the side of the house and into the bright, sunny kitchen, where coffee and biscuits were already laid out on a table in an alcove with a window overlooking the garden. She listened open-mouthed as Sukey described her encounter with the gardener.

'But this is amazing!' she exclaimed. 'Are you saying you think it was Arthur who damaged the picture? But why on earth would he do that? What has Digby ever done to him? He's a good employer, his staff respect him, he—' Already she was on the verge of tears, but she made a valiant effort to control them. 'This is like a dreadful nightmare; I can't believe it of Arthur; there must be some mistake.'

'Mrs Keene,' Sukey began and was immediately interrupted.

'Please, call me Miranda.'

'Thank you, Miranda; I'm Sukey. It's possible that the red paint under Arthur's nails got there when he was doing

73

something else, something completely innocent, although from the way he reacted when he realized I'd spotted it I think that's unlikely. Just the same, I think the police should know about it. If he did damage the picture he as good as accused Sir Digby of murdering Una May and they will want to know why.'

'But Digby didn't do it!' Miranda pleaded. This time the tears ran unchecked down her pale cheeks. 'He's as anxious for the murder to be solved as anyone. He swore to me he knew nothing about it and I believe him. I thought you believed it too, otherwise why are you here?'

'I came because I want to know why you're so sure of his innocence,' Sukey replied, 'but before we begin I have to make it clear that I can't answer any questions about the police investigation. I'd like to help you if I can, but you have to be honest with me. You hinted on the phone that there were things you wouldn't tell the police – are you prepared to confide in me?'

Miranda did not reply immediately. She dried her eyes and began drinking her coffee. She drank slowly; when she had emptied her cup she carefully replaced it on its saucer and said, 'If I tell you everything, you must swear not to repeat it to the police.'

Sukey shook her head. 'I can't do that, not if you tell me something that might incriminate him.'

'It won't do that, but I'd like you to understand why so many people think he's guilty.'

'So many people? Who, for example?'

'Well, whoever slashed the picture obviously does. And the other people working here . . . Arthur's son and daughter, for example, and Arnie who found Una's body . . . and I know the people in the village do from the way they look at me and change the subject if I walk into the shop while they're talking.'

'Why do they think he did it?'

Miranda's colour rose slightly. 'He's . . . well, he does have a bit of a reputation as . . . as a ladies' man,' she admitted after a moment's hesitation. 'Maybe they think he was . . . well, carrying on as they say . . . with Una and that she was becoming a nuisance and he wanted to get rid of her.'

'And was he? Carrying on with her, I mean?'

'He told me he'd had a one-night stand with her, but that was all. He had these flings from time to time,' she went on defensively in response to Sukey's raised eyebrows, 'it was just the way he was, but he tired of them very quickly and he always came back to me.'

'Do the village folk know about you and him?'

'Oh no,' Miranda said earnestly, 'we've always been very discreet.' She appeared quite shocked at the question.

From what she knew of village life, Sukey was pretty sure she was deluding herself, but all she said was, 'Look, if you are right and Sir Digby didn't kill Una May, it's obvious that someone else did. Have you any idea who it might be? Do you know whose baby she was carrying?'

Miranda gave a horrified gasp and put her hands to her face. 'So they know about the baby,' she whispered.

'Yes. Strictly speaking, I shouldn't have mentioned it, but it obviously isn't news to you. I take it you haven't admitted that to the police?'

'No, I didn't dare, I thought it would look so bad for him.'

'So it was his baby?'

'He thinks it might have been.'

'Surely you both realize that it's only a matter of time before the police will be able to confirm paternity from a DNA test?'

'He . . . we didn't think. As soon as he saw her he said it was obvious she'd been strangled and we just hoped and prayed the pregnancy wouldn't come out. Anyway, she was trying to put pressure on him to marry her; he refused and they had a terrible row.'

'When was this?'

'The day of the party, after the unveiling of the picture. She followed him into the shrubbery, where her body was found, and told him about the baby. He says he didn't believe her at first and then when she insisted it was true and that it was definitely his, he told her to get rid of it. He says she was beside herself and wouldn't listen to reason. She swore she'd let everyone know what a bounder he was; she even crushed the glass she was holding in her temper.'

'If she was making such a scene, how come nobody heard them arguing?'

75

'The shrubbery's quite a distance from the house and the rest of the party had gone the other way to admire the gardens. In any case, he said she wasn't screaming or shouting, just sort of spitting out words at him. He said she was using some pretty strong language too.'

'That doesn't match the impression other people seem to have of her.'

'Oh no, she was the perfect little lady, wasn't she?' Miranda's lip curled. 'She had a tough side as well – I've heard her on the phone a few times to contractors or suppliers when she thought they weren't giving proper service.'

'Do you know if she had any other lovers?'

'*Other* lovers!' Miranda seemed outraged at the implication. 'Digby wasn't *her* lover, he was mine, has been for years. He never really cared for her; he swore the night he spent with her was just a one-off.'

'Forgive me for saying this,' said Sukey, 'but to have what you call a fling with a woman and then tell her to abort the resulting baby isn't exactly my notion of a kind, caring man who wouldn't hurt a fly.'

'Digby *is* kind and caring, but he admits he lost his temper for a moment because he felt cornered. He's convinced Una had deliberately led him on because she wanted to be Lady Kirtling. As for the abortion, he says he apologized immediately for what he had said and offered to support the child and keep her job open while she had it, but she said if he wouldn't marry her she certainly didn't want to be "saddled with his brat", as she put it. So he said if that was how she felt he'd pay for an abortion, but he wouldn't marry her and that was that. Naturally, he didn't want the story to go round the village and it might have upset some of the shareholders if the press got hold of it, but it wasn't as if he was a politician whose career might have been damaged by the scandal.'

'So he told her to publish and be damned,' said Sukey.

'You could put it like that – yes.'

There was a silence while Sukey considered the ramifications of what she had just learned while Miranda waited patiently, never letting her eyes stray from her face. At last Sukey said, 'I asked you a few minutes ago if you had any idea who might have killed Una May, but you didn't reply.

If it wasn't Sir Digby, then obviously it was someone else, and that someone must have a motive – a rejected lover, for example. Do you know if she'd been seeing anyone else?'

Miranda made a helpless gesture with her hands. 'I don't know anything about her private life; all I know is everyone round here thinks she's lovely.'

'But you've never really liked her, have you?'

'Not really, but I tried not to show it.'

'This may sound a bit cheeky, but I have to ask it. Were you jealous of her?'

'Of course I was; it's only natural, isn't it, when you know your man has been playing around with another woman. But not enough to kill her, if that's what you're implying.'

'And you really have no idea who else might have done it?'

'None whatsoever. That's why I'm begging you to help us.'

'I'll think about it, but at the moment I really don't see what I can do. Tell me more about Arthur, by the way. How long has he worked for Sir Digby? Was he at the party?'

'He came to work here soon after Digby bought the property and had the gardens laid out. He wasn't at the party, but his son and daughter were because they're both in the picture. Tricia works here as a cleaner and Dick is a general handyman.'

'I see. Do you happen to know which of the figures in the painting Tricia and Dick sat for?'

'Oh yes; Dick is the young man in the straw hat and Tricia is the girl with the little dog sitting opposite him.'

'Ah yes; I remember thinking when I came to examine the damage that there was a certain likeness between them. Tricia must be a very pretty girl.'

Miranda shrugged. 'Yes, I suppose so,' she said, as if the thought had not occurred to her.

Sukey was a little surprised at the offhand response, but she let it pass. She stood up and said, 'I have to go now; thank you for the coffee. Would you mind walking down the garden with me? If Arthur's still there he might attack me again.'

'Certainly.' As they made their way down the garden, Miranda said hesitantly, 'Is there any way I can get in touch with you? Anne-Marie says your number's ex-directory and Fergus won't give it to her.'

'Fergus is quite right.'

'Will you give it to me? I promise not to pass it on to anyone, not even Digby. You've been such a comfort and if I felt I could have a chat with you if things get worse—'

Sukey hesitated, touched by the pleading expression on Miranda's pale face. 'I prefer not to give people my home number,' she said after a moment. 'Still, you could get me on my mobile.' She handed over one of her business cards. 'I may not be able to talk if I'm out on a job, but you can always leave a message and I'll call you back.'

'Thank you very much. And thank you again for coming to see me.'

The bonfire was still smouldering, but there was no sign of the gardener. 'You might take the opportunity of looking at his hands when you have a chance,' Sukey suggested, 'although as I'm pretty sure he noticed me looking at them he's probably cleaned the paint off by now.'

'I'll do that. Are you going to tell the police what you saw?'

'I'd rather you did it. I don't want them to know I've been here, remember?'

'I'm not sure Digby would want me to, but I'll think about it. The important thing is to clear Digby of a charge of murder. You will help us, won't you?'

'Like I said, I can't see there's much I can do. Anyway, he hasn't been charged yet, so don't give up hope.'

Twelve

On her way home, Sukey turned over in her mind everything she had learned about Kirtling's affair with the dead woman. Or rather, she mentally corrected herself as she waited at traffic lights in Cirencester, as much as Kirtling himself had thought fit to tell his long-term lover. Miranda had admitted to her that he was probably the father of Una May's unborn child, yet from her brief conversation with Jim that morning it appeared that he was stubbornly denying all knowledge of the pregnancy. She found it hard to believe that the pair had naïvely hoped for it to remain undetected but, on reflection, recognized that few members of the public were familiar with the procedure at a post-mortem.

Her first impression of Miranda Keene had been of a gentle, loving woman, so devoted to her man that, confident in the knowledge that he would quickly tire of his latest conquest and return to her, she was prepared to overlook his occasional 'flings'. Now she was beginning to question that impression. During their conversation, Miranda had betrayed more than a hint of hostility towards Una May and admitted when questioned that she did not like her. She had made a contemptuous reference to 'the perfect little lady' whose winsome manner concealed a hard, calculating streak. Could this be a case of the pot calling the kettle black?

Then there was the dismissive way she had brushed aside Sukey's comment about the attractiveness of the gardener's daughter. Did she suspect that Kirtling had been having – or possibly contemplating – a 'fling' with her as well? Did Tricia's father share those suspicions, or had he possibly observed something that confirmed them? If so, it could account for his frenzied attack on the painting.

In spite of Miranda's protestations, everything seemed to

79

point to her lover's guilt. On his own admission, he had had an encounter with the dead woman in the place where her body was found, and unless enquiries revealed other aspects of her life that pointed a finger elsewhere, he was the one with the strongest motive for wanting her out of the way. 'Sorry, Miranda,' she said aloud as she pulled up on her drive and switched off her engine. 'I'm afraid you'll just have to accept that your boyfriend did it. Unless, of course, it was you – but if that were the case you'd hardly be asking me to help clear him.'

She had been indoors for only a few minutes when Jim rang. 'Is there any chance you could feed a weary detective?' he asked.

'I'm just about to get my own lunch as it happens. It's only soup and cheese, but you're more than welcome to share it.'

'That'll be perfect.'

He was at the door within fifteen minutes. He gave her a quick hug and a kiss before following her into the kitchen and sinking onto a chair with a deep sigh.

'We've had to let him go,' he said.

'So there's no glass in the shoes?'

'Oh yes, we found a couple of splinters embedded in the soles – which had been thoroughly cleaned, by the way, so there were no visible traces of earth from the shrubbery or anywhere else.'

'Where were they?'

'At his London flat. He has a woman come in two or three times a week to clean the place, do his laundry and so on. Cleaning his shoes is one of her regular tasks and she's quite definite he gave her no special instruction about cleaning that particular pair. He'd left them with the rest of the clothes he wore to the shindig at the manor and she just cleaned them as a matter of course. She didn't recall seeing any earth on them.'

'Do the splinters match the fragments Mandy and I picked up at the murder scene?'

'There hasn't been time for the lab to examine them, but we didn't tell him that and in the event we didn't have to. As soon as we told him about the glass he changed his story. Up till then, all he would admit to was having a weakness for

80

pretty women and enjoying what he describes as "a bit of harmless dallying" from time to time. He then, under a bit more gentle probing, admitted that he "*might* have gone a bit far" in his dalliance with Una May that "*might*" have led the silly girl to think he was more serious than he intended.'

'He denies making her pregnant then?'

Jim raised an eyebrow. 'How did you know that? The news came through on your day off and we haven't told the press yet.'

'Mandy told me. We CSIs do take an interest in the progress of our cases, you know.'

'Yes, I've noticed,' he said dryly. He was, of course, making an oblique reference to certain previous cases where she had gone out searching for, and picking up, leads that he and his team had missed. She hoped he would not enquire how she had spent her morning.

'So what line did he take to start with?' she prompted as he took long, appreciative draughts from the glass of beer she handed to him.

'On the day of the party he noticed she'd been hitting the champagne rather hard and he was afraid she was going to make a scene in front of the others, so after the unveiling he escaped into the grounds with the idea of hiding from her until she'd had time to sober up. He claimed she followed him and started making up to him, trying to get him to admit that he loved her and wanted to marry her. He said he explained as gently as possible that there was nothing doing and hinted that if she continued to pester him she could find herself looking for another job. He said she got a bit shirty then and called him a few choice names, but he denied so much as laying a finger on her. He expressed outrage when we put it to him that he might be the father of the child she was carrying, denied even knowing she was pregnant. When he was told DNA tests were being carried out on the foetus he merely added to his long list of "no comments".'

Sukey had been listening carefully while stirring the pan of soup she was heating on the stove. Everything Jim had told her so far tied in with what Miranda Keene had said. It seemed clear that she and Kirtling, having realized that he might fall under suspicion, had agreed on what line they would take in

81

the event of his arrest: he would admit so much and no more while she would profess to know nothing.

'Anyway,' Jim went on, 'we're still pretty sure he was lying and so, it now appears, are at least two other people.'

'Two?' Sukey paused in the act of putting bread from the freezer into the microwave. 'Who else besides the person who slashed the painting?'

'Una May's sister Clara is convinced Kirtling's our man. She says she spent a few days with Una before going on holiday a week ago and she told her how much attention her boss was paying her. She even hinted that she was living in hopes of becoming Lady Kirtling.'

'Did she tell her sister about the baby?'

'Apparently not, but when we told her the result of the post-mortem her immediate reaction was that Kirtling must be the father but he wasn't prepared to marry her sister so killed her to avoid a scandal. She says she warned Una that he was probably just amusing himself with her and it seems they had a few words as a result. They didn't part on very good terms and ten days later she hears her sister is dead.'

'She must be heartbroken,' Sukey said sadly. 'Anyway, you said he changed his story when confronted with the evidence of the glass in his shoes.'

'Yes he did, but only marginally. He blustered a bit and then admitted that the conversation with Una May in the shrubbery got more heated than he'd told us earlier. He said she accused him of making her pregnant, which he strenu-ously denied, and then she lost her temper and broke the glass she was holding, but he still insists she was alive when he left her.'

'How about the DNA test on the foetus?'

'We've asked for it to be fast-tracked, but there was no way it would have come through before the extension expired. If it gives a match with Kirtling then obviously it will prove he's still not told us the whole truth and we can rearrest him.'

'What about the attack on the picture? Any progress there?'

'None of the prints you lifted give a match with any we took earlier.'

'Oh dear!' She pretended to sound dismayed. 'It's begin-ning to look as if you'll need my detective skills before long.'

He made a grab at her. 'Don't even think about it.'

'No? So what am I supposed to think about?'

'I'll tell you after we've eaten.'

It was nearly half-past four when Sukey woke. Jim was still sleeping soundly beside her; she snuggled up to him and put an arm round him, pressing her own naked body against his. He stirred, found her hand and squeezed it, then turned over and kissed her on the mouth.

'Happy, love?' he whispered.

'Ecstatically.'

For a while they lay still, drowsily content. Then she said reluctantly, 'I have to go to the bathroom.' She got out of bed and reached for her dressing gown. 'I think I'll have a quick shower before I get dressed.'

'Right,' he said, 'I'll go down and put the kettle on.'

He returned with two mugs of tea on a tray just as she emerged from the bathroom, mopping her damp hair with a towel. He had put on trousers but was naked to the waist and the sight of his tanned, muscular torso sent after-shocks of desire rippling through her. To her surprise, he did not return her smile, but pointedly looked down at the tray. Lying beside the mugs was her mobile phone.

'What's that doing?' she asked.

'It rang while I was making the tea. You were in the shower so I thought I'd better answer it in case it was urgent.' Something in his manner made her uneasy, but before she had a chance to speak he said, 'It was a woman; she sounded a bit taken aback when I answered, said she expected Mrs Reynolds and I said she had the right number but you were unavailable and could I take a message. She said to say Miranda called.'

'Is that all?'

'That's all. I brought the phone up in case you wanted to call her back.'

'There was no need,' she said, making her tone deliberately casual. 'I might give her a bell later, but I'll use the land line.' He knew she would do that, of course; bringing the phone had just been a ploy. It was the kind of trick his experience of dealing with suspects had taught him, something to give her a momentary jolt so that he could observe her reaction. He waited, his green eyes boring into hers. The atmosphere between them was charged with tension of a very different nature from the electricity that had made their recent passionate coupling so perfect. This was a rerun of previous moments when they had clashed over her involvement – or suspected involvement – with something in which, in his view, she had no business to be meddling.

'It wouldn't be Miranda Keene by any chance?' he prompted, as she remained silent.

She met his gaze defiantly. 'What if it was?'

'If it's anything to do with the Muckleton Manor case, it's your duty to tell me.'

'Are you suggesting I'm withholding information?' She tried to make her tone sound jocular, but it failed to draw a smile from him.

'It wouldn't be the first time,' he said.

'All right, if you must know, she tried to nobble me when I was at the manor yesterday. She was in a pretty distressed state and I felt sorry for her. I couldn't talk to her then, so I gave her my card and said she could ring me on the mobile if she wanted a chat.'

'What was she distressed about?'

'I imagine it was because Kirtling had been arrested. Her niece Anne-Marie was with her and, as you know, she told me about her aunt's affair with him. The two are pretty close.'

'So why would she want to talk to you?'

'I'll find out when I call her back, won't I? And in case you're wondering, that won't be while you're here breathing down my neck,' she added snappily.

In a sudden change of mood he took her mug of tea from her hands, put it on the tray and pulled her close. 'I'm sorry, love,' he said with genuine contrition. 'I know I get a bit heavy-handed at times, but I have these nightmares about you getting into a really serious scrape. You have to admit you've had some narrow squeaks in the past.'

'Maybe I wouldn't have had them if you'd listened to me earlier,' she retorted, pushing him away. 'Anyway, I can't see what harm there is in talking to Kirtling's housekeeper. She's not a suspect, for goodness' sake.'

'True, but her boyfriend is, and we've had to let him go for lack of evidence. For all we know he's told her a lot more about his relationship with the dead woman than he's admitted to us. In which case, if he finds out that she's been talking to you, he might see you as a threat.'

'Oh, do me a favour!' She reached past him for her tea, but he caught hold of her wrist.

'I've said I'm sorry,' he repeated, almost humbly. 'Can't we just forget it?'

'All right, as long as you promise to stop trying to keep me under surveillance all the time.'

'I promise.'

This time she yielded to his embrace and returned his kiss. The incident was not referred to again, yet they both sensed that some of the magic had gone out of the day.

Thirteen

After they were both showered and dressed, Jim said, 'Do you fancy a movie? The one at the Odeon this week is supposed to be very good. We could have an early meal first at that Italian restaurant we went to the other evening.'

Sukey hesitated. Normally she would have welcomed the prospect of a Saturday night out, but this evening it lacked appeal. 'To be honest, I don't really feel like doing anything special,' she said. 'It's been a hard week and I'm pretty tired. I'd be quite happy with a takeaway and then maybe watch something on the telly.'

'Anything you say,' he replied, 'and I won't stay late if you want to get an early night.' It was exactly what she did want, yet in some perverse way she felt vaguely irritated by his readiness to please her. Although the rest of the evening passed pleasantly enough, nothing was said about plans for the following day and she was conscious of a sense of relief when he left.

She had taken the precaution of switching off her mobile in case Miranda decided to call again. As soon as the door closed behind Jim she switched it on and found two messages. The first was from Fergus. 'Hi Mum, what are you doing tomorrow? I've found somewhere I can keep my car and Pete has offered to bring me over to collect it. Call me back when you get in and let me know if it's convenient.'

She had not been looking forward to a Sunday on her own and her spirits lifted at the prospect of seeing him. He had been gone only a couple of days, yet she was already missing his presence around the house. He answered promptly when she keyed in his number. He was in a local pub with some friends; he sounded relaxed and happy and it was against a background of chatter and laughter that they arranged for Pete to drop him off at about eleven the following morning.

'You'll stay for lunch, of course?' she said.

'I was hoping you'd say that. Will Jim be there?'

'I don't think so. He's very tied up with this Muckleton Manor case. What made you call me on my mobile, by the way? I've been at home all evening.'

'I called you on the landline during the afternoon and you were out. You'll find a message there as well.'

'Never mind, we've made contact now. See you tomorrow.' As she put down the phone, Sukey recalled being vaguely aware of a bell ringing during one of the most ecstatic moments of the blissful afternoon she had spent with Jim. In the light of what had passed between them since, there was something almost poignant about the recollection.

The second message was from Miranda. 'I hope I didn't call at an awkward moment,' she said, 'but I felt I had to try again, just to tell you the wonderful news.' She sounded breathless, apologetic and elated, all at the the same time. 'Digby is on his way home! He called to say the police have had to let him go because there simply wasn't any evidence against him. I knew all along he couldn't have done it; I told you, didn't I? Do call back when you have a moment; I'm sure he'll want to thank you personally for being so kind to me.'

'Not tonight I won't,' Sukey said to herself as she deleted both messages and switched off the phone. She had had enough of Muckleton Manor and its attendant complications for one day. Just the same, she could not dismiss the case from her mind. As she settled down in bed she found herself wondering whether Miranda had told her lover about the gardener's strange behaviour and the possibility that he was responsible for the damage to the picture. If so, how would Kirtling handle it?

In spite of her resolve, more questions piled up in her head. Had Arthur been included in the original house-to-house enquiries and, if so, what had he said? Surely, if it had been anything significant, Jim would have mentioned it. Certainly, he did not appear to have been questioned about the damage to the picture, presumably because, not having been at the party, he was unlikely even to have seen it. But he must have known of its existence because both his son and his daughter had featured in it. And as a worker on the estate he might well have been able to slip into the house undetected.

Most important of all, if for reasons of their own Kirtling and Miranda decided to keep quiet about the traces of paint she had noticed on the old man's hands, what – if anything – should she do about it? It seemed clear that if indeed it was the gardener who had vandalized the picture, he must be convinced of Kirtling's guilt. Was it just a gut reaction or did he know something? Miranda had insisted that her lover was a good and fair employer, but this could be no more than an emotional judgement based on her unquestioning devotion to him. The more Sukey thought about it, the more convinced she became that the police should be told. Yet how could she arrange for the information to reach them without revealing her own involvement? In the end, she fell asleep without having found any solution.

She slept until nearly nine o'clock and awoke feeling physically refreshed but with her mind still in turmoil. She had a quick breakfast before calling Muckleton Manor. Miranda answered the phone.

'Oh, Sukey, thank you for ringing back,' she said. Her voice sounded flat and lifeless, with no trace of the euphoria of the previous day. 'Sir Digby would like a word with you. He's . . . he's in his study . . . I'll call him. Will you hold on a moment, please?'

There was a murmur of voices in the background before a man's voice said, 'Mrs Reynolds? Kirtling here. Good of you to come over yesterday; thank you.'

The formal expression of appreciation was not matched by any warmth in the tone. 'Really, it was nothing,' Sukey replied politely. 'I just gave a bit of moral support, that's all.'

'Yes, quite so. I apologize for my gardener's aggressive behaviour. I've given him a ticking off, but I'm sure you'll appreciate he was only acting in my interests. He's very security conscious but he's not really a violent chap. He assures me he was just bluffing and had no intention of harming you. By the way, I understand from Mrs Keene that your visit here was unofficial and you don't want your superiors to hear about it.'

'If you mean, am I going to lodge a complaint against your gardener, the answer is no,' Sukey replied, 'but I expect Miranda . . . Mrs Keene . . . told you about the paint on his hands?'

'What paint? I didn't see any. You must be mistaken. I suggest you consider the incident closed and put it out of your mind.'

Sukey hesitated. From the start of the conversation there had been something about his manner that made her uneasy. It had a hectoring, almost menacing quality, as if he were practically ordering her to keep quiet about what she had seen. Was this his normal way of dealing with people he considered his underlings, or was there a more sinister reason behind it? To ensure that the police would not question Arthur, for example? If so, why? Jim's warning during their spat the previous evening flashed into her mind. She had poured scorn at the time on his suggestion that any involvement with the Muckleton Manor case could possibly involve her in personal danger, yet the notion no longer seemed quite so absurd. It would seem prudent to avoid antagonizing him.

'I'm sure I wouldn't dream of interfering in your dealings with your employees, Sir Digby,' she said.

'Quite so,' he said curtly. There was a click the other end of the line as he put down the phone, leaving her more confused than ever.

She spent the next hour making preparations for lunch. Just before eleven o'clock Fergus and Pete arrived. She gave them coffee and listened to their descriptions of their first few days in their new environment. The more she saw of Pete, the more she warmed to him. There was something four-square about his weather-beaten face and steady blue eyes that inspired confidence. Although she was anxious to have some time alone with Fergus she found herself inviting him to stay for lunch; he thanked her politely but said his parents were expecting him and left shortly afterwards.

'So, how are things with you, Mum?' Fergus asked as he returned to the kitchen after seeing his friend to the door. 'Solved any good crimes since I left home? What about Murder at Muckleton Manor?' He pronounced the words with a dramatic flourish, as if they were the title of an Agatha Christie novel.

'Give me a chance!' she retorted. 'You've only been gone a couple of days.'

'And here I am, back again. The car was only an excuse,

of course. The real reason I'm here is so you can consult me on aspects of the psychology of criminal behaviour.'

'Oh yes? I'm sure you've learned a lot since Thursday. Just the same, it's funny you should say that,' she continued more soberly. Ever since she had begun her work as a Scenes of Crime Officer nearly five years ago, he had not only taken an active interest in her more unusual cases – which meant, in practical terms, anything connected with murder – but had on occasions made useful suggestions, especially when her fascination with detective work brought her into conflict with Jim. The chance of talking over her current dilemma was too good to miss.

He listened with close attention while she told him of Miranda Keene's desperate plea for help, her clandestine visit to Muckleton Manor and her encounter with the irate gardener. He gave a sympathetic grin when she told him of Jim's suspicious attitude over the call from Miranda Keene, but grew serious again on hearing of the conversation with Sir Digby Kirtling.

'So you think he's going to keep quiet about what you saw?' he said after she had finished her story.

'I'm convinced of it,' she said. 'And not only that, he's very anxious that I should do the same. I shall probably hear on Monday that he's told the police he's found the person who damaged the painting and is dealing with them personally.'

'D'you reckon they'll call off their investigation into that particular incident then?'

'I don't know, but I'm sure that's what Kirtling wants and it's not out of consideration to a loyal employee. I've a hunch that he's worried about what might come out if the gardener is questioned.'

'Then the police will have to know about it; it could make a difference to the whole line of investigation. You have to tell them, Mum, even if it means getting into hot water with Jim.'

Sukey sighed. 'That's the trouble. If he'd only be sensible it wouldn't be a problem, but knowing him he's going to make the most idiotic fuss and accuse me of going behind his back. You know what he's like.'

90

'You could call Crimestoppers and leave an anonymous message,' Fergus suggested.

She shook her head. 'Someone would be sure to recognize my voice. No, I'm afraid I'll have to brave Jim's wrath – unless of course you can come up with some cunning scheme.'

The problem was still unresolved when Sukey arrived at the station the following morning. Bracing herself for a stern reprimand from Jim, she went straight along to his office to report on her visit to Muckleton and the conversation with Kirtling, but he was not there, nor was he in the CID general office. Resolving to catch him later on, come what may, she went along to the CSIs' office to report for duty. Moments later, Mandy entered with three mugs of coffee on a tray.

'Morning, Sukey. Morning, Sarge,' she said as she handed them round. 'Did we all have a good weekend?'

'I did some tidying up in the garden and took the lad to a football match on Saturday,' replied George Barnes as he spooned sugar into his mug. 'How about you, ladies?'

'I took Mum to the seaside for the day,' said Mandy. 'The weather was lovely and she really enjoyed it.' She turned to Sukey. 'Did you do anything special?'

'What?' Sukey started. She was still mentally rehearsing what she was going to say to Jim and had barely heard the exchange. 'Oh, er, nothing very exciting,' she said. 'That is, Gus came to lunch on Sunday, which was nice. What have you got for us this morning, Sarge?' she went on hurriedly, aware that Mandy had given her a curious glance.

'Not a lot,' said Barnes. 'The most spectacular is a theft from an art gallery in Cheltenham.'

Sukey's pulse gave a blip. 'Which art gallery?' she asked.

Barnes squinted at the printout. 'Odd sort of name. Begins with a P. The theft was reported by the owner, Philip Montwell.'

'The Phimont Gallery?'

'Is that how you pronounce it?' He held the paper out for her to see.

'I don't believe it!' Sukey's voice rose to a squeak in her excitement. The chance of a meeting with the man whose work must have given him at least some insight into the set-up at Muckleton Manor was like the answer to a prayer.

Anything she picked up from him could quite legitimately be reported to CID without her having to reveal her own part in the affair. 'Can I have that one, Sarge?'

'If you like.' He handed her the printout. 'What's your interest?'

'Philip Montwell is the artist who painted the picture for Sir Digby Kirtling at Muckleton Manor – the one that was damaged.'

'So?'

'I . . . well . . . it was a brilliant copy of a picture I've always loved and I . . . I'd like a chance to tell him how much I admired it,' she said. It was a pretty lame excuse but it was the best she could think up on the spur of the moment. She was relieved when the conversation turned to the remaining assignments.

On their way down to the yard to collect their vans, Mandy said, 'You're up to something. I recognize the signs. Want to tell?'

'Not now. Maybe later.'

Fourteen

When Sukey arrived at the Phimont Gallery the front window had been boarded up and Anne-Marie was shovelling a heap of broken glass into a plastic dustbin. On seeing Sukey she put down the shovel, rushed over and flung her arms round her.

'Isn't it terrible!' she exclaimed. 'The Matisse – the one with the dancing figures that I was telling you about – has gone. Philip is absolutely devastated.'

'When did it happen?'

'Some time in the small hours of this morning. The alarm went off and the police were called, but by the time they arrived the burglars had got away with the picture. He'd only just finished it and the client was due to collect it today; it was worth a huge amount of money.'

'Is that all they took – just that one?'

'Philip thinks so, but he's so upset I don't think he's checked properly. Everything in the gallery is catalogued and when he's calmed down we're going to go through it together. It's a dreadful thing to happen to him, but I'm so glad I'm here and can be of some service to him,' she added with an earnestness that Sukey found touching, but at the same time faintly disturbing.

'Shouldn't you be at a class or something?' she asked.

Anne-Marie shook her head. 'My course doesn't start until Wednesday, but even if it had I'd stay to help Philip. He needs someone to give him support. He's on his own, you know; he had a sister but she died.'

'Poor chap. Well, I'll leave you to get on with your cleaning up and go and see what I can do to help.'

Sukey pushed open the door and found herself in a thickly carpeted but otherwise unfurnished area the size of an average living room. It was arranged like a miniature art gallery with pictures on all three walls, illuminated by a series of carefully positioned spotlights. In the space behind what had been the front window was a narrow platform on which lay an over-turned easel. Beside it, among the shards of glass that had fallen inwards, was a picture of a ruined temple, which, together with a tall Greek vase that had rolled into a corner, had presumably formed the window display. Both appeared undamaged.

A buzzer sounded, probably activated by a switch under the doormat. A man's voice shouted, 'Coming!' and the next minute a tall, spare figure emerged from a back room through a curtained door directly opposite the entrance. He stared at Sukey and said, 'Who are you?' Both his voice and his manner were suspicious, almost hostile.

'Susan Reynolds, Crime Scene Investigator,' she replied crisply, holding out her ID.

He glanced at it briefly before saying, without any visible thawing in his attitude, 'I was told to expect you, but I don't really see the point. Your superiors have already had a good look round.'

Sukey did her best to conceal her resentment at the hint of condescension in his response. 'I imagine you're referring to the police officers who attended the scene, sir,' she replied coolly. 'My job is to make a forensic examination of the prem-ises in the hope that the thief or thieves have left some traces that will help us establish their identity and, we hope, recover your property.'

'Footprints and fingerprints, I suppose,' he said dismiss-ively. 'It was obviously a professional job so I doubt if you'll find any, but I suppose you have to go through the motions. Where do you propose to start?'

'In here, if that's all right with you.'

'Feel free. I daresay you'd like more light before you start crawling about on the floor.' He pressed a switch and a crystal chandelier blazed down from the ceiling.

'Thank you, sir, that's a great help. I understand that so far as you know only one item was taken. Can you tell me where it was kept?'

'In the room behind me.' He gestured over his shoulder at the door through which he had entered.

'Right; I'll check in there when I've finished here.' She was still standing just inside the door and she remained for a moment studying the space between the shattered window and the point he indicated, trying to assess the probable route taken by the thieves. 'Can you give me some idea of how many people have trodden on that part of the floor – ' she indicated the open space in the centre of the room – 'since the theft was discovered.'

'I don't think anyone has. When I arrived the police were waiting in the street and I let them in through the front door. My first thought was for the Matisse so I led them straight through to my office and saw at once that it was gone. It took me weeks to do and had personal as well as professional associations.' His voice wavered on the final words; for the first time Sukey detected a sensitive and vulnerable human being beneath the surface arrogance.

'And I take it the front door was still locked when you arrived. Is there a back door to the premises?'

'Yes, but it's still locked and bolted. It hasn't been touched.'

'So presumably the thieves left the way they came, through the broken window?'

'It would appear so.' Once again the tone was faintly condescending, as if he considered her remark a statement of the obvious. 'The police said not to touch anything, but it was all right to have the window boarded up so long as it was done from the outside.'

'Right, I'll get started.' She put down her bag and began unpacking her equipment. She had half expected him to disappear and leave her to it, but he leaned against the wall with his hands in the pockets of his dark green corduroy trousers and watched her every movement from deep-set eyes set beneath strong brows on either side of an aristocratic nose. It was easy to understand Anne-Marie's devotion, Sukey thought; he had a charisma that, despite his arrogant manner, would make him well-nigh irresistible to an impressionable young woman.

She marked out a wide strip of carpet between the window and the far door with tape and got down to work. She took samples of loose dirt and fibres from the carpet and with her powerful torch made a careful examination of the shattered

95

remains of the window, but could detect none of the kind of evidence commonly left by amateurs such as traces of blood, cigarette butts or marks left by the tools used to force entry. As Montwell had remarked, it looked like a thoroughly professional job.

When she had labelled and bagged such samples as she felt worth taking she said to Montwell, 'Now perhaps you will show me where the picture was kept?'

Without a word he held the curtain aside and beckoned her through. The next room was smaller and more intimate than the first. It was lit by a small single window through which Sukey caught a glimpse of what appeared to be a conservatory. In one corner was a Regency-style desk, on which the sole item was a photograph of a young woman in a silver frame, and beside the desk a filing cabinet of matching design. Two of the walls were lined with shelves, obviously custom-made, containing dozens of books. Many of these were in large format and looked like the catalogues Sukey had seen in art galleries she had visited with Paul in the early days of their marriage, while others had the names of well-known artists on their spines. The only other furniture consisted of two comfortable armchairs and a large coffee table, where no doubt prospective clients would sit browsing through lavish reproductions of some of the world's most famous paintings and discussing their choice with the artist.

In a space in front of the desk was an empty easel. Montwell pointed. 'It was there,' he said, and once again she heard the emotion that he just failed to conceal. 'All they had to do was grab it and run.'

Sukey felt an unexpected wave of sympathy for the man. It was almost as if he was suffering a bereavement, but she could think of nothing to say that would not sound trite and trivial. At that moment Anne-Marie, who had finished her task and slipped past them almost unnoticed through a door at the back of the room where they were standing, reappeared behind him and said timidly, 'Is there anything else I can do for you, Mr Montwell?'

He swung round and barked, 'Yes, you can bring some coffee out to the studio.' He turned back to Sukey. 'I don't imagine you'll find many clues here, but I suppose you have to complete the job.' Plainly, he considered the whole exercise a waste of time. 'If there's anything else you need from me, tell the girl and I'll come back,' he added and left the room, followed by Anne-Marie.

Although, by now Sukey shared Montwell's opinion that it was unlikely the thieves had left any valuable evidence, she made her normal thorough examination. Since nothing else appeared to have been taken and the thieves had obviously known exactly where to find the picture, it had almost certainly been stolen to order. As she worked she tried to imagine who would be interested in dishonestly acquiring a painting that, compared to the original, was worth only a modest amount of money. It seemed to her that there were two possibilities: first, that the client had arranged the burglary to avoid having to pay for it; second, that someone else had taken it in the belief that they could sell it, possibly even pass it off as an original to an unscrupulous collector with more money than expertise. It would be interesting to know how many people were aware of its existence. She had been tempted to ask Montwell, but no doubt the police had already questioned him on the subject. Dalia might know; she would have a word with her later.

She had just finished and was packing away her equipment when a timid voice behind her said, 'Did you find anything?' She looked round and saw Anne-Marie standing there with a steaming mug in her hand. Her eyes were moist; evidently, she shared her employer's distress.

'Nothing dramatic, I'm afraid. I've taken a few samples to send off to the lab, that's all I can tell you.'

The girl sighed. 'Oh dear,' she said in a sad little voice. 'I thought you might like this,' she added, holding out the mug.

'Thanks, that's kind of you.' As she sipped the coffee, Sukey turned and pointed to the photograph. 'You mentioned Mr Montwell had a sister who died. Is that her?'

'Yes.'

'Do you know what happened to her?'

'I believe she OD'd on some drug or other. I wasn't working here at the time, but I remembered reading about it in the *Gazette*. It must have been terrible for Philip; as far as I know she was his only surviving relative.'

'Do you know if it was accidental or deliberate?'

'I've no idea. The paper never said and I wouldn't dare ask him.'

'No, of course not. Does he ever speak about her?'

'Never. When I first came here I admired the photo and asked if it was his girlfriend. I know it was a bit cheeky but it sort of slipped out. He nearly bit my head off at first and then he sort of apologized and said it was his late sister. It was only then that I remembered reading the report; I felt absolutely dreadful as you can imagine. Do you think you'll be able to get the picture back for him?' she added wistfully.

'We'll do our best.' It was her stock reply, although in this case, as in so many others, she was not optimistic.

When Sukey returned to headquarters at the end of her shift she went in search of DS Chen. She found her in the canteen, chatting to a uniformed officer, PC Jean Forbes, whom she had last seen comforting an hysterical woman who had just discovered a headless torso in a ditch. 'May I join you?' she asked.

'Of course.' Dalia picked up her handbag from the empty chair beside her and put it on the floor. 'Jean was just asking me about the Una May murder. She's interested because she was called to a break-in at the gallery belonging to the artist who painted the picture that our prime suspect commissioned at Muckleton Manor. She was wondering if there might be a connection.'

'Funny you should mention it. That was one of my assignments this morning and I wanted to have a word with whoever dealt with the break-in. I thought you might know the answer to that one.'

'I didn't deal with it personally,' said Dalia, 'but I heard about it of course and it does seem as if there's a jinx on the work of the artist. First one of his canvases is damaged and then another is stolen. I gather it's a copy of a Matisse that had been commissioned.'

'Yes, *La Danza*. It obviously meant a great deal to him; he was almost in tears over losing it.'

'I noticed he was pretty upset,' said Jean. 'I thought it was on account of the money he wasn't going to receive from the client.'

'I think it was more than that,' said Sukey. 'Just out of interest, Dalia, do you know how he reacted when the boating party picture was slashed?'

'We did have a word with him after it happened, just to see if he could throw any light on it, but he couldn't. So far as I know, he didn't show any particular concern, probably because he'd been paid.' Evidently, Dalia shared Jean's cynical assessment of the man's motives.

'So what did you want to ask about the break-in?' asked Jean.

'I was wondering if you'd found out how many people knew about the Matisse – other than the client, of course.'

'Naturally, we asked him about that. Apparently he'd told a business associate called Athena Letchworth about the commission – in fact, he said she'd been the one to put him in touch with the client – and the young student who works for him part-time knew as well. She probably told half her friends at the art college.'

'Anne-Marie,' said Sukey. 'My son knows her and I've met her several times. She told me as well and there didn't seem to be any secret about it. She went on at length about how much she admired the original and how wonderful she thinks Montwell is. The poor kid has a hopeless crush on him and he treats her like dirt.'

'She'll get over it,' said Dalia dismissively. She picked up her bag and pushed back her chair. 'I have to go now,' she said.

'Me too,' said Jean.

Left alone, Sukey found her mind dwelling less on the disappearance of the picture than on the sad fate of the artist's sister. It was difficult to see how there could be a connection, yet she was convinced that something more than mere pecuniary loss had caused that hastily stifled display of emotion. Not, she concluded, that it could possibly have any bearing on the motive for the theft.

Fifteen

Sukey lingered for several minutes over her cup of tea after Dalia and Jean had left the canteen. Eventually she faced up to the fact that she could put off no longer her showdown with Jim and returned to the CSIs' room. It was a relief to find it empty, especially as Mandy appeared to have cleared her desk and gone home. Mandy would almost certainly have detected the tenseness she was feeling, no matter how hard she tried to conceal it. She completed her report, checked over the samples she had taken during the day and put them in her out-tray. Then she made her way along to DI Castle's office. She had her hand raised to knock on the door when it opened and Jim emerged with a file in his hand.

'Ah, Sukey,' he said with a frown. 'I'm afraid I can't see you now. Something's come up in the Muckleton Manor case and I have to see DCI Lord right away.'

'As a matter of fact, this concerns the Muckleton Manor case as well, sir. I think I know who damaged the painting.'

He fixed her with a penetrating stare and said, 'Oh you do, do you? Who then?'

'The head gardener, Arthur Andrews. I suppose he wasn't questioned because he wasn't at the party so he might not even have seen the picture before it was damaged. He must have known about it, though, because both his son and daughter figure in it.'

'Why should that make him a suspect?'

'It wouldn't necessarily, not by itself, but the fact that he had traces of red paint on his hands seems suspicious, don't you think?'

'It might indeed, but how come you know about it?'

'I saw it for myself when I spoke to him in the gardens at the manor on Saturday morning.'

His jaw dropped for a moment before his look of astonishment hardened into anger as the significance of her reply dawned on him. For a moment she thought he was about to forget where they were and give her a verbal roasting on the spot, but the explosion never came. He merely said curtly, 'Then you'd better come with me and tell Chief Inspector Lord about it.' He vented his feelings by slamming his office door behind him and striding off down the corridor, leaving her trailing in his wake.

DCI Lord was sitting at his desk studying an open file when they entered. 'Ah, Jim,' he said. 'Sit down. You too,' he added with a friendly nod in Sukey's direction. 'Do I take it you're both here on the same errand? Something important, Carole said.'

'Yes, sir,' said Castle. 'It's about the Muckleton Manor case. The DNA report has just come through and it confirms that Digby Kirtling is the father of Una May's unborn child.'

'No surprises there, then. I take it you'll be bringing him in again straight away?'

'As it happens, there may be a slight delay as we aren't sure where he is at the moment. He spends the week in London attending to his business and at present his mobile phone seems to be switched off. His secretary was out of the office when we called and we've left a message saying we need to contact him urgently. I've detailed a team to go and pick him up the minute we locate him, but in the meantime – ' at this point Castle gestured at Sukey, who had been sitting quietly beside him – 'Mrs Reynolds claims she has observed something suggesting that Kirtling's gardener might be the person who vandalized the picture and virtually accused his employer of the murder.'

'*Has* she?' Lord sounded impressed. He turned to her and said quietly, 'Let's have it then.'

Whereas she could sense the hint of resentment in Jim's tone, Sukey was reassured by Lord's encouraging response.

'It happened when I called at the manor on Saturday morning, and it might help if I start by explaining what I was doing there,' she began. Lord listened intently while she told him about Miranda's pathetic belief in her lover's innocence and her plea for help in proving it. She felt bound to reveal that the woman knew about and condoned her lover's occasional infidelities; however, since it had now been officially confirmed that he was responsible for Una May's pregnancy, there seemed no need for her to mention the fact that, despite his denials when being questioned by the police, he had admitted the possibility to his mistress.

'I was really impressed by her passionate belief in him,' she went on. 'She insisted he's never lied to her and that he solemnly swore to her that he didn't kill Una May. She was adamant that there's no violence in his nature and she begged me to help prove his innocence. I kept saying I didn't see there was anything I could do, but she wouldn't be put off and she didn't want to talk over the phone, so in the end I agreed to go and see her. I made it quite clear that it would be as a private individual, that I couldn't discuss the investigation and, in any case, my part in the enquiry was to all intents over. I also warned her that if she told me anything that would incriminate Kirtling, I'd be bound to report it. She insisted that all she was trying to do was make me understand why so many people – by which she meant the locals and of course the person who slashed the picture – supposed him to be guilty.'

'And why do they?'

'Because of his reputation as a ladies' man with a string of what she called "little flings" – women he dallied with for a while and then got tired of.'

'And did she tell you anything incriminating?'

'She didn't tell me anything that you don't already know, sir,' Sukey replied. Well, it's true now even if it wasn't at the time, she thought to herself. Just the same, she was on shaky ground and it was a relief when Lord did not press her further. She shot a brief glance in Jim's direction, but he was staring stonily ahead of him and she could tell by the set of his jaw that he was still angry with her.

'All right, I get the background to your visit,' said Lord. 'Now tell me about your encounter with the gardener.'

'Well, sir, when I arrived at the manor he was at work in the grounds and I noticed that he had what looked like red paint on his hands. It occurred to me immediately that he might have been the one to damage the painting. Mrs Keene seemed very surprised when I told her and said she could think of no reason why he should have done such a thing. Naturally, I assumed she would see the man for herself after I left and then inform the police immediately.'

'Let me get this straight,' said Lord. 'You went to Muckleton in response to a plea from Miranda Keene, Kirtling's house-keeper, and when you arrived the gardener was working in the grounds and you noticed red paint on his hands.'

'To be precise, there were traces of some red substance under his fingernails, sir. I couldn't be certain it was paint, of course, or that it had got there when he attacked the picture, but I felt it was worth mentioning.'

'You must have been standing quite close to him to see it – or did you approach him for some reason?'

'No, sir, he approached me. He asked me what I was doing there.'

'Why do you suppose he did that? It's hardly the job of a gardener to challenge visitors to his employer's house.'

In an attempt to avoid giving a straight answer, Sukey said, 'He jumped to the conclusion that I was from the press, coming to snoop round. I explained that Mrs Keene had asked me to call, but he didn't believe me.'

Lord sat back in his chair and fixed Sukey with a pene-trating stare. His eyes, almost as black as his moustache, were no longer friendly and reassuring.

'For what reason, do you suppose?' he said. 'I understand we still have a police guard on the house.' He shot an enquiring glance at Castle, who gave a brief nod. He turned back to Sukey. 'So you must have satisfied the officer on duty of your bona fide visit. Didn't you tell the man that?'

It was no use; she would have to come clean. She swal-lowed nervously and said, 'No, sir. The fact is, I had entered the grounds by climbing over the wall at the bottom of the field behind the house. He was working there and he took me for an intruder. He wouldn't listen to my explanations; in fact, his manner was quite aggressive.'

'You climbed over a wall into a field at the back of the house,' Lord repeated slowly, as if to make sure he had heard correctly. Sukey nodded. 'No doubt you had a reason for this unconventional method of entry.'

'Mrs Keene suggested it, sir. The fact is,' she stumbled on, anticipating his next question, 'I had made it clear to her that I did not want to be seen by the police guard.'

'I see. Do I take it that was because you might have been recognized and it might have got back to this chap?' Without taking his eyes off Sukey, Lord tilted his head briefly in Castle's direction. She thought she detected a twinkle in the depths of his eyes and felt marginally reassured. He knew not only that she and Jim were an item, but also about his overprotective attitude coupled with an almost obsessive desire to keep their affair secret. When she did not reply, he went on, 'So you decided to leave it to the housekeeper to inform us about the paint on the gardener's hands without mentioning your visit. Is that it?'

'Yes, sir. I didn't hear any more until Sunday, when I returned a call from Mrs Keene. She was over the moon because Kirtling had been released without charge. She called him to the phone and he thanked me for my visit. He apologized for his gardener's behaviour and said he had spoken to the man and rebuked him for his attitude towards me. When I mentioned the red paint he denied having seen it and made it clear that he wanted the matter to be considered closed.'

Lord frowned and plucked at his moustache. 'Wasn't this the moment when you should have reported it to us?'

Sukey felt her colour rise. 'Yes, sir, in fact I intended to, but it was the weekend so I decided to leave it until today. I looked for DI Castle when I got here this morning but I couldn't find him so I'm afraid I left it until I came back at the end of my shift. When I went to his office to see him and to explain what it was about he said I'd better come with him and report directly to you.'

'That's right,' Jim said, almost grudgingly she felt, in response to a questioning glance from Lord.

'I take it your team took a statement from the gardener on the day of the murder, Jim?'

'No, sir. My information is that he wasn't at work that day. Kirtling had given him the day off.'

'Any idea why?'

'I believe it was so he could visit a sick relative.'

'Where does this relative live?'

'Offhand I can't answer that one, sir.'

'Get all the details, find out if he actually went and then bring him in for questioning. Okay,' Lord went on without giving Castle time to respond, 'thanks for bringing me up to date. Let me know the minute you locate Kirtling.'

'Of course, sir.'

Both Castle and Sukey stood up to go, but Lord detained her with a gesture. She sat down and waited uneasily as the door closed and the sound of Jim's footsteps in the corridor grew fainter. Then Lord said, 'Don't be scared, Sukey, I'm not going to eat you. Just the same, you should have reported what you saw straight away. You know that, don't you?'

'Yes, sir.'

'I'm mindful of the fact that you've put in some very useful work in the past by picking up information that for some reason hasn't reached us through what we'll call the usual channels, but I don't recall any occasion when you've deliberately withheld information. See that it doesn't happen again.'

'It won't, sir.'

'I know that chap,' Lord jerked his head in the direction of the door through which Castle had just left, 'gets a bit shirty with you when you go off on your own, but it's only because he's concerned about your safety.'

'Yes, I know.'

'Just on a point of interest, when you had that encounter with the gardener, you said he became aggressive. In what way?'

'He chased me with a garden fork, sir.'

For a moment she thought he was about to burst out laughing, but he managed to compose his features before saying, 'Yes, well, I can understand why you omitted to mention that. Still, it proves Jim's point, doesn't it? Just watch it in future.'

Sixteen

The route from the CSIs' office to the exit from the building took Sukey past DI Castle's office. She was hoping his door would be shut so that she could slip past unnoticed, pick up her car and go home. She was feeling tired and a little bruised; the last thing she wanted at the moment was another argument with him. To her dismay, the door was wide open; even worse, he was standing there talking to DC Derek Page. As she approached, she heard the young detective say, 'Right, sir,' before making off down the corridor. The next moment, Sukey found herself inside the office with the door closed behind her and Castle facing her from behind his desk.

'I think we'd better have this out right away,' he said.

'Do we have to?' she said wearily. 'I've already given DCI Lord an undertaking not to delay passing on information in future.' After a moment's thought, she added, 'Although I think he understands the reason why I did it in this case.'

'I daresay he does, and in a way I suppose I do too, although I wish you hadn't done it.' His expression was hurt rather than angry. He lowered his voice and said, 'Sook, didn't you give a thought to the risk you were taking? A woman was murdered in those grounds a few days ago and you never know who might have been lurking around. You said that fellow became aggressive – supposing he was the killer? He might have attacked you and with no one within earshot, heaven knows what could have happened. It doesn't bear thinking about.'

'With your prime suspect under arrest? I hardly think so.'

'You know as well as I do that we always keep an open mind until we've got enough evidence to charge anyone. We might be pretty sure Kirtling's our man – this latest bit of evidence strengthens the case against him – but we still can't rule out other possibilities.'

'Well, I don't think that old boy is the killer type – although,' she added mischievously, 'as it happened, he did wave a spiky fork around in a rather threatening manner, so I decided not to argue and I ran away instead. The thing is,' she went on hurriedly, realizing from his expression that her attempt at levity had fallen flat, 'none of it would have happened if you didn't insist on monitoring my every move all the time.'

'That's not fair,' he protested. 'I said I was sorry for upsetting you on Saturday. You should have told me then about the paint on the gardener's hands.'

'Yes, I know,' she admitted, 'but things between us were still a bit edgy and I was afraid it would only set you off again. In any case, if Miranda had reported it as I expected, you'd never have found out I'd been there. Okay, it was very stupid and I've already admitted as much to DCI Lord. When Kirtling denied seeing the paint and made it clear in no uncertain terms that he wanted the matter dropped, I knew I had to report it, and I did.'

'Yes, two days after you'd spotted it. The old boy had plenty of time to clean it off, which could explain why Kirtling didn't notice it. On the other hand, it's quite likely he did notice it, but was anxious that we shouldn't find out about it.'

'That's exactly what occurred to me. He was probably afraid the gardener would make some damaging allegations that would help you build a case against him. All right, I know I shouldn't have waited till this morning, but I did try and see you first thing. It wasn't my fault you weren't available.'

'That's no excuse. You could have told someone else in CID. DS Chen, for example.'

'I thought of that, but she wasn't in the office either. In any case, it would have meant having to explain to her why I didn't report it straight away. I didn't think you'd appreciate that, knowing how you feel about other people knowing about us. Something's just occurred to me, though,' she added slyly.

'What's that?'

'That particular hang-up of yours could turn out to be an advantage in this particular instance.'

'How d'you work that out?'

'Well, if I hadn't known you'd object to my going to see Miranda Keene I'd have gone there quite openly through the front door instead of climbing over the wall and I wouldn't have encountered the gardener. In fact,' she went on, her confidence growing as she realized she had scored a point, 'it's quite possible I've opened up an important new lead for you. I hope you'll bear that in mind when you get a bouquet from the Super for solving the case.'

In spite of his obvious efforts to look stern, his features relaxed and after a moment he lifted his hands in a gesture of surrender.

'Sook, you're incorrigible!' he said.

'It'll be interesting to see how the gardener spells "murderer", won't it?' she went on, pressing home her advantage. 'If he gets it wrong a check on his clothes should be enough to prove he was the one who vandalized the picture.'

'There doesn't seem much doubt about that,' he said. 'What's more to the point is why he did it? If he has some information about the killing, we'll want to know why he hasn't come forward.'

'That's something I'd like to know too. You will keep me in the picture, won't you?'

His expression grew serious again. 'Provided you give me your word you'll stay out of the case from now on.'

'If you're sure you can manage without my help,' she said cheekily.

Before he had a chance to retort, his telephone rang. He picked up the receiver; after a few monosyllabic responses to the caller he said, 'Right, I'll be downstairs in five minutes,' and hung up. He got to his feet and began clearing his desk. 'I have to go now,' he said. 'They've located Kirtling and there's a team standing by to go and pick him up. I don't have to tell you to keep that information to yourself until we release it officially. And remember, if from now on you come across so much as a mote of dust that might have some bearing on the case, you report it at once. Understood?'

'Yes, sir,' she said demurely. She got up and went to the door.

He put on his coat, picked up his briefcase and followed

her. Their eyes met as he reached past her to open the door; for a moment she thought he was about to forget where they were and make some gesture of affection, but he simply said, 'I'll be in touch,' and hurried off down the corridor.

Sukey followed him more slowly. Her feelings were mixed; the rift between them appeared to have been healed, which was a relief, but she was still conscious that she had handled the whole episode very badly. By the time she drove out of the yard the rush-hour traffic was at its height; an accident at a busy junction delayed her still further and it was almost six o'clock when she reached home. Already the sun was setting; at the end of the month the clocks would go back and it would be dark by this time. The thought made her even more depressed. She went into the kitchen and dumped her bag in a corner. Thinking a drink might help to lift her spirits, she took out a bottle of wine, removed the seal and rummaged in a drawer for the corkscrew. Then she changed her mind and put the bottle away again. There was no fun in drinking alone.

She checked her phone for messages. There was just one, from Fergus, left an hour or so earlier. 'I've been wondering whether you told Jim about your visit to Muckleton,' he said. 'I hope he wasn't too mad at you. Have there been any other developments? Give me a bell when you have time.'

Feeling marginally more cheerful, she called him back. 'Hi, got your message,' she said when he answered. 'What sort of day have you had?'

'Went to a very interesting lecture this morning. Slightly potty old prof with hair like a bird's nest, but he certainly knew his stuff. How about you? Did you emerge unscathed from the lion's den or did you chicken out and send an anony-mous note?'

'Chicken out? As if I would! It was a bit of an ordeal, espe-cially as I had to make my confession in front of DCI Lord.' She gave him a run-down on the interview without revealing the most recent developments, ending with, 'I think Jim's forgiven me, but I won't be seeing him this evening because he had to dash off and . . .' she was about to say 'make an arrest', but to avoid further questions settled for '. . . see someone urgently.'

'Never mind, I'm sure you'll see him soon and everything

will be hunky-dory again. You will keep me posted about the Muckleton murder, won't you?'

'You'll read about any developments in the paper,' she said. 'I've been told very firmly to stay away from it.'

'But won't Jim tell you what the old gardener has to say?'

'I doubt it. I'm putting the whole thing out of my mind. I've already told Miranda Keene there's nothing I can do to help. Like I said before, she'll have to accept the fact that lover-boy is guilty.'

At the briefing on Wednesday the press were informed that Sir Digby Kirtling had been charged with the murder of Una May and would appear before magistrates the following morning. The news was announced on the radio at midday; an hour later Sukey received a call from Anne-Marie.

'Oh Sukey, isn't it terrible about Sir Digby being charged?' she exclaimed without preamble. 'Auntie M is absolutely frantic; the phone hasn't stopped ringing and there are photographers ringing the bell and peering through the gates.'

'Yes, I can imagine. I'm very sorry; it must be awful for her.'

'Can't you do anything to help?'

'All I can suggest is that she goes into hiding somewhere. Could she stay at your home for a little while, just until the heat's off?'

'Yes, I suppose so. Mum and Dad are away on a cruise, but I'm sure they wouldn't mind. Auntie M's too upset to talk to you herself, by the way, that's why she gave me your mobile number. I hope it's all right – and I hope this isn't an awkward time for you.'

'As it happens, I'm sitting in the van eating my lunch so it doesn't matter, but I prefer not to receive personal calls while I'm at work.'

'I'll remember that another time,' Anne-Marie promised.

'I see no reason why there should be another time,' said Sukey. There was a little gasp on the other end of the line and she immediately felt guilty at having replied so sharply. 'I'm sorry, that must have sounded rude, but my involvement in this case has caused me a few problems.'

110

'Oh dear, what sort of problems?'

'Never mind that. What you and your aunt have to understand is that there must be some pretty solid evidence against Sir Digby or he wouldn't have been charged.'

'Yes, I suppose so,' the girl admitted. 'It's hard for her to accept; she loves him so much and trusts him so completely—'

'I know she does, and I really do sympathize,' Sukey said gently. 'It's a good thing she has your support. By the way,' she went on, 'do you know if Mr Montwell's picture has been recovered?'

'I was going to ask you. I thought you'd know.'

'I'm not kept informed about the progress of every incident I deal with,' Sukey explained patiently. 'I just examine the scene of the crime and pass on any evidence I find there for experts to deal with. If there's a result I might get to hear of it, but it doesn't follow.'

'Oh dear, I was hoping I might have some good news to pass on to Philip. He's really upset about it.'

'I'm sure the police are doing their best.' Sukey glanced at the clock on her dashboard. 'I have to go now; I've got several more jobs to attend to.'

'Yes, of course. Thanks anyway. Goodbye.'

Sukey put her mobile back in her pocket, finished her sandwiches and set off on her next assignment. On the way she found herself wondering how much Philip Montwell would charge to make a copy of a Matisse. A thousand? Two thousand? It could hardly be a fortune, surely? It would be interesting to find out.

Before setting off on her first assignment the following morning, Sukey went in search of DS Dalia Chen. Finding her at her desk in the CID office, she said, 'Have you got a moment, Dalia?'

'Sure. What is it?'

'Jim tells me you know about art,' Sukey began.

'A bit. What do you want to know?'

'That picture that was stolen from the Phimont Gallery – Montwell's copy of *La Danza* by Matisse. I think I mentioned how upset he was about losing it. I suppose he was thinking of his fee. Would you have any idea how much he'd have charged?'

'None whatever, I'm afraid.' Dalia's tone was dismissive.

'How would it compare with what Sir Digby paid him for the boating party picture, for example?' Sukey persisted. 'I imagine you know how much that was?'

Almost pointedly, Sukey felt, Dalia evaded the question. 'If you compare the two pictures, I'd say the Matisse would be a lot simpler and quicker to copy than the Renoir so he wouldn't charge so much,' she said. 'I can understand the man getting upset at having his work stolen, but he was probably insured.'

'Yes, I suppose so. Do you know if there are any leads?'

'I've no idea,' Dalia said flatly. 'If you'll excuse me, I—'

At that moment DI Castle put his head round the door and said, 'Ready, Dalia?'

'Coming, sir.' Dalia picked up her bag and left the room. Sukey had a strong suspicion that she had had instructions not to discuss any ongoing cases with her and felt aggrieved at the thought. She resolved to tackle Jim about it at the earliest opportunity. Meanwhile, the fact that he was going on some assignment with Dalia did nothing to improve her mood.

Seventeen

Sukey was thankful to find no messages when she returned home at the end of her shift on Thursday. Ever since Fergus left she had been missing his presence round the house, but this evening she was tired and a little jaded and for once found it a relief to have the place to herself. She showered and put on a clean pair of jeans and a sweatshirt before preparing her evening meal, which she ate in the kitchen while listening to a comedy programme on the radio. Later, having decided that there was nothing worth watching on the television, she switched the sitting-room radio to a music programme and settled down with a book. For the first time since her brush with authority on Monday she felt totally relaxed.

She had read only half a dozen pages when the phone rang. Jim was on the line.

'Are you doing anything special?' he asked.

'Just having a quiet read.'

'Does that mean you don't want company?'

'That depends what sort of company we're talking about. I'm not in the mood for any more arguments.'

'Oh come on, Sook, I thought we'd got everything sorted. You asked to be kept up to speed about the Muckleton case and I thought you'd like to know what we found as a result of your visit to the manor. Of course, if you're not interested—'

'Don't talk rot; you know jolly well I'm interested. Have you eaten, by the way? I could do eggs and bacon—'

'Don't worry; I had a steak and a pint in the Bear with Andy Radcliffe. He's been telling me about his current case – it sounds a humdinger. Some quite well-known heads are going to roll. And before you ask, it's also very hush-hush,' he added in a mock stage whisper.

113

Putting on her most innocent voice, Sukey said, 'Whatever makes you think I'd ask?'

'I can't imagine. Is it okay if I come round for a while, then?'

'Yes, of course.'

He arrived half an hour later bearing a large bunch of flowers. 'Peace offering?' she said mischievously as she accepted them.

'Just a token of my esteem.' He kissed her briefly on the mouth but, unusually, he made no attempt at a more ardent embrace. She sensed, with a secret twinge of satisfaction, that he was uncertain how she would respond.

She put the flowers in water and carried the vase into the sitting room. 'Would you like some coffee?' she said.

'No thanks. Just come and sit down while I talk. I'm not staying long – I have to make an early start in the morning.'

'On another case?'

'No, still gathering evidence against Kirtling. That's what I've come to tell you about. We interviewed your friend, the gardener, and it wasn't long before he admitted he was the one who vandalized the picture. When he realized you'd spotted the paint on his hands he did his best to remove it, but we found the clothes he'd been wearing and there was plenty on them.'

'So why did he do it?'

'It seems he overheard Kirtling and Una May having an argument about a week before the party. They were in her office, which is on the first floor of the house; the window was open and he was working immediately below. He couldn't hear what Kirtling was saying, but at one stage he heard the woman raise her voice and say something like, "Don't you threaten me! I don't care who hears, it's true and you know it!" He can't recall the exact words, of course, but Derek Page is convinced he was telling the truth.'

'So why didn't he come forward?'

'He blustered at first when Page put that to him, said he would have done if he'd been asked but he hadn't been questioned – which was true, of course. Anyway, we ran a check on him and found he's got form for GBH. He got into a drunken brawl, knocked out a few of someone's teeth and got a six months' suspended sentence. It was several years ago but, needless to say, he didn't tell Kirtling about it when he applied for the job here. He was afraid if it came out he'd get the sack and it would be difficult to find another job. Anyway, he agreed to make a statement, which of course helps our case no end. So, many thanks for putting us on to him, Sook.'

'All in the line of duty, Guv,' she said airily. She grew serious again as she said, 'He must have been pretty angry to go into the house and slash the picture like that. It's almost as if he had a personal grudge against Kirtling.'

'In a way, he felt he had. His daughter Tricia works at the manor as a housemaid – she's the pretty girl with the dog in the picture, by the way – and she told her father she'd had to fight Kirtling off more than once. We had another word with her; she didn't like talking about it but eventually admitted that she'd told her father and he told her to give in her notice. She was afraid to speak to Kirtling so she went to Miranda, who asked why she wanted to leave. When she gave the reason, she said Miranda seemed "a bit put out" but promised to arrange things so that she was out of the way when Kirtling was at home.'

'I take it you checked that with Miranda?'

'Naturally, and according to Page there were two interesting things about that interview. First, she tried to make out that she didn't believe the girl's story and then, when pressed a bit further, said if anything Tricia had led Kirtling on.'

Sukey nodded. 'Meaning, she knew jolly well it was true, but she wasn't going to admit to anything damaging to her blue-eyed boy.'

'That was Page's impression.'

'What was the other interesting thing?'

'Page reported seeing the remains of a bruise on the side of her face and another on her arm. Does that ring a bell?' he said as she gave a slight start.

'It might do. She left a message on Saturday – that was one of the ones I didn't retrieve while you were here – to tell me Kirtling had been released and was on his way home. She sounded absolutely over the moon and asked me to call back some time so he could thank me for the support I'd given her.

When I returned the call on Sunday she sounded . . . well, different, deflated almost . . . I'm not sure how to describe it.'

'It looks very much as if he took exception to her having confided in you,' Jim said dryly. 'That would have taken the gilt off the gingerbread, wouldn't it? Needless to say, she wasn't going to let on he'd knocked her about.'

'So how did she account for the bruises?'

'She claimed she'd fallen off a stepladder while rehanging some curtains that had just come back from the cleaners, but Page said it sounded pretty lame and he had no doubt she was lying.'

'You reckon Kirtling did it?'

'We're sure of it. We put it to him, of course, but all we got was "no comment".'

'That figures. I suppose when he heard about the conversations she had with me, instead of being grateful to her for trying to enlist my help in proving he didn't kill Una May he lost his temper at the thought of what she might have let slip. No wonder he was keen to keep my visit secret from the police.'

'Exactly.'

'He assured me he'd given the gardener a ticking off. Was that true?'

'Not according to Andrews; Kirtling declined to comment. The fact is that little by little we're building up a very different profile of our man from the one Miranda Keene would like us to have. We've re-interviewed all of the staff and they all say more or less the same thing – she's completely devoted to him, but at the same time she's more than a little afraid of him. In fact, I get the impression he gives all his employees a hard time if they step out of line.'

'I'm surprised they stay with him.'

Jim shrugged. 'It can't be too bad; he's away most of the week and he pays good wages, so they say.'

'What about his employees in London?'

'Basically, very similar reactions. He provides good working conditions and pays them well; in return he rules with a rod of iron and doesn't hesitate to use bullying tactics if anyone dares to challenge him.'

'A man who can turn violent when crossed,' Sukey said

thoughtfully. 'It's a bit surprising, when you come to think about it, that he didn't dish out the same treatment to Una May. I don't imagine he'd have taken kindly to being threatened. Were there any bruises on her body, by the way?'

'None, but it's hardly surprising. The argument Andrews overheard took place when there could have been other people within earshot, which of course is why he was so anxious for her to keep her voice down. By all accounts she was the kind of girl who wouldn't hesitate to bring a charge of assault if he laid a finger on her.'

Sukey nodded. 'And in the end she pushed him just a bit too far. Poor girl, she might have been a little schemer, but she didn't deserve that. And I suppose the row with Miranda took place at the weekend when none of the other staff were on the premises.'

'Exactly,' said Jim. 'Oh, and one other thing; Athena Letchworth, the glamorous interior designer, told us he'd pestered her for a date ever since she started working for him. She got his measure pretty quickly and made sure she was never on her own with him. Then he commissioned the picture and was very keen for her to appear in it. She made the excuse that she didn't have time to sit for hours posing for it, but he was very insistent, offered to drive her to the studio and take her out to dinner after the sitting and so on. She saw through that, of course, and said the artist could just as easily work from a photograph. She said he was pretty angry at being thwarted, but she stood her ground and there wasn't much he could do about it because the work of decorating and furnishing was well under way.'

'I gather it was through her that Montwell got the commission.'

'That's right. We think they're an item, although it hasn't any bearing on the case. By the way, I understand you wanted to know how much Kirtling paid for the picture.' His tone was casual, but there was a familiar searching look in his greenish eyes.

So Dalia's been telling tales again, Sukey thought, but she managed to conceal her irritation and said casually, 'I was curious because Montwell seemed so upset at losing the copy of the Matisse that I assumed he expected to be paid a lot of money for it.'

'Maybe he was thinking of the amount of work that had gone into it. Artists are pretty temperamental people. Anyway, he was probably insured.'

'Yes, that's what Dalia said.'

Jim glanced at his watch. 'I really should be going. What are you doing at the weekend?'

'No special plans. What do you suggest?'

'I'm not sure how I'm going to be fixed. I'll be in touch.'

His goodnight kiss was warm and affectionate, but not passionate. She had a strong impression that there was something going on that he didn't want her to know about, and that the missing picture was in some way involved.

The next day was Friday and it passed uneventfully. At the end of the afternoon, as the CSIs were making out their reports and preparing their samples for despatch to the various departments for examination, Mandy complained that it had been a pretty dull week.

'All run-of-the-mill stuff,' she sighed as she sealed up her report and dropped it into the out-tray. 'No murders, no armed robberies, no muggings or beatings up – what are today's villains coming to?'

Sukey gave a sympathetic chuckle. 'Perhaps they've decided that too much excitement isn't good for us,' she said.

'So what are you planning at the weekend?'

Sukey hesitated. There had been no word from Jim and she had no intention of sitting around at home waiting for him to call. 'I thought I'd do some shopping in Cheltenham. The cold weather's coming and I need some new sweaters and things. I could take Gus out to lunch if he hasn't got anything else fixed.'

Sukey was disappointed to learn that Gus had arranged to drive to Stratford with some friends, so she set off on her shopping expedition alone. After a couple of hours spent battling her way through the Saturday morning crowds in Cheltenham, she returned to her car, locked her purchases in the boot and went in search of lunch. She was trying to decide between several small restaurants in Regent Street when someone called her name. She turned and found herself face to face with a woman wearing a long coat, dark glasses and a hat with a wide brim pulled down over her eyes. It took her a moment to recognize Miranda Keene.

'Mrs Reynolds . . . Sukey . . . I hope you don't mind my speaking to you. I saw you there . . . are you looking for somewhere to have lunch?'

'Yes I am, as it happens.'

'I wonder if I could join you. I promise not to pester you to do anything about . . . you know . . . it's just that with Anne-Marie at college all day and my sister and her husband away . . . I'm all alone in the house and—' Her voice faded to a whisper; she was plainly on the point of breaking down.

Touched by her distress, Sukey replied, 'It'll be a pleasure! I've had a pretty tiring morning trailing round the shops and it'll be nice to have some company. Can you recommend any of the restaurants along here?'

'Last time I was in town I had a very nice meal in the Country Kitchen.'

'All right, let's go there.'

When they were settled at a corner table Miranda took off her hat and glasses. 'You're probably wondering why the disguise,' she said with a faint smile. 'It must sound a bit paranoid, but there have been photographers hanging around ever since,' her voice wavered again but after a moment she carried on bravely, 'Digby's arrest. They seem desperate to get a picture of me; I can't think why.'

Feeling that it would be tactless to point out that reporters were always hungry for anything sensational, and no doubt they had gleaned from talking to the locals that Miranda Keene was more than just a housekeeper to a man on a murder charge, Sukey picked up the menu. Miranda did the same, but after a moment she gave a sudden exclamation and whispered, 'Look who's just come in.'

Sukey half turned and saw two people being shown to a table behind them: Philip Montwell and a strikingly beautiful woman whom she recognized from the painting as Athena Letchworth. As they sat down, the woman said something to her companion; Sukey did not catch the words, but the artist's reply, although spoken quietly, was clearly audible. 'Don't worry, we'll celebrate in style when it's all over,' he promised with a smile.

Sukey turned back to Miranda and was astonished to see that she was glaring at Montwell. Her face was scarlet and she was baring her teeth like an angry dog. 'How dare he!' she hissed. She pushed back her chair, stood up and grabbed her belongings. 'I'm not eating in the same room with *him*!' She swept past Sukey and made for the door, brushing aside a waitress who was approaching to take their order.

With an apologetic gesture at the startled woman, Sukey hurried after her.

Eighteen

By the time Sukey reached the door Miranda was already running along the street as if pursued by the crowd of reporters she had taken so much trouble to avoid. When Sukey caught up with her she stopped short and put her hands to her face. Her shoulders were heaving and it was several seconds before she managed to control herself. Eventually, she took out a handkerchief, wiped her eyes and said, 'I'm sorry; you must think I'm quite mad.'

'Not mad, just very upset,' Sukey said gently. 'You've been under a lot of stress lately.' She thought for a moment and then said, 'Did you drive here?'

'No, I came by bus.'

'In that case you can have a drink. I think you need one,' she insisted as Miranda shook her head.

'I'm all right, really. I'm sorry to mess you about,' she went on hurriedly, 'but on second thoughts I'll forget about lunch.' She glanced at her watch. 'I was going to do some shopping and get the four o'clock bus, but there's one in half an hour; I think I'll get that.'

'You'll do no such thing,' Sukey said firmly. 'You need something to eat, but first of all you need something to help you unwind. There's a pub over the road; let's go in there. I need a visit to the loo anyway.' Ignoring Miranda's feeble protests, she steered her into the bar, found the ladies' room and waited while she tidied her hair and renewed her make-up. 'Right, let's go and get that drink. We can order our food at the bar at the same time.'

They settled at a corner table. Miranda drank slowly and in silence for a few minutes before saying, 'I suppose I owe you some sort of explanation.'

'If you feel like giving it,' Sukey replied. 'You've obviously taken against Montwell in a big way. I don't want to pry, of course—' though I'm dying to know what you've got against him, she added mentally. She waited patiently while Miranda continued to sip her brandy, still apparently deep in thought.

'I suppose there are two reasons why I took a dislike to him,' she began. 'I'm sure he's a brilliant artist, and I know artists are said to be temperamental creatures, and Digby doesn't know much about art, of course – but it's nothing to be ashamed of. He's an expert in his own field and he doesn't look down on people who don't share his knowledge of business. He admitted his ignorance about art to Montwell at their first meeting. He didn't put it quite like that, of course; he said something like "I don't know much about your old masters and all that stuff, but I do know what I like". I saw Montwell's lip curl and it spoke volumes.'

'I know what you mean,' Sukey said sympathetically. 'Some people who have a particular expertise look down their noses at people who don't know as much as they do. It makes them feel superior when dealing with ordinary folk like us.'

'Superior?' Miranda said scornfully. 'Contemptuous would be a better word in that man's case. At first he made excuses not to take on the commission at all, made out it was too big and he didn't have time. When Digby put pressure on him, he quoted a figure that he probably thought would be turned down, but Digby agreed to it. He knows what he wants and he doesn't give up easily.' The last words were spoken with a hint of pride.

'Are you sure Montwell wasn't speaking the truth when he talked about pressure of work?' Sukey asked. 'The boating party is a pretty big picture – it would take quite a long time to copy.'

'Of course I'm sure; I was there. I thought his curt, offhand manner was most offensive and I said so to Digby after he left, but Digby just laughed and said it was an old dodge to squeeze more money out of him. He was so determined to get what he wanted that he was prepared to pay over the odds for it. Eventually, Montwell agreed; Digby poured drinks and then insisted on showing him over the house. It was almost embarrassing; there was Digby boasting about how much he was spending on having the place done up and praising the

Letchworth woman to the skies, while Montwell was making snide remarks like, "yes, you will need a few nice pictures to complement the decor". There was a sort of sneer in his voice; I could feel the contempt he had for Digby and I remember being very angry on his behalf. She's as bad; she didn't say anything objectionable but once or twice I caught them exchanging glances and almost smirking.'

'How did Digby react to the jibes?'

'That's the sad thing. I don't think he noticed and I didn't have the heart to tell him. In a way, you see, Montwell was right. That's what he did want; it was part of the image of himself he was trying to build up as a member of the landed gentry. I suppose you could describe that as his Achilles heel; he's as tough as they come over anything to do with the business.'

Or his personal relationships, was the thought that flashed into Sukey's mind. While they were in the ladies' room, Miranda had combed her hair back from her face before rearranging it and there was still a trace of bruising near the left eye.

'You said you had two reasons for disliking Montwell,' said Sukey. 'What's the other?'

Miranda hesitated before replying. 'I'm no expert, but it so happens that years ago – just before I started working for Digby – I was in Washington DC with my previous employer. He was a great art lover and he took me to the Phillips Collection and showed me the original of *The Luncheon of the Boating Party*. It's absolutely stunning; it had a wall to itself and the light just seemed to blaze out of it. I mentioned it to Digby when he first got the idea of having a copy of an old master made for the sitting room; as it happens, he'd seen it too and he agreed that it would be perfect to go over the mantelpiece in the big sitting room. When he heard that the people in the picture were friends of the artist he was tickled pink and insisted on adopting that idea as well.'

'And I suppose you saw Montwell laughing behind his hand?'

'No, it wasn't that, although I'm sure he was. What makes me so angry is the quality of the painting. As I mentioned, he charged Digby a huge fee for it, but even I could tell that

123

it wasn't up to the standard you'd expect from an artist whose work has been known to fool the experts. It seemed like just another expression of his contempt; I could imagine him saying, "That's good enough for that ignoramus."''

Miranda had emptied her glass and was gripping the stem so hard that Sukey feared it would snap between her fingers. She reached out and gently took it from her. 'I know how devoted you are to Digby, and how badly his arrest has affected you,' she said, 'but don't you think you're being a bit OTT about this? It's quite likely Montwell takes the same sort of attitude when dealing with anyone who doesn't know much about art. I remember Anne-Marie telling me how he slapped her down when she ventured to pay him a compliment about his work.'

Miranda frowned. 'Yes, she told me that,' she admitted.

'Doesn't that prove my point?'

'Not a bit, it's just another example of his arrogance. My niece made excuses for him, of course. The poor child is quite besotted with the man. She says we should make allowances for him because of some tragedy in his life a few years ago.'

'Yes, she told me how he'd lost his only sister in rather tragic circumstances,' Sukey said. 'It must have been dreadful for him.'

'That doesn't give him the right to go round gloating over other people's misfortunes. You heard what he said about "celebrating in style when it's all over", didn't you?'

'You aren't suggesting that's got anything to do with Digby being charged with Una May's murder, surely?'

'I certainly am.'

'Oh come now,' Sukey protested, 'surely no one would be as spiteful as that just because someone they despised was in trouble. Anyway, what makes you think they were talking about Digby?'

'I just feel it in my bones,' Miranda seethed. 'Well, they'll laugh on the other side of their faces when he's acquitted.' Her mouth set like a steel trap; it was plain that her mind was closed to reason. At that moment a waiter brought their food, and to Sukey's relief the subject was dropped in favour of more general topics.

When they had finished their lunch and paid their bill, they went out into the street. Miranda put a hand on Sukey's arm and said hurriedly, 'I do hope you'll treat what I've said as confidential.' She dropped her voice and began speaking in hurried, jerky sentences, with frequent glances over her shoulder as if she was afraid of being overheard. 'People are saying such dreadful things about Digby . . . they're all lies, of course, and his lawyer has warned me to be very careful about what I say to the police . . . and in a way you are the police, but . . . just remember I've been talking to you as a friend. Please!' There was a pathetic pleading in her voice that contrasted sharply with the recent anger.

'Don't worry, I'm sure nothing you've said this afternoon could possibly have any bearing on the case,' said Sukey.

The response seemed to satisfy Miranda and her face cleared. 'No, of course it couldn't. Thank you for being so sympathetic. Goodbye.' She turned and hurried off in the direction of the High Street. Sukey followed more slowly on her way back to the car park.

When she reached home she unpacked her shopping, made a cup of tea and sat down at the kitchen table to drink it while making a few notes about her chance encounter with Miranda Keene, the incident in the restaurant and Miranda's subsequent outburst against Athena Letchworth and Philip Montwell. Despite the assurance she had given, Sukey knew from experience that even the tiniest scrap of information could prove significant in an investigation and despite Miranda's plea she resolved to tell Jim about it at the earliest opportunity. That came sooner than she expected; at six o'clock, just as she was about to start preparing her evening meal, he rang.

'Have you had a good day?' he asked.

'Very interesting. I'm glad you rang; I wanted a chance to have a word with you. I went into Cheltenham to do some shopping and I bumped into Miranda Keene. We had lunch together.'

'And?'

'Athena Letchworth and Philip Montwell came into the restaurant just after we'd sat down and Miranda nearly went berserk.' Reading from her notes, Sukey gave a brief rundown of the incident.

When she had finished, Jim said, 'It doesn't surprise me really – she's insisted from the start, in the face of all the evidence, that Kirtling is just a big softie with a crusty exterior, although we're uncovering a very different picture of the man. As for Montwell's attitude towards his client – well, we gathered at the first interview that he didn't exactly hold him in high esteem, but there doesn't seem to be anything personal in it, just an arrogant condescension towards someone he considers his intellectual inferior. Miranda's probably blown it up in her mind because of her fanatical devotion to Kirtling. Her attitude towards Athena Letchworth doesn't surprise me either in view of the way Kirtling was making passes at her.'

'Fanatical is the word. She's convinced herself that the talk of celebration was in anticipation of a guilty verdict on Kirtling.'

'Poor woman. She really needs help, but there's nothing you can do for her. I do hope she isn't going to keep pestering you.'

'Me too,' Sukey said fervently. 'Anyway, that's enough about me. Where are you calling from?'

'At the station but, thank goodness, I've finished for the day. Do you fancy going out for a meal?'

'That would be lovely.'

'I hoped you'd say that. I've taken a chance and booked a table at that Greek restaurant we found a month or so ago. I'll pick you up about seven.'

'I'll be ready.'

He arrived with more flowers and the recent coolness between them melted away as he swept her into a lingering embrace and told her she looked and smelled divine. During the short drive to the restaurant, while they were waiting at traffic lights, she said casually, 'I've just realized I was so busy telling you about Miranda that I forgot to ask what sort of day you've had. And there's something else I want to ask you—'

'Let it wait. I'm off duty and tonight there are more important things to think about.' For a brief moment before the lights changed he leaned towards her and put his hand on her knee. Her flesh tingled under his touch; his breath was warm on her cheek and the tone of his voice put his meaning beyond doubt. Of course her question could wait. She snuggled down happily in her seat with all thoughts of Miranda and her obsessions driven from her mind.

Nineteen

Over breakfast the following morning, Sukey said, 'Jim, I've just remembered, I wanted to ask you something.'

He looked up from his plate of eggs and bacon and said, 'What was that?'

'It's about something Miranda said while she was babbling on about how everything she'd told me was in confidence and all that. She said something like, "people are telling dreadful lies about Digby" and went on to say that his lawyer had warned her about not saying too much to the police. I was wondering what sort of lies – would it just be village gossip, or is there something more sinister that you haven't told me about?'

Jim put down his knife, picked up his mug of coffee and took several swallows before replying. Then he said, 'Sook, don't take this the wrong way, but I'd like your assurance you aren't going to let Miranda drag you into any more of her attempts to find proof of Kirtling's innocence.'

She reached across the table and put a hand on his arm. 'I promise you that's the last thing I intend to do,' she said earnestly. 'To be fair to her, I think she's already got the message; she didn't even mention it yesterday. Reading between the lines, I'd say she probably knows in her heart that he did kill Una May, but can't bring herself to admit it or say anything to help the police prove their case.'

'We've come to that conclusion as well,' Jim agreed. 'The fact is, we've been turning up a great deal of stuff about Kirtling's private life that paints a rather different picture of him than the one Miranda would have us believe.'

'What sort of stuff?'

'Stuff we found on his computer, for a start. Some of it he'd downloaded from porno websites, but there were some very interesting shots apparently taken with a camera rigged up in his London flat. They show him and Fiona having fun together.'

'Fiona? Isn't she his PA in London?'

'That's right. She's been much more forthcoming than Miranda about Kirtling's sexual appetites and when she was confronted with the evidence she didn't attempt to deny doing a spot of overtime. She's quite definite he's never threatened her with serious violence, although there were some simulated S & M sequences that she said she'd not been too keen on at first but eventually agreed to if he paid her extra.'

'She sounds quite a tough cookie.'

'Yes, but she admitted she was always careful not to push him too far. In fact she more or less confirmed the general consensus – he can be ruthless and intimidating in order to get his own way, even quite frightening on occasions. Just the same, she insisted she'd never heard of him physically attacking anyone. She seems genuinely shocked by his arrest for Una May's murder.'

'Have you told Miranda about the porno websites?'

'Oh yes – and needless to say she refuses to believe it. She maintains it's something we've invented to turn her against him.' Jim laid down his knife and fork and stared moodily at his empty plate. 'The fact is, we're a hundred per cent sure that Kirtling's our man, but we still haven't been able to find any copper-bottomed evidence to confirm it. We believe our case is strong enough to convince a jury, but we still don't know if the CPS is going to allow it to come to court.'

'Yes, I can see your problem,' Sukey said thoughtfully. 'You're dealing with a man who is known to have a voracious sexual appetite and a ruthless side to his character, a man who fathered an illegitimate child and refused to marry the mother. The mother of that unborn child was subsequently found murdered in the garden of his own home and there's no evidence pointing to anyone else who might have had a motive to kill her.'

'Or to indicate a tendency to violence – apart from a few unusual sexual requirements that his PA obligingly satisfied,' Jim added.

'There is the bruise on Miranda's face, of course,' Sukey

pointed out. 'I know she swears she got it by falling off a stepladder, but if that's the truth she must have had a real purler. I saw the remains of the bruise when we were in the ladies' room and it's still quite noticeable.'

'Yes, we questioned her about that very closely. She contradicted herself several times about which room she was in when hanging the curtains and how high she'd had to reach, how far she fell and what she landed on and so on. It was obvious she was making it up, but she still stuck to her story.'

'Of course, even if he did take a swipe at her in the heat of the moment, it doesn't itself prove he's capable of murder.'

'No, of course it doesn't, although it does show he's capable of lashing out if he's pushed too far. But since they were alone in the house at the time there was no one who could even testify that they heard them having a row.'

'No gardener lurking in the bushes to overhear them,' said Sukey with a wry chuckle. 'By the way, what was Kirtling's reaction when you tackled him about what you found on his computer?'

'All he did was shrug his shoulders and say something like, "well, it's not exactly a hanging matter, is it?" I think his lawyer was a bit shocked; he asked for the interview to be suspended so that he could have a quiet word with his client.'

'And?'

'When they came back, the solicitor pointed out that Kirtling had freely admitted possessing the material in question, but he maintained it had no bearing on the crime with which he'd been charged and had nothing further to say about it at this stage. He suggested if we wanted to pursue it we should treat it as a separate offence. He was quite right, of course.' Jim sat back in his chair and gave a weary sigh. 'This is turning out to be a real cow of a case.'

'I'm sure you'll crack it in the end.'

'Let's hope so. What bothers me is that if it gets to court and he's acquitted, and we subsequently come across some really hard evidence against him, it'll mean he's got away with it. We just have to keep on digging in the hope of turning up something to clinch our case.' Jim stood up and began clearing the table. 'Come on, let's forget about it for now. It's going to be a nice day – how about a country walk and a pub lunch?'

'Great idea.'

As they were getting into their outdoor things, Sukey said suddenly, 'I know you'll think this is a daft question, but is there absolutely no possibility that someone else did it? Someone completely outside the frame that you haven't even considered or heard about?'

'You think we haven't thought of that? We've gone pretty thoroughly into Una May's past – and that of everyone else known to have contact with her – in the hope of finding a lead, but we've got absolutely nowhere. No, it's got to be Kirtling.'

They drove a few miles to a village high in the Cotswolds, parked the car and set off for their walk. The sky was blue and cloudless; the late October sunshine infused the stone houses with a hint of pale honey and set the woodlands aglow with multiple shades of bronze, copper and gold. Here and there a tractor-drawn plough moved like a clockwork toy across the gently undulating landscape, turning fields into patchworks of faded straw and rich brown. As they explored footpaths and lanes they met and exchanged greetings with other walkers, some in pairs, some in groups, some with children and dogs – all, like them, revelling in the chance to escape into the countryside.

They returned to the car invigorated, refreshed and relaxed. They drove to a favourite pub for lunch; by the time they had finished the day had begun to wane, with a touch of chill in the air to remind them that winter, although still a few weeks ahead, was nevertheless on its way.

'I rate that the best weekend we've had for a long time,' Jim remarked as he drew up outside Sukey's house. 'How about you, Sook?'

'It's been lovely,' she said softly.

He squeezed the hand she slipped into his and whispered, 'Let's go indoors and make it perfect.'

Later, as he was about to leave, she said, 'By the way, that case Andy's been working on – the one you told me was so hush-hush – how is it progressing? All right, I'm not asking for details, just interested,' she added as he put a finger to his lips in a mock gesture of secrecy.

'I haven't had much chance to talk to him for a couple of

days, but I get the impression they're moving in for the kill,' he said, adding mysteriously, 'I think you'll be quite surprised when it breaks.'

'I can't wait!'

After he had gone home and she was locking up the house for the night, it occurred to her that there was one further question she might have put to him. It had no particular relevance to the Kirtling case, but it would have been interesting to know if he had come across the answer during his investigations. It seemed unlikely, and in any case he was too busy to be bothered with red herrings. Maybe she would make a few enquiries of her own, if for no other reason than to satisfy her own curiosity. There was no earthly reason why he or anyone else should object to that.

Every time her phone rang during the next couple of days Sukey found herself wondering if Miranda was going to be on the line and experiencing a sense of relief when she wasn't. At about midday on Wednesday, as she was eating her lunch, Fergus rang.

'Hi Mum,' he said breezily, 'how are things?'

'Okay, thanks. How about you? Is your course going well?'

'Yes, fine. I'm sorry I haven't been in touch. Life's sort of full these days.'

'I understand. How was the trip to Stratford?'

'Oh, brilliant. We saw the new production of *Macbeth*. I felt mean turning down your offer of lunch – you sounded a bit jaded. I hope you found something interesting to do?'

'I spent most of the weekend with Jim except Saturday morning when I did some shopping in Cheltenham. While I was there I happened to bump into Miranda Keene and we had lunch together.'

'*Did* you?' His voice indicated both surprise and interest. 'I imagine she told you all about how the wicked police are trying to blacken the name of her innocent lover?'

'She hinted as much although she didn't go into details,' Sukey said cautiously. 'Anyway, how did you know about that?'

'Anne-Marie told me. Did Miranda try to re-enlist you as her personal private eye, by any chance?'

'Certainly not, and I'd have turned her down flat if she had. Gus, I have a feeling this is leading to something. What is it?'

'So Miranda didn't mention that her niece has picked up your magnifying glass and deerstalker hat and set off on a trail of enquiry of her own.'

'You're kidding!'

'It's true. On top of that, she confided in me yesterday that she thought she was getting somewhere. And, before you ask, she didn't give me the slightest hint of where she's been looking or what she's found out.'

'I suppose Miranda put her up to this,' Sukey said. 'It's too bad; the poor kid's too young to be lumbered with the obsessions of a paranoid aunt. Just the same, next time you see her, try and get her to go into a bit more detail. If she really has turned up something significant, she should tell the police right away.'

'I told her that and she promised she would. As a matter of fact, I'm hoping to see her at lunch today.'

'Then be sure and tell her what I said. What are you doing this evening, by the way?'

'Going out with Pete for a Chinese.'

'That's nice. Give him my regards, and keep in touch.'

When she reached home that evening she went into the sitting room with a cup of tea, turned on the television and settled down to watch the news, but realized after a few minutes that she had grasped very little of what was happening on the screen. Her mind was busy speculating on what Fergus had said about Anne-Marie and her mind went back to the question that she had forgotten to ask Jim on Sunday. She wondered whether the girl had picked up on the same point and, under pressure from her aunt, turned it into something with more sinister undertones. It would be interesting to find out.

Twenty

After leaving the station at the end of her shift on Thursday afternoon, Sukey called in at the office of the *Gloucester Gazette*. A middle-aged woman sat behind the desk, reading the latest edition. The headline on the front page read: 'Art Treasures Stolen From Stately Home'.

When Sukey entered the woman looked up with a friendly smile, put down the paper and said in a warm Gloucestershire accent, 'Good afternoon, can I help you?'

'I'd like to look at some back numbers, please.'

'Certainly. You'll find the most recent ones over there.' She pointed to a table on which lay several heavy binders.

'What about earlier ones?' Sukey asked. 'What I'm looking for happened some time ago.'

'How long ago?'

'I'm not sure. A couple of years, perhaps – maybe longer.'

'In that case you'll have to check on the microfiche. Those only go back to the beginning of last month.'

'Oh, right. Where can I do that?'

'The viewer is in the corner. I'll come and set it up for you; where would you like to start?'

Sukey chose a year at random. While the woman was fiddling with the machine, she scanned the first few pages of a copy of that evening's edition lying on the table. The lead story concerned the theft of two pictures from a well-known property in a neighbouring county, but it was something on one of the inside pages that caught her eye. A headline reading: 'Local Tycoon Freed' was followed by a brief statement that Sir Digby Kirtling had successfully appealed against the magistrates' original decision not to grant bail.

The woman turned from the machine and said, 'There you are. Let me know if—' Spotting the item Sukey was reading, she broke off and commented tartly, 'I suppose it's his money that got him out. If he wasn't rich he'd still be locked up, wouldn't he?'

'I don't think it's quite as simple as that,' Sukey said and added, 'I see he's not allowed to return to Muckleton Manor, though.'

'Afraid he'll do it again, I suppose.'

Time was passing and Sukey did not feel like wasting it in speculation as to what bail conditions might have been imposed on Kirtling, so she thanked her, sat down and began the daunting task of scrolling through page after page of news items. After half an hour of fruitless searching she leaned back and closed her eyes. This is crazy, she told herself. It could have been five, even ten years ago. You're wasting your time, and anyway, what's it to you? But she refused to give up and the minutes ticked away as the search took her further and further back into the past.

At a quarter past five the woman came over to her and said, 'The office closes in fifteen minutes. If you haven't found what you're looking for by then I'm afraid you'll have to come back another time.'

Sukey passed a hand across her forehead. 'To be honest, I've absolutely no idea when the thing I'm looking for happened.'

'If you could give me some idea of what it was about I might be able to help you,' the woman said. 'I like to keep up with the local news myself so I read the paper most days. Of course, I can't remember everything, but—'

Sukey hesitated for a moment before telling herself that there was nothing particularly secret or confidential about her enquiry. 'That would be a great help,' she said. 'It was about a young woman who died of a drug overdose. Her brother is an artist who owns a gallery in Cheltenham.'

'I remember that!' the woman exclaimed. 'It was such a sad case. Let me see now, it was two, no probably three years ago, in the summer. I particularly remember because it was my mother's birthday and we took her to a matinee at the Everyman. May I?'

'Please do.'

Sukey moved aside to let the woman sit down at the machine.

After a couple of minutes she gave a little cry of triumph and said, 'Yes, here's the first report. Look.' She indicated a front-page headline reading: 'Corpse Found in Luxury Flat', followed by a brief account of how the as yet unidentified body of a woman had been discovered by a concerned neighbour.

'Brilliant!' Sukey exclaimed. 'Yes, that must be the one. I take it there were further reports?'

'Oh yes, there were several during the next week or so. They found out who she was – you're right, her brother was an artist and the poor man had to identify the body. I don't think they ever managed to establish exactly what had happened; there was some evidence that she'd been seen with some known drug addicts and been experimenting with drugs herself. They came to the conclusion that she must have taken an overdose by accident, although I seem to remember there was a rumour going round at the time that she might have been upset after a row with a boyfriend.'

'I suppose the boyfriend was one of the junkies she'd been mixing with?'

'I don't think they ever found him. Someone living in the same house said they'd heard her having an argument with a man, but I don't think he ever came forward. The press hinted at something sensational at the time, but you know what reporters are like; what they don't know they make up. I suppose I shouldn't say things like that, seeing as I work for a newspaper,' the woman added with an apologetic smile. She glanced at the clock. 'You have another few minutes if you want to take a quick look.'

'I'd quite like to know the full story, but there isn't time now.' Sukey made a note of the date the first report had appeared and picked up her bag. 'Thank you very much for your help. I'll pop in again tomorrow.'

Friday morning brought only routine jobs. During the after-noon Sukey was called to a break-in at the home of an elderly couple who had returned to their house from their weekly visit to the supermarket to find a patio window smashed and a number of items stolen, including a recently acquired digital television. The husband was comforting his wife, explaining that they had been looking forward all the week to a showing of an old black and white film that evening.

'It meant so much to us; it was the one we saw the first time we went to the pictures together,' the old man explained while his wife wept on his shoulder. 'And just look at all the mess. Our carpet has been ruined – we'll never get it clean.'

'It's mostly just broken glass and trodden in dirt,' Sukey said. 'Perhaps a neighbour will give you a hand.'

'But look at all the blood.' He gestured at the stains on the carpet. 'I suppose they cut themselves getting in.'

The woman raised her head, hiccupped and said brokenly, 'I hope they bleed to death,' before bursting into a fresh bout of sobbing.

'Now love, that's not a Christian thing to say,' he reproved her gently.

'It might comfort you to know that the blood could be a great help in tracking down the villains,' Sukey said as she settled down to collect samples. 'If they've been arrested previously they'll be on the DNA database.'

'There you are, love; there's always a bright side. Let's get out of the lady's way while she does her job. I'll make a cup of tea,' he said over his shoulder as he led his wife from the room.

When she had finished, Sukey politely declined the offer of tea. She still had two more jobs to do; she returned to the station, wrote her report and checked all her samples and it was nearly five o'clock before she reached the *Gazette* office. The receptionist looked up from her paper and said, 'Hello, back again? There's someone using the microfiche at the moment, but I see she's just finishing.' She nodded in the direction of a young woman who was pushing a notebook into a bag lying on the floor beside her. As she straightened up and turned round, Sukey recognized her.

'Anne-Marie!' she exclaimed in surprise. 'Fancy seeing you here.'

The girl flushed and said, in a slightly breathless voice, 'Oh, hello, Mrs Reynolds. I'm just doing a little research.'

'Something to do with your art course, I suppose?'

'Er, yes, sort of.'

'How's it going?'

'Fine, thank you. It's nice seeing you; excuse me, I've got to dash.'

Her manner was evasive and Sukey's suspicions were aroused. Remembering Fergus's reference to the girl 'picking up her magnifying glass and deerstalker hat' she caught her by the arm as she made for the door. 'I'd like a word, but it's a bit confidential,' she said in a low voice. 'Shall we go outside?'

With evident reluctance, Anne-Marie agreed. 'I'm not doing anything wrong,' she said defensively the minute they were out in the street.

'I'm not suggesting that you are. It's just that Fergus told me your aunt was upset when I said I couldn't help her so you'd decided to ferret around to see if you could find anything that might help clear Sir Digby.'

Anne-Marie looked taken aback. 'Oh ... yes, that's right,' she said after a momentary hesitation.

'And have you found anything?'

'Well, not exactly. I just—' She broke off in such evident confusion that Sukey had a strong impression that she was thinking on her feet. 'I know Una May had a sister,' she hurried on. 'I thought perhaps she might know of some other man Una had been seeing that no one else knew about ... I was looking up the reports to see if I could find out where she lives so I could go and see her.'

'And did you? Find out where she lives, I mean?'

'Oh ... er, no ... that is, I've had to leave it for now; perhaps I'll come back another time.'

'I can understand you wanting to help your aunt,' Sukey said gently, 'but there really isn't any mileage in this. The police will have questioned the sister very thoroughly, and in any case—' She was on the point of going on to say that she had information that the woman had unhesitatingly named Kirtling as her sister's killer. Realizing that if such an indiscretion got back to Jim or DCI Lord she would be in serious trouble, she merely said, 'I'm sure Sir Digby's lawyers will have thought of it as well. Did you know he's been released on bail, by the way?'

'Yes, of course; Auntie M is thrilled, but she's upset that he's not allowed home. I feel so sad for her, although I do get a bit cross when she says awful things about Philip.'

'I suppose she told you about the encounter in the restaurant.

She did get up quite a head of steam – it was rather embarrassing.'

'I know. She really has got her knife into him, and it's so unfair.'

'Has he got over the loss of his picture?'

For some reason, Anne-Marie appeared momentarily thrown by the question. 'I . . . I suppose so,' she stammered. 'He hasn't mentioned it since.'

'So you're still working for him?'

'When I can fit it in; the money comes in useful. As a matter of fact, I'm going tomorrow and I'm taking something I've been working on at college to show him. He's being very kind, helping me with my assignments. I pointed this out to Auntie M, but all she said was, "so he should be after all the trouble he's caused". Look, I really must go or I'll miss my bus and I've got a date this evening. Maybe I'll take your advice about going to see the sister.'

'That's good. Take care.'

Sukey went back into the office and walked over to the microfiche. It was still switched on at the page Anne-Marie had been studying. She was not surprised to find that the report had nothing to do with the death of Una May. It was a recent feature about a police hunt for a gang of art thieves.

Her first task on reaching home was to call Fergus. 'Hello, what sort of day have you had?' she said when he answered.

'Good, thanks. How about you?'

'Boring from the work point of view, otherwise quite interesting. Listen, Gus, did you see Anne-Marie today?'

'No; she wasn't in the refectory at lunchtime. Why?'

'I was wondering . . . you told me she seemed to think she'd found something out . . . about Una May's death, I mean.'

'Oh, that. Yes, I'd forgotten. Do you think it's important?'

'I don't know, but I found her in the *Gazette* office this afternoon looking through back numbers. She claimed she was trying to track down the dead woman's sister to see if she could help, but it turned out she'd been looking into something quite different.'

'How odd,' he said after she had explained. 'She never said anything about that to me. I wonder if she's picked up something to suggest this gang might be responsible for nicking Montwell's painting.'

'That occurred to me. If that is the case I think someone should warn her it's not a good idea to tangle with people like that.'

'You're right; I'll have a word with her next time I see her. Anyway, what were you doing in the *Gazette* office?'

'Trying to find out what happened to Philip Montwell's sister.'

'What's that to you?'

'That's what I've been asking myself,' she admitted. 'It's just that I keep thinking about how cut up the man seemed about the loss of the painting. The officers who dealt with the break-in were quite cynical about it, thinking it was only the money he was thinking of, but I had the impression – and so, incidentally, did Anne-Marie – that he was really suffering, as though it was more personal than that. According to Jim, he's an arrogant so-and-so, and you should have heard Miranda Keene bad-mouthing him the other day, but beneath all that he's just as vulnerable as the next man. I feel really sorry for him – I can't explain why, but it's been bugging me ever since I met him.'

'Well, don't let Jim know you're hankering after another man or he'll get in a real froth.'

'Don't be daft, Gus, I'm not hankering after him. Just the same, I'd be obliged if you didn't mention it to Jim.'

'Trust me,' he said with a chuckle.

'And remember to tell Anne-Marie what I said.'

'I will,' he assured her. 'Mum, what are you up to at the weekend?'

'I'm having a meal with Mandy and her mother this evening and tomorrow and Sunday I'm hoping to catch up with some household and gardening chores. Jim's visiting some relatives in Scotland; he suggested I go with him, but I turned it down. How about you?'

'Actually, Pete and Lester have asked me to join them on a walking trip in Wales.'

'That sounds a lovely idea. The forecast is good; you should have a great time.'

'You're sure you don't mind being on your own?'

'Of course not, silly. Have fun, and give my regards to Pete and Lester. I must have a shower and change now; I'm due at Mandy's in an hour.'

Later, when she returned home after an enjoyable evening, she found a message from Jim to say he had reached his destination safely and would call when he returned on Sunday. She slept soundly and awoke refreshed. On Saturday, after a morning occupied with housework and laundry, she spent a satisfying afternoon tidying up the back garden before settling down to watch a movie with her evening meal on a tray and a glass of wine at her elbow.

On Sunday morning she decided to tackle the front garden. While she was working out there a couple about her own age, who had recently moved into the house next door, emerged with their dog and asked if she could recommend a walk ending in a country pub which would allow them to bring their dog while they had lunch. A friendly discussion ensued, which ended in Sukey putting away her gardening tools and donning her walking boots before the three of them set off together.

By the time they returned it was almost four o'clock. Sukey and her new friends parted with mutual expressions of pleasure in one another's company and a firm promise to go on similar expeditions in which Jim would also be included. She went indoors in a relaxed state of mind she had not experienced for some time. Since Fergus had started at university there had been a change in her lifestyle to which she was still adjusting, and recent tensions between her and Jim had not made things any easier. It was as if a cloud had lifted; she hummed a tune as she took off her outdoor things and went into the kitchen to fill the kettle.

The red light on her answering machine was flashing. It was Jim, no doubt, to say he was on his way home. Perhaps he would call in to see her. She picked up the phone with a happy sense of anticipation.

But it was not Jim, it was Miranda, and she sounded distraught. 'Sukey, please call me as soon as you get this message,' she said, her voice so unsteady it was difficult to make out the words. 'Something awful has happened – Anne-Marie has disappeared!'

Twenty-One

In an instant, Sukey's mood changed from mild euphoria to dread. She sank into a chair, closed her eyes and thought back to the scene in the *Gazette* office on Friday afternoon in the hope of recalling something – anything – Anne-Marie had said that might give some clue to her movements that evening. She recalled the girl's apparent confusion at seeing her and the stammered excuse – exposed a few minutes later as a fabrication – she had given for being there. What else had she said? Something about being in a hurry to catch her bus and having a date that evening, but nothing of any real significance. There was, however, the clue she had inadvertently left on the microfiche; perhaps Miranda could shed some light on that.

After a few minutes she picked up the phone. It was answered in an instant; evidently Miranda had been sitting awaiting her call, any call. 'Oh Sukey, I'm so thankful to hear from you!' she said in a tremulous, barely audible whisper. 'I'm nearly going out of my mind ... I don't know what to do ... who to turn to—' Her voice broke into a series of short, staccato sobs. When she had managed to control herself she continued, 'my sister's due home tomorrow and her daughter is missing ... what shall I tell her? What can it mean?'

'Suppose you tell me exactly what happened?' Sukey suggested. She had a cold feeling in the pit of her stomach and her own voice was none too steady. 'When did you last see her?'

'On Friday evening, just before she went out with her friends. She's been staying with me here this week but she was going home that night so that she could do a bit of tidying up in the house, ready for Priscilla and Roy when they come back from their holiday. She was going to ring me some time on Saturday and we were going shopping together to stock up with food and so on, but she didn't phone and she didn't answer my calls . . . and I went to the house, but she wasn't there . . . it's not like her; something terrible must have happened!'

'Have you tried ringing her mobile?'

'Of course I have, but she doesn't answer.'

'Did you inform the police?'

'Not right away; I kept telling myself she'd probably gone to a friend's house and just forgotten our arrangement, but it wasn't like her. When she still hadn't got home this morning I rang and reported her missing. They sent two officers straight away; they asked a lot of questions about her friends and where she was going with them and so on, but all I could tell them was that someone picked her up in a car and they were going . . . "clubbing", I think she said. She was so happy and looking forward to her parents coming home . . . and that's the last time I saw or heard from her and I'm so frightened. Sukey, please help me!'

'I don't really see what I can do that the police can't do much more effectively,' Sukey said gently. 'They've got all the resources and—'

Miranda cut in before she had a chance to finish. 'You know Anne-Marie,' she pleaded. 'You've talked to her . . . I was hoping she might have said something to you that might—' Her voice died away on a thin note of despair.

'As it happens I saw her on Friday afternoon; I expect she told you?'

'No, she didn't mention it. What did she say?'

Sukey made the split second decision that anything she had gleaned from the encounter was best kept from Miranda for the time being. It would only add to her natural anxiety; the best thing to do the moment this call ended would be to get in touch with whoever was in charge of the investigation. Aloud, she said, 'Nothing special. We didn't chat for long because she was in a hurry to catch her bus.'

'A bus?' Miranda's voice registered surprise. 'I don't under-stand. A friend of mine who lives in the village brought her home in her car.'

'Perhaps this lady saw her by chance at the bus stop and gave her a lift?'

'No, it was all arranged. Sheila came to dinner here on Thursday evening and Anne-Marie happened to mention that she had to go to some art shop in Gloucester after college. Sheila works in Gloucester so she very kindly offered her a lift home.'

'Oh well, I must have misheard her,' Sukey said, although privately she was confident she had done nothing of the kind. It was obvious that Anne-Marie, in her anxiety to avoid being questioned further, had blurted out the first excuse to end the conversation that came into her head. 'Miranda,' she went on, 'have you spoken to Sheila? Did Anne-Marie say anything to her on the way home about her plans for Friday evening?'

'The police asked her that, but she couldn't help them much. She's here with me at the moment. She's being so kind; she stayed with me last night.'

'Will she stay tonight?'

'No, she can't, but the police have arranged for someone to keep me company and she's going to stay until they arrive. I think I'd go mad if I had to be here alone. Sukey, can you find out what's going on? The police promised they'd do everything possible to find Anne-Marie, but I haven't heard a thing since they left.'

'I can probably find out who's dealing with the case and have a word with them, but I can assure you that—'

'Oh please!' Miranda begged before Sukey had a chance to finish. 'Anything . . . anything . . . oh, just a minute, there's someone at the door.' There was a murmur of voices in the background followed by a short interval before she returned to the phone. 'It's the lady who's going to stay with me. I'd better go now,' she said and hung up.

Sukey had barely put her own telephone down when it rang. Jim was on the line. 'Hello, my love!' he said, and the sound of his voice brought immediate comfort. 'I thought I'd let you know I'm safely home.'

'Thank goodness for that!' she exclaimed, and she could hear the relief in her own voice.

'How was your weekend?' he asked, and without waiting for a reply went on, 'I've had a wonderful time with the aunties – perfect weather, lashings of superb Scottish food and—'

'That's great,' she broke in, 'but listen, Jim; I've just had a very disturbing phone call from Miranda Keene.'

'Not her again! I thought you'd made it clear—'

'This isn't anything to do with the Kirtling case. It's her niece, Anne-Marie – I think you've heard me speak of her; she was at school with Fergus. She hasn't been seen since Friday evening and Miranda's in a fearful stew.'

'Oh no!' Jim's voice sank to a horrified whisper. 'What have they done?'

'I don't follow you,' she said. 'What have who done?'

'The magistrates – letting Kirtling out on bail. We weren't happy about it because of our suspicions that he'd shown violence to Miranda Keene and might do so again. That's why we asked for it to be conditional on his staying away from the manor, but we never for one moment—' He broke off; Sukey pictured him as she had so often seen him before in a crisis, his hawklike features tense and grim, his green eyes narrowed in concentration. 'Is Miranda there on her own?' he asked after a brief silence.

'No, there's a Family Liaison Officer with her. Jim, do you really think Kirtling might be responsible? What motive could he possibly have for harming Anne-Marie?'

'None that we know of, but we do know he has a weakness for nubile young women and some strange sexual tendencies, which is why we felt he'd be better locked up. But he appealed and his counsel made a convincing case and got a psychiatrist to support him. The magistrates accepted his evidence so there wasn't much we could do except ask for him to be kept away from Muckleton, which they agreed.'

'So where's he been staying since he was let out?'

'At his London flat.'

'Jim,' Sukey said, 'is there any reason to believe that Kirtling is mixed up with this gang of art thieves?'

'Not that I know of. Why do you ask?'

She told him of her encounter with Anne-Marie in the office of the *Gloucestershire Gazette*. 'I don't like the sound of this at all,' he said. 'If it's okay with you I'd like to come round and have a more detailed talk about it. Say in half an hour or so?'

'Yes, fine.'

When he arrived he gave her a perfunctory embrace, walked straight into the kitchen and sat down at the table with a notebook in front of him.

'Would you like a drink?' she said.

'Maybe later.' He gestured at the chair opposite him and she sat down. 'Right, let's go over it again from the beginning.'

He listened intently while she repeated her story, interrupting from time to time with a question. When she had finished, he closed the notebook and sat for a few minutes without speaking. Then he said, 'This is worrying, Sook. I'm afraid that girl has blundered into a very dangerous situation.'

'You reckon it is something to do with the recent reports about art thefts?'

'It looks like it to me. Incidentally, that's what Andy Radcliffe and his team are working on.'

'The one you mentioned the other day – the one you said was so hush-hush?'

'That's right. The thing is, it so happens that the son of someone they suspect of being part of the gang is a student at the art college.'

'And you think maybe Anne-Marie's got hold of something she thinks might have a bearing on the thefts, told the son of her suspicions and—'

'—he mentioned it to his father, who passed it on to whoever's been masterminding the scam,' Jim finished as Sukey broke off in horror at the picture her words had conjured up. 'Yes, I think it's more than likely.'

'And you reckon Kirtling might be mixed up in it?'

'Who knows what pies he's got a finger in? It's a very odd coincidence that Anne-Marie should disappear within days of his being released from the nick.' He put away his notebook and stood up. 'I'll be on my way now, Sook.'

'You won't stay for a drink and something to eat later on? I had a pub lunch so I'll only be having something light, but I can easily—'

'Not this time, thanks, love. I'd like to pass all this on to Andy right away, as well as to the team looking into the girl's disappearance. No doubt they'll be in touch with you; in the meantime, think carefully and see if you can remember anything else that might help.'

'I'll do my best,' she promised, without a great deal of hope. 'Fergus might remember something though. He probably knows who some of her friends are. He's on a different course, but I know he meets her in the refectory now and again.'

'Fine. Have a word with him; you don't need me to tell you that every scrap of information helps us build up the picture. It would be better if you didn't mention the art scam, by the way.'

It was only after he had left that she realized he hadn't bothered to ask about her own day, not even when she mentioned the pub lunch. Normally after he'd been away he expressed an interest in what she had been doing in his absence. This case must be a pretty big one, she thought as she set about preparing her supper.

It was gone ten o'clock that evening when Fergus responded to the message she had left on his mobile, saying she needed to speak to him urgently.

'What's up, Mum?' he said when she answered his call.

'It's Anne-Marie. She hasn't been seen since Friday evening when she went out with some friends and she hasn't been in touch. Her aunt has reported her missing.'

'That's awful! Any idea where they were going?'

'It seems not. No one seems to know at the moment who might have been with her. You see her from time to time; do you know who she hangs around with?'

'Let's see . . . I've heard her mention a girl called Flo, and I've seen her talking to a chap who wears a black beret – I think I heard someone call him Pablo, but I don't know whether that's his name or because they reckon he thinks he's a wannabe Picasso.'

'Flo and a guy in a black beret,' Sukey repeated. 'That could be very useful, Gus, thanks. I'll pass it on to Jim; he was here earlier and he's very concerned.'

'Is he on the case then?'

'Not exactly, but he thinks it might be connected with something bigger. I can't tell you any more at the moment, Gus, and it would be better if you didn't say anything to anyone about this conversation.'

147

'If you say so. Everyone at college is going to be devastated if anything's happened to Anne-Marie. She's a lovely person, and talented too. How did you hear about it? Was it on the news?'

'I haven't heard the news this evening; I got it from her aunt. She rang me up earlier in a fearful state.'

'I can imagine. You'll let me know the minute you hear anything, won't you?'

'Yes, of course. I'll say goodbye now; I want to pass this on to Jim right away.'

As she got ready for bed, it occurred to Sukey that there was at least one other person who was going to be sadly affected by Anne-Marie's disappearance.

Twenty-Two

When Sukey reported for work on Monday morning she found the place buzzing with speculation about the disappearance of Anne-Marie. It had somehow leaked out that she had paid an unofficial visit to Muckleton Manor soon after Sir Digby Kirtling had been detained for the first time in connection with the murder of Una May, and the minute she arrived she found herself being plied with questions. Even Sergeant George Barnes, who normally tended to discourage gossip in the office, showed an interest. She brushed aside the suggestion that she had any inside knowledge of the case by saying that she had merely been responding to a frantic plea from Miranda Keene.

'She was absolutely distraught when he was arrested,' she explained. 'She insisted that it simply wasn't in his nature to kill anyone and she got it into her head that I could help her find the real murderer. When I asked her why she was so sure of his innocence – ' here Sukey allowed herself a minor deviation from the truth – 'she wouldn't tell me on the phone and begged me to go and see her. It was Saturday, I didn't have anything special to do and I was curious, so I went.'

'And what did she tell you that was so sensitive she wouldn't talk about it on the phone?' asked Mandy.

'Not much, really; I think she was just desperate for someone to talk to. It seemed to me that she's so potty about him she believes anything he tells her. She won't accept that he's guilty even now he's been charged.'

'You don't reckon she might be having second thoughts?' Mandy persisted. 'He gets bail and her niece disappears – coincidence or what?'

Sukey shrugged. 'She didn't mention him but, knowing how she feels, she wouldn't entertain the idea for a moment.

Anyway, there's no suggestion Anne-Marie is pregnant, or even that he's shown an interest in her.'

'What made Miranda think you could help?' asked George Barnes.

Sukey gave a sigh of exasperation. 'Gus knows Anne-Marie from college and he planted the idea in her head that I'm some kind of Sherlock Holmes, solving cases that have the police baffled. I had quite a job to convince them that there was nothing I could do for them.'

'Well, I wonder where your son got that idea,' Barnes said provocatively, but Sukey ignored the jibe. She had been struck by a horrifying thought: if only, instead of merely telling Fergus to warn Anne-Marie that what she was doing might be dangerous, she had contacted someone in CID right away to tell them about the encounter on Friday afternoon at the office of the *Gloucester Gazette*. Would they have taken it sufficiently seriously to get in touch with the girl immediately? And if so, might she still be alive? The possibility was to haunt her for many days to come.

'I take it that's a "no comment"?' Barnes taunted, as Sukey remained silent. 'Well troops, that's enough of the chit-chat. We might learn a bit more during the day; meanwhile, let's get on with some work, shall we?'

He distributed the day's assignments and the team sat down to plan their itineraries over the first mug of coffee of the day before setting off. On the way down to the car park, Mandy grabbed Sukey by the arm and hissed in her ear, 'I've noticed you being quite mysterious lately and I have a notion you know more about this than you're letting on.'

'What makes you think that?'

'We've worked together for a long time and I recognize the symptoms. Am I right or am I right?'

They had reached the yard where their vans were parked side by side. Sukey glanced round to make sure no one was within earshot before saying in a low voice, 'I'm pretty sure something big is going to break pretty soon and, yes, I have got some idea what it's about, but—'

'But your lips are sealed,' Mandy finished as Sukey broke off, uncertain how to continue. 'I suppose you've picked up something on your hot line to CID and it's all very hush-hush, but surely you can tell me. I won't breathe a word.'

Sukey let the oblique reference to her relationship with Jim Castle pass without comment. 'I'm sorry, you'll just have to wait for developments,' she said firmly. 'Have a good day. I'll see you later.' She got into her van and drove off.

Both her first two assignments were close to the city centre: a break-in and the theft of cigarettes from a corner shop in the Barton Street area and a burglary at a ground floor flat a few streets away where the occupant had carelessly left a window open. By the time she had finished checking the scenes, taking samples and bagging them up she felt in need of a break, so she had a quick drink of coffee from her flask while checking the local radio station for the latest news. A brief bulletin stated that the police were concerned for the safety of an eighteen-year-old woman named Anne-Marie Gordon, who had not been seen since parting from her friends after leaving a club on Friday night. They were appealing for anyone who might have seen her to come forward.

When the bulletin ended she switched off the radio and sat for several minutes, going over for the umpteenth time the meagre hints that Jim had let drop concerning the girl's possible, almost certainly inadvertent involvement in a dangerous situation connected with a gang of art thieves and swindlers. She had a vague notion that something someone – it might even have been Anne-Marie herself – had said to her, something that had no apparent significance at the time, might have a bearing on the case. Or it might have been something she had picked up elsewhere. She racked her brains, but found no answer. Maybe it would come to her later. Meanwhile, she had work to do.

Her last assignment of the day was at an Indian restaurant in Cheltenham that had been seriously damaged by fire. The officer in charge of the crew who dealt with the blaze suspected it had been started deliberately and his suspicions were confirmed when Sukey found traces of an accelerant in the kitchen. After taking numerous photographs and collecting and labelling samples from the debris she had to spend some time comforting the proprietor and his wife, whose limited command of English was compounded by the fact that they

151

were both in a state of shock. The husband had suffered burns to his face and hands in a futile effort to extinguish the flames; an ambulance had been summoned and was waiting to take him to hospital, but he made it clear with frantic signs that he feared a further attack and refused to leave his premises unattended, although he reluctantly allowed Sukey to photograph some of his injuries. Eventually a patrol car arrived in response to Sukey's call confirming that the fire was suspicious, the police took charge and between them they persuaded him to go and have his injuries treated.

By the time she left to return to Gloucester it was after four o'clock. To avoid the build-up of traffic leaving the town centre, she turned down one of the side streets leading off the Bath Road. Her route took her past Philip Montwell's gallery; as she waited at a junction a young man in denims emerged and began walking along the road ahead of her. From the portfolio he was carrying she guessed that he was an art student. She caught a quick glimpse of a thin, bearded face before her eyes fastened on the black beret he wore over his long, straggly hair. On impulse, instead of turning right she drove straight on, stopped the van a short distance ahead of him, pulled into the kerb and jumped out.

'Excuse me,' she said, 'are you a student at the university here?'

He eyed her suspiciously and replied in a slightly defensive tone, 'What about it?'

'I saw your portfolio and you came out of the Phimont Gallery so I thought you might be an art student.'

'So?'

'A friend of mine is doing an art course,' Sukey hurried on. 'Mr Montwell has been helping her with her project and I thought he might be doing the same for you. She said something once about one of the students being nicknamed Pablo because he wears a black Basque beret like Picasso. Would that be you by any chance?'

His manner changed yet again. 'Are you taking the piss or what?' he said aggressively.

'No, of course not,' she assured him. 'I just—'

'So what the hell's it got to do with you what my friends call me?'

'My friend's name is Anne-Marie Gordon. Do you know her?'

The question appeared to startle him and he hesitated before saying cautiously, 'I've seen her around.'

'Do you know she's gone missing?'

His eyes narrowed and he hesitated again before replying, 'I heard about it.'

'She was with some friends at a nightclub last Friday and she hasn't been seen since. Were you with the same crowd?'

'There were a lot of us from the art department. I can't remember all of them.'

'Well, I do hope you'll think very carefully and tell the police if you think of something that might help them. We're all very worried about her.'

For a fraction of a second she detected a tightening of the muscles round his mouth at the mention of the police, but he responded coolly enough, 'Yes, I'll do that.'

He was about to move on, but she detained him by saying, 'Is Mr Montwell helping you with a project as well?' She pointed to the portfolio he was carrying.

This seemed to take him by surprise and he looked down at the portfolio as if he had only just noticed that he was carrying it. 'Oh ... er ... yes, that's right,' he said.

'I think it's very good of him to encourage young artists, don't you?' she went on. 'Does he do it for many of the students?'

'I ... I'm afraid I don't know. If you'll excuse me, I have to go now,' he said, and hurried away before she had a chance to say anything further.

Back at the station, Sukey found that Mandy had already gone home and George Barnes was handing over to another sergeant whom she knew only by sight. She checked her samples and wrote her report; by the time she had finished Barnes had left and his relief had followed him from the room muttering something about tea and a sandwich without giving her a chance to ask about developments in the hunt for Anne-Marie. She went along the passage to Castle's office and tapped on the door. He was seated at his desk talking to Andy Radcliffe. They broke off when she entered and Castle said, 'Yes, Sukey, what is it?'

'I was wondering if there was any news of Anne-Marie?'
she said.

Both officers shook their heads. 'I'm afraid not,' said Castle.
'We've spoken to several of the students who were with her
last Friday, but she seems to have got separated from them
when they went their separate ways. The lad who was supposed
to take her home was having trouble with his car and several
of them were trying to fix it. It took quite a while and by the
time they got it going she'd disappeared. They didn't take it
too seriously at the time . . . they just assumed someone else
had given her a lift.'

'Which is probably exactly what did happen,' Sukey said
grimly. 'Did you by any chance speak to Pablo?'

Both men looked perplexed for a moment before Radcliffe
said, 'Oh, you mean the one who wears the black beret? No,
not yet; it seems he wasn't in class today and he wasn't at
home when we called at his lodgings.'

'Well, I've beaten you to it,' Sukey said, a little smugly,
and she told them of her encounter outside the Phimont Gallery.

'That's very interesting,' said Castle when she had finished.
'Perhaps you'd write out a detailed report and let one of us
have it tomorrow.'

'Yes, of course.' She turned to go, but Radcliffe said, 'Just
a moment, Sukey. I get the impression that you have some
doubts about the project this guy's supposed to be doing?'

She thought for a moment. 'Not doubts, exactly . . . I mean,
I'm sure he's got a project on the go the same as the others
on his course. It's just that for a split second he seemed sort
of taken aback at the notion that there was a connection
between it and his visit to Montwell's gallery.'

'You think it was a pretext for being there if he should be
challenged?'

'Not even that. After all, a portfolio is a normal thing for
an art student to be carrying. I'm inclined to think he was
there for a different reason altogether.'

'Such as?' It was Castle speaking this time and she felt his
eyes boring into hers. 'Come on, Sukey; if you know anything
it's your duty to tell us.'

'I don't *know* anything,' she replied. 'I just thought . . .
could there be some connection between Pablo and the disap-

pearance of Montwell's copy of the Matisse picture a week or so ago? I mean –' here she recalled that Jim had given her in confidence the information she was about to refer to and in consequence chose her words carefully – 'supposing this gang of art thieves Anne-Marie seems to have been researching is somehow connected with someone at the art college . . . and that Pablo somehow knew about the picture? And supposing Montwell is working on a copy of another masterpiece the gang might be interested in?'

Radcliffe stared at her. 'Are you suggesting that Montwell is in on the scam?'

'Oh no, not when I think how upset he was when his Matisse was nicked. Just the same, I understand he produces some extraordinarily accurate copies.'

'That's true,' Castle said, 'and we believe this mob has been involved with at least one case of a copy being traded off as the genuine article.'

'One thing puzzles me,' Sukey said. 'How does he manage to produce such accurate copies in his studio? I'd have thought he'd need to spend hours working in front of the original, and I believe the original of *La Danza* is in the Hermitage Museum in St Petersburg.'

'Fancy your knowing that.' Castle sounded impressed and Sukey, who had spent some time researching the artist on the Internet, felt a small glow of satisfaction. 'I think I know the answer to your question though,' he went on. 'When I interviewed his girlfriend, Athena Letchworth, she treated me to a mini-lecture on his working methods. She claims he has a photographic memory and only has to stand and contemplate a canvas for a couple of hours and make a few notes and every detail is indelibly printed on his brain. It's a rare gift she assured me, with pride.'

'I'm sure it is and I reckon he's lucky not to have had other works nicked,' Radcliffe commented. 'Thanks for the tip about young Picasso, Sukey.'

It was clear that both men considered the conversation at an end. Had Castle been on his own she would have asked him if anyone had spoken to Kirtling about Anne-Marie's disappearance. As it was, she said, 'You're welcome,' and left.

Twenty-Three

The house stood in a tree-lined street in a quiet part of the town not far from the main university campus. DS Radcliffe, accompanied by DC Patrick Burns, a recent addition to the CID team, climbed the staircase to the first-floor flat and rang the bell. The door was opened by a thin, ashen-faced girl with heavy eye make-up and severely cropped black hair.

'Good evening, Flo. Remember us?' She nodded mutely as Radcliffe held up his warrant card and Burns did the same. 'We had a chat yesterday about the missing student, Anne-Marie Gordon. You and your friend Sally were very helpful. There's no need to look so alarmed,' he went on, seeing her apprehensive expression, 'we just want to have a word with your friend Noah – the one nicknamed Pablo. He was out when we called. Is he here now?'

'I think he's in the shower. You'd better come in.' She opened the door to admit them and closed it behind them before saying, 'We're all worried sick about Anne-Marie. Is there any news?'

Radcliffe shook his head. 'I'm afraid not. We're following up one or two possible sightings, but we've had no luck so far. The problem seems to be that your crowd were so busy trying to help get Matthew's car started that it was some time before you all realized she wasn't with you.'

She gave a little groan and her eyes filled with tears. 'It's so awful! We looked around but there was no sign of her so we just assumed she'd gone home with someone else.'

'It was a natural assumption,' he said gently. 'You mustn't blame yourselves.'

She put her hands to her face. 'Poor Matt, he's absolutely devastated. He keeps having nightmares about it; we've all

156

been telling him it's not his fault, but he feels terribly responsible just the same because it was his job to see she got back safely. I don't know what he'll do if anything's happened to her; it doesn't bear thinking about.'

She was on the verge of breaking down and Radcliffe waited until she was calmer before saying gently, 'We understand that and we've done our best to reassure him. I promise you we're doing everything we possibly can to find Anne-Marie. Noah – the one you call Pablo – is the only one of your crowd we haven't been able to talk to yet and we're hoping very much he'll be able to help.'

'He keeps saying he doesn't know anything, but that's how we all feel.' She made a helpless gesture with her hands.

'But he was there with you on Friday?' She nodded. 'Did you see him talking to Anne-Marie?'

'I remember seeing them dancing together, but—' She broke off as a door at the far end of the passage opened and a young man came out clad only in a bath towel wrapped sarong-fashion round his waist. He pulled up short at the sight of the two detectives and then quickly disappeared into an adjacent room.

'Is that him?' Radcliffe asked. The girl nodded. 'Right, we'll go and have a word. Thank you for your help, Flo.' She muttered something unintelligible and clapped her hand over her mouth before diving through another door and slamming it behind her. Seconds later they heard unmistakable sounds of throwing up.

'Poor kid, she's really cut up,' Burns commented.

'It'll hit her and the others even harder if it turns out the worst has happened,' Radcliffe responded grimly. 'Right, let's go and have a word with our budding Picasso.'

He strode along the passage and rapped on the door. It opened a crack, revealing a thin, bearded face.

'Who is it?' the apparition demanded.

'Noah Dawden?' He nodded. 'Detective Sergeant Radcliffe and Detective Constable Burns. We'd like a word with you about the missing student.'

'If you mean Anne-Marie, I don't know anything . . . and I'm not dressed.'

'No need for modesty, there's no ladies present,' the

157

detective interrupted, pushing past him and entering the room with Burns at his heels.

Dawden kicked the door shut behind them and stood with his back to it, sullenly towelling his thin, unhealthily white naked body. 'Bloody cheek,' he muttered under his breath.

'Just take your time getting dressed.' Radcliffe strolled over to the window, adding over his shoulder, 'we're in no hurry.'

'Thanks for nothing.'

The room was typical of those in other Victorian houses in the town converted for student occupation. It was narrow, almost cell-like in its proportions, but it was newly decorated and had a pleasant outlook over the garden. Against the right-hand wall was a bed strewn with books and an assortment of rumpled garments that looked none too clean and, under the window, a desk on which papers and artist's materials were spread out. There were shelves on the wall opposite the bed with a chest of drawers below, a recess served as hanging and storage space and a small partitioned area with a half-open door that revealed a toilet and washbasin.

A track from a recent rock album was blaring from a radio on top of the chest. Radcliffe switched it off and waited while Dawden threw aside the damp towel and pulled on under-pants, jeans and a sweatshirt. Then he took the chair from beneath the desk, cleared a space on the bed for himself and Burns to sit facing it and said amiably, 'Why don't you sit down and make yourself comfortable while we have our chat?'

'Thank you very much,' said Dawden sarcastically. He slumped on to the chair and sat with his hands in his lap, staring at his bare feet. There was an interval during which Radcliffe deliberately remained silent and Dawden appeared increasingly uneasy. At length he raised his head and said, 'All right, what do you want to know?'

'We'd like your account of the evening Anne-Marie was last seen,' said Radcliffe. 'What can you tell us about it?'

'I can't tell you anything ... I mean, I didn't see her go and I've no idea where she went.'

'She didn't say anything to you that might help us to find her?'

'No ... I hardly spoke to her that evening. I don't know her all that well anyway.'

'Really? Isn't she on the same course as you?'

'Well yes, but she isn't a particular friend.'

'But you were with her the night she disappeared?'

'She was in the mob I was with, that's all. We didn't spend any time together . . . I mean, she was just there with Flo and some other girls and I was talking to my own mates.'

At a sign from Radcliffe, DC Burns pulled out a notebook and made a show of consulting it. 'According to statements we've taken from other members of your crowd,' he said, 'both you and Anne-Marie were among the group who arrived at the Oasis night club around nine o'clock and left together around midnight. Several of them saw you chatting to her earlier and you were also seen dancing with her.'

Dawden stared at the floor. 'I suppose that's right if they say so,' he muttered. 'I'd had a few drinks before we got to the Oasis.'

'Oh yes? Where was that?'

'At Jojo's bar in the High Street.'

'On your own?'

'No, with a couple of mates . . . the others joined us later and we all went on to the Oasis together. I can't remember everyone I talked to there and I didn't notice Anne-Marie leave,' he added with a touch of defiance.

'But we understand you were both outside the club when one of your friends, Matt Goddard, was having trouble starting his car?'

'I was. I didn't see her. Some of us tried giving him a push, but it didn't work.'

'You weren't too drunk to remember that, then?'

'Never said I was drunk, did I? I'd just had a few.'

'So tell me what happened about the car. You tried pushing and it didn't work. What happened next?'

'Someone had some jump leads in his car and he went to fetch them.'

'And that did the trick?'

Dawden shrugged. 'I suppose so. I don't know about cars. I left them to it.'

'But you said, "some of *us*".' Radcliffe deliberately emphasized the pronoun.

159

Dawden shifted his feet and looked uncomfortable. 'All right, I meant some of *them*. Slip of the tongue, wasn't it?'

'And you appear to know what jump leads are.'

'I just heard them talking.'

'You seem to be able to remember quite a lot about what happened at the end of the evening, but not much about what happened earlier.' Dawden shrugged, but made no reply. 'All right, we'll leave that for now. Anything else you'd like to ask?' he said to Burns.

Burns nodded. 'Just one thing. Did you leave the Oasis at any time between arriving and leaving with your friends?' he asked.

'No, why should I?'

'Maybe to get a bit of air . . . or make a call on your mobile, for example?' Burns continued. 'I don't suppose you get a signal inside, and what with all the noise going on—' He left the question hanging in the air, but Dawden declined to comment. 'All right, so tell us how you got back here.'

'I walked. I'd planned to anyway. The Oasis is in the town centre and it's only a mile or so away.'

'Was anyone with you?'

'No.' He spoke the monosyllable with another show of defiance. 'And I didn't see Anne-Marie and I don't know where she went or who she went with or what happened to her.'

'Yes, I think we've got the message.' Radcliffe picked up the questioning again while Burns made notes. 'Perhaps you can tell us a little about yourself, Noah. You're in your first year at the college, I believe.' Dawden nodded. 'And I understand your father is the head of the art department?'

'What's that got to do with anything?'

'Nothing special. Just making sure I've got the facts right. I've heard that Mr Dawden senior is considered to be something of an expert on art, particularly what are loosely referred to as "old masters".'

'Some people say so.'

'You don't sound very sure.'

'All right then, he knows quite a bit. It's his job, isn't it?' Dawden glowered resentfully at the detectives. 'Look, are you accusing me of something? Because if you are, I want a solicitor.'

160

'All right, calm down,' said Radcliffe soothingly. 'No one's accusing you of anything, Noah; we're just asking for your help. A girl is missing and we're trying to find out what's happened to her. We'd like to think you're as concerned for her safety as the rest of her friends.'

'Of course I am, but I've told you all I know. I'm sorry it isn't much help.' Dawden got up, went to the door and opened it. 'Do you mind leaving? I'm going out later and I want to get some decent clothes on first.'

'All right, we'll go now, but we may want to talk to you again. Oh, one more thing. I believe you know Philip Montwell, the artist who owns the Phimont Gallery.'

If Radcliffe had hoped to disconcert his witness, he was disappointed. Dawden looked him straight in the eye and said, 'Sure I know him. He gives occasional lectures at the college and sometimes he gives advice to individual students about their work.'

'Is that why you were at his gallery yesterday afternoon? Getting some advice about your work?'

Again, Dawden showed no surprise at the question. 'That's right. He was a great help.'

Radcliffe nodded. 'Very good of him, I'm sure. And did you know that he produces unusually accurate copies of famous paintings for sale to private clients – paintings that have been known to deceive the experts?'

This time Dawden's gaze flickered, but he answered steadily enough, 'I had heard.'

'Have you ever seen any of his work? A copy of a canvas by Matisse, for example?'

Dawden swallowed and hesitated before saying, 'No. Why would he show it to me?'

'No reason,' said Radcliffe blandly. 'Did you know it was stolen recently?'

'Of course. Anne-Marie told us.'

'Oh, so you do talk to her sometimes?'

'She told the whole class. She was quite upset about it.'

'So I understand,' Radcliffe said smoothly. 'Did you know she worked part-time at Montwell's gallery?'

This time there was a significant hesitation before Dawden replied, 'She might have mentioned it – I'm not sure.'

The detective pursed his lips and nodded. 'I see. Right, that's all for now, Noah. Enjoy your evening.'

There was no response. The two detectives quietly let themselves out of the flat and went downstairs to the street. 'What did you make of that, Patrick?' asked Radcliffe.

'There's something he's not telling us,' Burns replied without hesitation. 'He may be telling the truth when he says he didn't see Anne-Marie leave the group, but he was distinctly uncomfortable when you started questioning him about his father and I reckon he knows all about the Matisse even if he hasn't actually seen it.'

'Maybe he knows his old man is up to his neck in this art scam and is afraid there's some link between that and the girl's disappearance,' said Radcliffe. 'Supposing she saw the picture, talked about it at college and it somehow got back to Dawden senior?'

'Or Junior did see it and couldn't wait to tell Daddy about it. He admits he visits Montwell's gallery as well,' Burns pointed out.

'True. I think we can safely say that through one or the other, information about the picture got back to the gang and then it was nicked.'

The two men exchanged glances as a frightening possibility took shape in both their minds. 'Maybe that girl suspected a link and found something significant in the press reports that put her on to some other source of information?' Burns suggested. 'She might have confided her suspicions to someone.'

Radcliffe nodded. 'Young Picasso, for example,' he said sombrely, 'knowing his old man's reputation as an art expert and thinking his expertise might be useful in tracing the missing picture. He keeps insisting that he hardly spoke to her, but they were seen dancing together and she might well have said something then. He could easily have slipped out and called Daddy on his mobile. That's pure guesswork at the moment, of course, but someone might have noticed and it ties in with something DI Castle was saying earlier. We'll have to ask around. Meanwhile—' He turned and headed back to the house. 'I think we should have another word with our young friend. Well, there's a bit of luck – here he is!'

162

As he spoke, the front door of the house opened and Dawden emerged. At the sight of the two detectives barring his way he turned and bolted indoors, but Burns sprinted after him, grabbed him halfway along the passage leading to the back door and marched him outside. 'What's the rush, sunshine?' he said.

'I told you, I'm going out – I've got a date,' Dawden said angrily. 'You've no right—'

'We only want to ask a few more questions and the quicker you answer them the sooner you can meet the girlfriend. It's getting chilly out here so we're going down to the station where it's nice and warm.'

'You can't do this, I've done nothing wrong,' Dawden protested as they bundled him into the car.

'How about withholding information from the police for starters?' Burns suggested.

'I told you, I'm not answering any more questions without a solicitor.'

'That's no problem,' Radcliffe assured him as Burns started the engine. 'We can fix you up with one, or maybe you'd rather call your father and get him to send his own legal eagle along to take care of you. It's your choice.'

Dawden maintained a sullen silence during the drive back to the station. Once there, he was escorted to an interview room and seated at a table opposite the two detectives. It was while the formalities were being explained to him that Radcliffe received a message from DCI Lord to say he wanted to speak to him urgently over a serious development in the case of the missing student.

Twenty-Four

Sukey's phone rang shortly before ten o'clock on Monday evening. Jim was on the line.

'Sorry to call so late, but something's come up,' he said. 'You might be able to help so I'll pop by on my way home if that's okay.'

'Is it urgent? I've just got out of the bath and I was hoping to get an early night—'

'This won't take long,' he cut in almost brusquely. 'See you in about fifteen minutes.' He hung up before she could utter another word.

'Cheek!' she muttered as she put down the phone, unconsciously echoing Noah Dawden's response to the unceremonious incursion into his room a few hours previously. 'So you think you can come barging in here whenever it suits you,' she grumbled aloud as, after drying herself, she applied a lavish quantity of seductively perfumed body lotion. 'I'll show you!'

By the time he arrived she was swathed in her most becoming bathrobe with her short hair brushed into a cap of dark chocolate-brown curls. As on his previous visit he walked straight into the kitchen, except that this time he did not give her so much as a peck on the cheek in passing. 'Do come in,' she muttered under her breath in response to his monosyllabic greeting.

He was already seated at the table with an open notebook in front of him when she entered. 'Come and sit down,' he said, pointing to the chair opposite.

'Thank you so much,' she said sweetly, but if he detected the sarcastic edge to her voice he gave no sign.

'Sukey, I want you to think carefully about this,' he said, and at the sight of his expression she felt a flicker of unease. 'When did you last speak to Miranda Keene?'

'On Sunday afternoon. I told you, she left a message—'

'Yes, I know she did and I know it was because she was in a state about the girl going missing, but can you remember if she said anything . . . anything at all . . . to suggest that she'd been in touch with Kirtling since he was let out on bail?'

'No, she never mentioned him. As a matter of fact, if Andy Radcliffe hadn't been there this afternoon I'd have asked if any further information about him had turned up. Jim, what's this leading up to? What's happened?'

'Kirtling hasn't been seen since Friday morning, when he reported to his local station in London in accordance with his bail conditions. He wasn't in his office today; he had appointments he didn't keep but his secretary didn't know where he was and his car's missing from the garage. We suspect he's made his way back to Muckleton Manor, but Miranda flatly denies having seen him and his car isn't in any of the outbuildings. It's just occurred to me that you might be able to shed some light on the mystery.'

'Why me?'

'That time you made an unauthorized visit to the manor and used an alternative point of entry—' Castle unfolded a large-scale Ordnance Survey map that he had placed on the table at his elbow. 'Here's the village, here's Crook Lane and this,' he indicated with an index finger, 'is Muckleton Manor. As you can see, the house is surrounded on three sides by fields and woodland.' He pushed the map towards her. 'You said you climbed over a wall into a field; can you show me exactly where that was?'

Sukey studied the map briefly before pushing it back. 'That's easy,' she said, pointing. 'It was here. I drove up that narrow lane – it's not much more than a cart track really – parked about fifty metres along and walked through the trees to the boundary wall. I climbed over into that field and walked up to the house. It's only a short distance, although as you can see from the contours it's quite steep.' A sudden recollection of herself charging and panting up the incline with the gardener in pursuit, brandishing his fork, brought a momentary smile to her face. Fortunately, Jim failed to notice.

'That's what we figured,' he said, 'but we couldn't find anything to suggest anyone's come that way recently and there's no sign of a car. There are several acres of woodland; we'll have to organize a more far-ranging search tomorrow.'

'What makes you so sure Kirtling's been at the manor?'

'Chiefly on account of Miranda's attitude under what began as the usual sympathetic questioning by our people about Anne-Marie's movements. At first she was completely open, although naturally very distressed and emotional, but when they asked if she'd mentioned the girl's disappearance to Kirtling she began hedging and said she couldn't remember exactly the last time she'd heard from him, although she admitted that he rings her up from time to time. Then they asked if he'd visited her since his release on bail and she became really flustered. Eventually they asked if he was actually in the house, whereupon she started going on about police harassment and told them to search the place if they weren't satisfied.'

'And did they?'

'Oh yes, but they didn't find any trace of Kirtling. Except for one thing, although it's not enough to count as evidence. One of the officers claims to have an unusually sensitive nose and she swears she detected a hint of cigar smoke in one of the rooms. Unfortunately, the officer who was with her has a cold and couldn't smell a thing.'

'Did the officer mention it to Miranda?'

'Naturally, but she insisted she must have imagined it.'

'So what's your theory?'

'Briefly, we're beginning to wonder if Kirtling is somehow mixed up in the stolen art scam.'

'You're joking! Even Miranda admits he doesn't know the first thing about art.'

'That doesn't mean he wouldn't be above making a fast buck or two out of it if the opportunity arose. We've been delving into his history and although he's never been known to be directly involved in any shady deals, not all his business associates are squeaky clean. He's sure to have heard about Montwell's copy of the Matisse and it so happens that one of his cronies is a collector of somewhat dubious reputation.'

'But surely—' Sukey began, but he silenced her with an impatient gesture.

166

'We believe Anne-Marie said something to her aunt on Friday evening – after you saw her at the *Gazette* offices, that is – to suggest she'd picked up clues to the identity of one or possibly several members of the gang. We think Miranda mentioned it to Kirtling and that he panicked and hurried home with the intention of preventing the girl from passing damning evidence to the police.'

'You're suggesting Miranda knows what Kirtling is up to and warned him that Anne-Marie might be on to him? Jim, I can't believe she'd do anything to put that girl at risk . . . she's her sister's child, for goodness' sake, she thinks the world of her.'

'I don't suppose she suspects him for a moment, but they've almost certainly kept in regular contact since he was granted bail. If they spoke on Friday, after the girl went out, she may have let it drop in all innocence.'

'So at the precise moment Anne-Marie is hanging around in the middle of Cheltenham some time after midnight waiting for a lift home, the gallant Sir Digby appears out of the blue, apparently galloping to her rescue like a knight in shining armour but in reality with murderous intent?' Sukey felt herself losing patience. 'Honestly, Jim, don't you think this is all a bit far-fetched?'

'Murders have been committed for less,' he insisted. 'And there's another thing; we've been assuming the reason he killed Una May was because her pregnancy threatened to be an embarrassment, but supposing she knew about the art scam as well and was using that knowledge as an additional weapon to force him to marry her?'

'I suppose you could be right,' she admitted reluctantly, 'but just the same, something tells me you're barking up the wrong tree.'

'Have you got a better theory?'

'No,' she admitted, 'but it occurs to me that your frustration at seeing Kirtling let out on bail against police advice might have clouded your judgement a little.'

For a moment she thought he was going to snap at her, but instead he passed a hand over his eyes and said wearily, 'To be honest, Sook, things get more complicated by the hour. At first we thought we had two separate cases: the murder of

Una May and the spate of art thefts. We believe Kirtling is our man in the former, but now we have to consider the possibility that he's involved in the other one as well, which would put him in the frame for Anne-Marie's disappearance.'

'Well, as you know, my personal knowledge of him has been limited,' said Sukey, 'but from what you've told me he does seem to be a thoroughly tricky piece of work. Incidentally, do you know when Muckleton Manor was built?'

'I've no idea. Why do you ask?'

'It's just occurred to me that if parts of it go back far enough there might be a priest's hole or something where Kirtling could be hiding.'

Castle brightened a little at the suggestion and made a note. 'I'll look into that,' he said. He gave a deep yawn and stood up. 'Thanks for your help, love. I'll get along home now.'

'I'm not sure I've done much, but you're welcome anyway.'

At the door he put his arms round her and nuzzled her neck. 'Mmm, you smell delicious,' he murmured. 'Were you hoping to lure me into your bed by any chance?'

Earlier, her intention had been to get her own back at him for blatantly taking her for granted by leading him on and then showing him the door, but in view of the seriousness of the situation she dismissed the notion as frivolous and unworthy. Besides, it was still not quite eleven o'clock. She found herself relaxing against him; chemistry took over. 'Why not?' she whispered.

She was on her way to her first assignment the following morning when she received an emergency call from George Barnes.

'We've had a report of a woman's body being found in woodland on the Muckleton Manor estate,' he said. 'Will you drop what you're doing and go straight there, please?'

Sukey caught her breath. 'Oh no! It's not Anne-Marie?'

'We don't know for certain, of course; we'll have to wait for the formal ID, but first info suggests it's highly likely. The victim's in a hut some distance from the house, by the way, so there'll be an officer standing by to direct you. I'm contacting Mandy as well; she'll join you there and CID are on their way.'

Half an hour later, Sukey was standing outside a ramshackle shelter about the size of an average double garage. It was in a clearing at the end of a rutted track in some fairly dense woodland and was partly occupied by a trailer that, from a scattering of sawdust and chippings on its wooden bed and the surrounding earth floor, appeared to have been used for hauling sawn timber. The remaining space was empty except for a heap of sacking in the corner.

At first, she could see no sign of a body. Then the uniformed inspector in charge said, 'She's right at the back, behind the trailer.' He pointed. 'If you duck down you can just see her foot.'

'Is the doctor here?'

'Not yet; he should be here soon.'

'Right, I'll get on with protecting the scene before anyone else goes trampling around. Could one of your men give me a hand, please?'

'Sure.' He detailed one of his men to return with her to the van and help her carry stepping boards, which she laid along the right-hand wall of the shed while taking care to disturb the ground as little as possible. It was not until she reached the far corner that she was able to see the entire body. It lay prone in deep shadow beneath the back of the trailer; in the dim light she could just make out a typical student's outfit of trainers, jeans and a brightly coloured T-shirt topped by a mass of blonde curls. The face was half hidden by an outstretched arm, but Sukey knew with a sickening certainty that she was looking at the body of Anne-Marie.

'Who found her?' she asked the inspector when she had finished her task.

'Some drunk who staggered in to sleep it off after a night on the tiles. He's over there, giving a statement.' He gestured at a police car where a white-faced, dishevelled young man was sitting in the back seat. 'It seems he saw the sack and took it to use as a blanket, but didn't notice the body until he got up at first light to relieve himself. When he'd recovered from the shock he made a 999 call on his mobile. He wasn't at all sure where he was and it took us a while to locate him.'

'What on earth was he doing there? He doesn't look like a vagrant.'

He chuckled. 'It was his stag night and his mates nicked his car keys and his trousers and dumped him on the edge of the wood to find his own way home.' He glanced at his watch and remarked, 'CID are taking their time. How come you got here so quickly?'

'I was already on my way to another job in the next village. That's them now,' she added as through the trees she saw DI Castle approaching with DS Chen.

'And that'll be the doctor,' the inspector said as a car pulled up at the end of the track and a young, prematurely bald man carrying a stethoscope got out. He hurried to meet them while Sukey stood back and waited. Mandy arrived a few minutes later and after exchanging brief greetings the two CSIs waited in sombre silence a short distance away while the doctor carried out his examination. When he emerged to confer with the officers, they edged closer to hear what he had to say.

'At a rough guess she's been dead for three to four days,' he told them. 'Any idea of the cause of death?' said Castle.

'That's for the pathologist to decide, but there's a wound to the head that suggests she might have been shot.'

Twenty-Five

'Shot?' Sukey repeated. In her astonishment, she almost blurted out, 'Are you sure, Doctor?' Realizing just in time that the information was not intended for her ears, she bit back the words, but could not resist muttering under her breath, 'Try fitting that into your theory, DI Castle.'

Mandy pounced. 'I knew there was something you weren't telling me,' she hissed in Sukey's ear. 'What theory?'

'Never mind that now,' Sukey hissed back. 'We've got work to do.'

'We can't start until Eagle Eyes and his acolyte have given us the go-ahead,' Mandy said, with a hint of waspishness in her tone that made it clear she was offended by her colleague's refusal to confide in her.

'We can be getting the rest of our stuff ready,' Sukey replied. 'The light's pretty poor in there; I'll have to get you to hold the lamp while I do the photography. And I'll tell you later what I meant, only you must promise not to talk to the others about it,' she added in a low voice.

'You know you can trust me,' said Mandy, squeezing her arm.

The doctor departed and Castle came over to where the two CSIs were waiting. His face was grave. 'We can't be sure because of the way the body's lying, but it looks very like the missing woman,' he said. 'You can go ahead and take your pictures and samples now, and I want you to pay particular attention to the ground. There are tyre tracks outside and some disturbance to the dust and debris on the floor inside that suggest a vehicle might have been left in there recently. We'll have to try and trace it; it may belong to one of the workers on the estate, of course, but we'll need to check for elimination purposes. And that piece of sacking

171

will have to go to forensics for a thorough examination. As soon as you've finished you can liaise with Inspector Tether about having the body collected.' He hurried away, followed by DS Chen, leaving Sukey and Mandy to get on with their sad task.

'From a preliminary examination, Sergeant, I'd say she died from a single gunshot wound to the left temple.' The pathologist, Doctor Blake, glanced up from the naked body lying on the stainless steel table in the mortuary. 'A very small calibre weapon – probably a .22 fired at close range. It was smart of Doctor Seymour to spot it,' he added. 'The entry wound was almost completely hidden by the hair – look for yourself.' He took the head of the dead girl between his hands and tilted it sideways.

DS Hill, attending his second post-mortem within a matter of days, swallowed hard and took a deep breath before moving closer to peer at the point Blake's gloved forefinger indicated among the tumbled mass of blonde curls. 'That's a gunshot wound?' he exclaimed, surprise overcoming the feeling of nausea. 'But I thought—'

'Expected to see a smashed skull and plenty of gore, I suppose?' Blake said with a dry chuckle. 'You've got a lot to learn, my lad. That sort of weapon leaves a very small hole and –' he turned the head back so that the sightless eyes stared once again at the ceiling – 'as you see, no exit wound. I imagine your people will want more pictures before I set about digging out the bullet.'

'Yes, of course.' Hill beckoned to Sukey, who stood awaiting instructions a short distance away. 'Will you do the necessary?'

'Right.' She moved methodically round the body, taking shots from various angles. After a few minutes she said, 'We'll need a clearer shot of the wound please, Doctor. Could you possibly –' it was her turn to swallow back a wave of nausea – 'cut away some of the hair?'

'No problem. I'll have to do it anyway.' Blake's tone was almost breezy as he wielded the razor.

When she had finished, Sukey went straight back to the station to prepare her photographs for processing. She was on her way back after delivering them to the laboratory when she met DI Castle in the corridor. 'I can't talk now,' he said with a glance at his watch. 'We're meeting the press in five minutes.'

'Any news of Kirtling?'

'Not a sign. We'll be going public with mugshots and a description; he should hit the TV screens for the early evening news bulletins. See you!' He hurried away and she went slowly back to the CSIs' office. It was gone two o'clock and she had not eaten since breakfast. She took her packet of sandwiches from her bag, unwrapped it, pulled a face and put it away again.

'Feeling a bit queasy?' George Barnes looked up from his computer with a concerned expression.

'I thought I was all right, Sarge, but the sight of the food turned my stomach.' She put her hands over her eyes. 'I keep seeing that poor girl lying on the slab and thinking of her family, especially her parents. Fancy coming home to that awful news, plus having to face the fact that the aunt's boyfriend is wanted for murder.'

'Two murders now,' Barnes pointed out.

Sukey frowned and shook her head. 'I'm not sure about the second. The first doesn't appear to have been premeditated, but it looks as if someone hunted Anne-Marie down and shot her in cold blood. That takes a different type of killer.'

'But why would Kirtling abscond, if he didn't do it?'

'I admit it makes him look guilty, but—' She made a helpless gesture. 'My head's reeling. I think I'll have a coffee and a biscuit and then get on with some of the jobs you gave me this morning.'

'Forget those; the others have sorted everything between them. You go home and have a rest.'

'Thanks, Sarge. See you tomorrow.'

'Mrs Keene,' DS Dalia Chen said gently, 'we do realize that this tragedy is very distressing for you and your family, but it's essential that we speak to Sir Digby and we're having some difficulty in contacting him. DC Page and I,' she indicated the officer sitting beside her, 'think you may be able to help us.'

173

Miranda Keene, ashen-faced and red-eyed, gazed back at her and whispered, 'I'll try.' She had an air of helpless resignation, as if she had finally accepted the inevitability of her lover's guilt. She glanced round the small sitting room where, no doubt, she and Kirtling had sat together on countless occasions. Something in her expression suggested to the waiting detectives that she was mentally asking herself how much longer she would be living in the house.

'We have reason to believe,' Dalia continued, 'that Sir Digby was here at Muckleton over the weekend. Can you confirm this?'

'Yes.'

'When did he arrive?'

'It . . . it was quite late on Friday night. I don't remember the exact time. As a matter of fact, I was asleep.'

'So it was more likely to have been in the small hours of Saturday morning?' There was no response, and after a moment Dalia said, 'You were expecting him, though?'

'Yes, but he never said what time he was coming, except that he'd leave it until after the pub in the village closed so that no one would see him drive by.'

'Did he not understand that in coming here he would be breaking his bail conditions and would be rearrested if the police found out?'

'Of course. I tried to talk him out of it, but he insisted on coming. He said he was miserable being cooped up in London, he was missing me and wanted to spend some time with me before he had to report to the police again.'

'You say you tried to talk him out of it – I assume this would be during a telephone conversation?' Miranda nodded. 'Which took place when?'

'On Friday evening.'

'Would that be after Anne-Marie left with her friends?'

Mention of the name brought a rush of tears to Miranda's inflamed eyes; she nodded, gave a muffled sob and fumbled for a handkerchief. Liz Preston, the liaison officer who had been assigned to the family, gave her hand an encouraging squeeze and whispered, 'You're doing fine. Just answer in your own time.'

After allowing her a couple of minutes to steady herself

and drink a sip of water, Dalia said, 'So what time on Friday did Sir Digby call you?'

'It must have been about eight o'clock.'

'Could you please tell us as much as you can remember of the conversation?'

'It was about everyday things to start with; he always wanted to know how I was and how things were on the estate.'

'And then?'

'He asked what I was doing for the weekend and I told him I was going to help Anne-Marie – ' she stumbled over the name, pulled herself together and continued in an unsteady voice – 'do some shopping and a bit of laundry and house-work so the place was tidy for when her parents came back from their holiday.'

'Did you mention that Anne-Marie was going straight home afterwards . . . in other words, that you would be alone at Muckleton for the rest of the weekend?'

'Yes.'

'What else did you tell him?'

'I . . . can't remember exactly.'

'You didn't happen to tell him that your niece was very excited because she thought she knew who was behind the recent spate of art thefts?'

Miranda gave a start. 'You know about that?'

'Did you?' Dalia persisted.

There was another long silence. Then Miranda drew a deep, shuddering breath and said, 'Yes, I did mention it.'

'Did you have a particular reason for telling him?' Miranda shook her head. 'It wasn't by any chance because you suspected he might be involved in some way and wanted to warn him?'

'Of course not!' Miranda said indignantly. 'That never entered my head. It was just . . . I told him in passing.'

'How did he react?'

It was several seconds before Miranda answered. At last she said, 'I don't remember him making any comment.'

'Did you also tell him at which nightclub Anne-Marie and her friends planned to spend their evening?'

'I may have done . . . I don't remember . . . she mentioned several places where they'd talked of going.'

175

The recollection brought another rush of tears and Dalia waited for a moment before saying, 'Was it at that point in the conversation that he talked about coming down to see you?'

Miranda's mouth opened but no sound came out. It was clear from her expression that she could see the implication behind the question. She nodded, put her hands to her mouth and broke down completely.

'This might be a good time to break for a few minutes.' Dalia turned to DC Page and indicated with a tilt of the head that they should leave the room. Outside she said, 'What do you make of that, Derek?'

'I think she's telling the truth so far,' he replied, 'but it may be a different story when we get down to Kirtling's detailed movements.'

'I agree. I'd like you to question her about that.'

Page nodded. 'Okay, Sarge.'

When they returned, Miranda appeared more composed and in answer to a question from Dalia Chen agreed to continue the interview.

'Mrs Keene,' said Page, 'we'd like you to tell us in your own words exactly what happened from the time of your telephone conversation with Sir Digby on Friday evening.'

The explanation took some time, with several interruptions at points where Miranda was on the verge of breaking down again. When she had finished, Dalia put a further question. 'Can you tell us where Sir Digby is now?'

Miranda glanced at the ormolu clock on the mantelpiece and said, 'He's probably in his office. Haven't you checked with his secretary?'

'Do I understand you haven't spoken to him since your niece's body was discovered?'

Miranda shook her head, once more close to tears. 'I left a message on his mobile the minute we got the news, but he hasn't rung back. I can't think why; it's not like him.' She looked appealingly at Dalia. 'Has something happened to him?'

'That's what we should like to know,' Dalia replied. 'The fact is, Sir Digby has not been seen since he reported to the police last Friday and we thought you might know where he is.'

Miranda Keene gave a despairing groan. 'I've absolutely no idea,' she whispered.

Twenty-Six

When she reached home Sukey went into the kitchen and made a pot of tea. After drinking her first cup she realized that she was hungry after all so she reopened the pack of sandwiches, but discarded them in favour of a poached egg on toast. When she had finished eating she went into the sitting room, sat down on the couch and almost immediately fell asleep. She was awakened by the telephone.

'Hi Sukey, it's Mandy. George Barnes said you were feeling groggy after having to cover the PM so he sent you home. How are you now?'

'Better, thanks. I had a bite to eat and then I dozed off.'

'Was it very gruesome?'

'It was a bit. Nigel Warren would normally have done it, but he's on leave.'

'Anyway, you're all right now?'

'Yes, fine thanks.'

'I take it you've seen the six o'clock news.'

Sukey checked the time; it was half-past six. 'Actually, no. I must have dropped off. I take it they covered Anne-Marie's murder.'

'Yes, and put out an appeal for anyone who's seen Sir Digby Kirtling to come forward. They showed mugshots as well, so they must be pretty keen to get their hands on him. It seems he's skipped bail.'

'Yes, I know.' The admission was out before she realized its implication.

'I thought you might,' Mandy said dryly. 'That's one of the reasons I'm calling – to remind you of your promise.'

'What promise?'

'To tell me about some theory of Eagle Eyes that you were

muttering about this morning. Is it okay if I pop round for half an hour?'

'Well, I—'

It was unlikely that Jim, no doubt fully occupied with the manhunt, would be calling round that evening. Just the same . . . but before she could think of an excuse, Mandy said, 'Are you expecting lover-boy?'

'Don't be silly,' Sukey snapped, and then added in a gentler tone, 'What about your mother? Surely you can't leave her on her own when you've been out all day? I could always . . .'

'She's got a friend here and they're playing Scrabble. She'll be fine. Don't worry; if he turns up unexpectedly I'll slide out through the back door.'

'Oh, all right then,' Sukey agreed resignedly.

She had barely put the phone down when it rang a second time. Fergus was on the line and he sounded in deep shock. 'Mum, I've just heard the news . . . about Anne-Marie. It's terrible . . . why in the world would Kirtling want to kill her?'

'I'm not at all sure he did, Gus.'

'The police seem to think so.'

'I know, but I have serious doubts.'

'Then why has he gone AWOL?'

'I don't know. Panic, perhaps, after breaking his bail conditions to visit his girlfriend.'

'Is that what he did?'

'It seems so.'

'But if he didn't kill her, who do you think did?'

'I've no idea at the moment; it's just that I've got this nagging feeling that we're all missing something. Tell you what,' she went on quickly, 'Mandy rang a few minutes ago to ask if she could come round and talk about it. She'll be here quite soon; why don't you join us? She won't be staying long and I'll get us both something to eat after she's gone.'

'Thanks, Mum. I need to talk to someone.' She could tell he was very close to breaking down and his voice was muffled as he said, 'See you,' and hung up.

Half an hour later the three of them were gathered round Sukey's kitchen table. She offered drinks; both visitors declined alcohol so she mixed three glasses of fruit cordial and they sat sipping in a sober silence for a minute or two before Mandy said, 'Is it true she was shot, then? I know that's what Doctor Seymour thought, but the cause of death wasn't released at the press briefing.'

'Oh yes; Doc Blake confirmed it.' Sukey shuddered at the recollection.

'Shot?' Fergus looked aghast. 'It didn't say anything about that on the telly. Does it mean Sir Digby's got a gun?'

'I don't know,' she replied. 'I suppose it's possible. Doc Blake said it was probably a .22, which is quite small – not the sort of weapon you'd expect a man to have.'

'Maybe he belonged to a gun club and managed to hang on to it instead of handing it in when the law was changed,' Mandy suggested.

'In that case it should be fairly easy to check, but it just doesn't add up to me.'

'Does Jim think he did it, Mum?' asked Fergus.

Sukey noticed Mandy's eyebrows lift at the familiar way her son spoke of the man she was in the habit of referring to as Eagle Eyes, but she made no comment other than to say, 'I haven't discussed it with him since the body was discovered, but I know CID suspect Kirtling of being mixed up with the art scam DI Radcliffe has been investigating, partly because he happens to be acquainted with some dodgy art dealer.'

'So apart from strangling Una May, he's now number one suspect for this latest killing,' said Mandy. 'He's a big-shot businessman, though,' she went on after a moment's reflection. 'He probably knows lots of people from all sorts of back-grounds besides the arty-tarty brigade.'

'Exactly. Anyway, I discovered quite by chance that Anne-Marie had been doing some private research into the case and naturally I passed this on to CID.' For Mandy's benefit she gave a brief account of the meeting in the offices of the *Gloucester Gazette*, but without mentioning her own reason for being there. 'What she'd discovered, or maybe simply suspected, we might never know,' she went on, 'but I believe that whatever it was made her a danger to the mob and that was the motive for killing her.'

'Her family must be absolutely devastated,' said Fergus. 'Have you spoken to Miranda, Mum?'

'Not since the body was discovered. I understand her sister and brother-in-law are staying with her at the manor and they're all being cared for by an FLO.'

There was a long silence. Then Fergus said, 'I take it you'll be sharing your thoughts about this with Jim?'

'If I have the chance, but I doubt if he'll take any notice except to tell me to keep my nose out of it.'

Mandy glanced at the clock and said, 'I'd better be going. Mrs Plackett doesn't like to be late home.' At the door, she said in a low voice, 'Thanks for putting me in the picture. So I'm right; you and, er, Jim,' she gave a mischievous smile and put an ironic emphasis on the name, '*are* an item, then? Have been for quite a while?'

'You won't say anything in the office, Mandy? He'd have kittens if he thought it was generally known.'

'You know I won't, but he must be a bit naïve if he really thinks no one has spotted it.'

'He's not naïve, he just kids himself.'

'Silly chap. He should be proud for everyone to know you're his.' Mandy gave her friend an impulsive hug. 'See you tomorrow.'

Sukey returned to the kitchen to find Fergus still sitting at the table, absently twisting his empty glass between his fingers. His face was drawn; she noticed with a pang that he looked several years older than the carefree nineteen-year-old who had embarked on his university course with such enthusiasm. 'Did you mean it when you said you had no idea who killed Anne-Marie,' he said, 'or is it just that you don't want to tell me?'

'I meant it, Gus, truly; all I have to go on is this nagging feeling that something doesn't add up.'

'What about Kirtling's sidekick – the chap who figures in the painting? The one Kirtling commissioned from the artist who runs the gallery?' he added as Sukey looked blank. 'Maybe he's in the scam as well, and Kirtling used him as a hit man to kill Anne-Marie because he was afraid to go near Muckleton himself in case someone recognized him,' he went on.

Sukey shook her head. 'I don't think that's one of your best ideas, Gus,' she said with a weary smile. 'Anyway, strictly between us, Jim is pretty sure Kirtling drove down from London to Muckleton late on Friday.'

'You mean he's been spotted?'

'Not that I know of, but Jim told me this on Monday evening and I've hardly spoken to him since. There may have been developments I haven't heard about.'

Together they prepared a light meal and later sat listening to music until ten o'clock, when Sukey switched on the radio for the news. The first item was an announcement that Sir Digby Kirtling had been arrested at a private hotel in Coventry and taken to an unidentified police station for questioning in connection with the murder of the Cheltenham student Anne-Marie Gordon.

'All right, Sir Digby, let's go over it again, shall we? You have told us that after speaking to Mrs Miranda Keene, your housekeeper, last Friday evening, when you learned that she would be alone in the house for the weekend, you decided to seize the opportunity of a few hours with her in the hope and belief that your visit would pass unnoticed.'

'That's right.' Kirtling stared defiantly back at DI Castle and DC Page across the table in the interview room.

'You were aware, of course, that such a visit was a breach of the terms under which you were granted bail after being charged with the murder of one of your employees, Una May, and that if the breach should be discovered it would almost inevitably result in your return to custody.'

'Of course.'

'And what decided you to take that risk?'

'You're a man of the world, Inspector. I would have thought that was obvious.'

'You mean Mrs Keene is your mistress and being separated from her was causing you a certain degree of, shall we say, frustration?'

'Exactly.'

'Sir Digby,' Castle made a show of referring to the file that lay open in front of him, 'it is true, is it not, that you also have a regular sexual relationship with another of your employees, Ms Fiona Slade?'

Kirtling turned a dull red and sat bolt upright in his chair. 'What the hell—' he began, but his solicitor, a middle-aged man called Whitlock who was sitting beside him, put a hand on his arm and he sat back, glowering.

Whitlock cleared his throat and said in a firm, authoritative voice, 'I cannot see that my client's sexual relationships are of any relevance to this enquiry, Inspector.'

'On the contrary, I believe in this particular case they are of considerable relevance,' Castle retorted. 'It is clear from previous evidence that there was no need for Sir Digby to travel to Muckleton merely to satisfy his sexual appetites and we believe he is not telling us the truth when he claims that was the sole reason for his visit last Friday.' He turned back to Kirtling. 'Sir Digby, during your telephone conversation with Mrs Keene on Friday, did she tell you where her niece was going that evening?'

'Only that she was going clubbing with some friends.'

'Did she tell you the name of the club where they planned to go?'

'How could she? I don't suppose she knew.'

'All right, I'll come back to that in a moment. You have no doubt read or heard reports of a number of recent thefts of art treasures in Gloucestershire and the neighbouring counties?'

'Naturally, but I don't see what this has to do with me.'

'And that there has also been at least one case where a fraudulent dealer attempted to pass off a fake painting as a genuine work by a well-known artist?' Castle continued as if he had not heard the interruption.

'I may have done.'

'Did Mrs Keene also mention during your telephone conversation that her niece had told her she thought she had identified one of the people behind the robberies?'

'No, why should she? It's of no interest to me.'

'You're sure about that?'

Kirtland thumped the table with his fist. 'Of course I'm sure,' he said angrily. How many times—'

'So it would surprise you,' this time it was DC Page who took up the questioning, 'to know that Mrs Keene has made a statement to the effect that she not only told you about her niece's discovery, but also mentioned the name of the night club where Anne-Marie would be that evening?'

Kirtling's jaw dropped and his colour faded. 'The stupid bitch!' he muttered.

'Did she?' Page persisted.

Kirtling cast a despairing look at his solicitor, who compressed his lips and shook his head before turning to Castle and saying, 'Inspector, I should like an opportunity to confer with my client.'

'Very well. Interview suspended at 9.30 am,' Castle said and switched off the tape recorder.

Half an hour later Whitlock informed the detectives that his client was prepared to give a full account of his movements from the time he left London on Friday evening until the time of his arrest, but that he wished to make it clear at the outset that he denied all knowledge of or responsibility for the murder of Anne-Marie Gordon.

Twenty-Seven

'**K**irtling's a broken man, Sook. I'm beginning to feel almost sorry for him.'

It was Wednesday evening. Drained and frustrated after hours in the interview room with the prisoner, DI Castle sank down on the couch in Sukey's sitting room and closed his eyes. 'You have to hand it to him,' he said wearily, 'he's a tough nut to crack. He's had to face questioning from one member of the team after another throughout the day, but we've made hardly any progress.'

'He's still denying everything, then?' she asked.

'Not quite everything. He's finally admitted being at Muckleton on Friday evening, but insists his sole reason for going was to spend a few hours in the arms of his ladylove. He categorically denies having seen Anne-Marie while he was there, or knowing anything about her disappearance. He says he left Muckleton in a hurry on Saturday night when Miranda Keene said she was going to contact the police to inform them the girl was missing. He knew that if it came out he'd broken his bail conditions he'd be back in the nick in no time.'

'What made him choose Coventry?'

'There doesn't seem to be a logical explanation other than the one he gave us – he simply panicked. He's already awaiting trial for murdering the woman who was carrying his child; next thing, another woman staying in his house goes missing while he's there himself.'

'It must have seemed a frightening combination of circumstances,' Sukey remarked. 'Lots of people have been known to behave irrationally in that kind of situation.'

'That's exactly what he's saying. He claims he simply went to pieces and his one thought was to hide away in a place where no one knew him.'

'Presumably he'd sworn Miranda to secrecy about his visit?'

'Naturally, but he must have been afraid she'd blurt it out under questioning. He says he realizes now that his best bet would have been to go home, hope that no one had missed him and that Miranda would keep quiet about his visit. As it turned out, of course, it wouldn't have made much difference in the long run. When the girl's body was found on his land he'd have been a suspect from the word go, especially as we already had a shrewd idea that he'd been at the manor.'

'But if he still maintains his innocence, why do you describe him as a broken man?'

'He believes Miranda has betrayed him and that seems to have affected him more than being suspected of a second murder.'

'Because she broke her promise and admitted he'd been at Muckleton Manor the night her niece disappeared?'

'Partly that, but mainly because she said in her statement that she told him about the girl's researches and where she was going on Friday night. At first he denied that she did any such thing and insisted he knew nothing about the girl's movements, but when we confronted him with her evidence all the bluster went out of him. Until then he believed – with good reason as you well know – that she was so besotted with him that he could get away with, if not literally murder—' Jim broke off and ran his long fingers through his hair in mute frustration; for the first time, Sukey noticed flecks of grey among the brown. 'He feels he's lost his sheet anchor,' he went on. 'It's almost as if he doesn't care what happens to him any more.'

'But he still maintains he knows nothing about Anne-Marie's murder?'

'Oh yes. We haven't been able to shake him on that.'

'What about Miranda? Does she believe he's guilty?'

'The poor woman doesn't seem to know what to believe. You don't need me to tell you that she's always refused to hear a word against him, even when the evidence that he killed Una May was stacking up. The first time we interviewed her after she reported Anne-Marie missing she stoutly denied he'd been to Muckleton since being granted bail. After the girl's body was found she broke down and admitted he'd been there, but said she believed him when he said it was because he was missing her so badly and simply wanted to see her. The fact that he took off late on Saturday leaving her to cope with her niece's disappearance on her own must have hurt, although she says she accepted his reason for it at the time and assumed he was going back to his London flat. It came as a shock to hear he'd done a runner.'

'Didn't it strike her as odd that he hadn't been in touch since he left?'

'You'd have thought so, wouldn't you, knowing how worried she was – but they seem to have had the sort of relationship where he came and went as he pleased. I suppose from one point of view it figures – after all, he is her employer. In any case, she claims she was so distraught at her niece's disappearance that she could think of nothing else.'

'How is she now?'

'Devastated. It must have been bad enough to know he'd gone missing, but learning he'd denied knowing anything about Anne-Marie's movements, when she knew jolly well she'd told him, must have raised serious doubts in her mind about his motives. The FLO says she's on the verge of a breakdown, although she's doing her best to be strong for her sister's sake.'

'Poor Miranda, what a reward for all that loyalty,' Sukey said sadly. 'So Kirtling's story is that he left London late on Friday night, drove to Muckleton, hid his car in the shed where Anne-Marie's body was found and sneaked up to the house via the field behind it the way I did?'

'That's right.'

'And left twenty-four hours later, having spent the whole time at the manor with Miranda?'

'That's what he claims, and Miranda confirms that part of his story.'

'But if it's true, Anne-Marie's body must have been there when he left. How come he didn't see it?'

'We put that to him, of course, but he claims he drove in and out without lights to avoid being spotted until he got to the road. It's feasible, I suppose; there was bright moonlight on both nights and it's his land so he knew the layout. In any case, the body was half concealed under the trailer and covered

187

with sacking. It could have lain there for ages without being discovered if that drunk hadn't blundered in.'

'Did you question him about the cause of death?'

'Naturally. He swears he's never possessed a gun and so far we haven't been able to prove otherwise. He admits he was a fool to go to Muckleton in the first place and then go to ground as if he was guilty, but that's all. The hard truth is, we simply haven't got any evidence against him.'

'So you've had to let him go?'

'No, he's still in custody for breaking his bail conditions. He's asked to see Miranda, but so far she's refused. I'd say that as far as he's capable of loving any woman, as distinct from a purely sexual relationship, she's the one. Dalia maintains he puts down her refusal to see him as proof that she believes he killed her niece and Una May as well. I've no doubt she's right,' Jim added, with what Sukey considered unnecessary warmth. 'That young woman shows a remarkable insight into the way people's minds work.'

With difficulty, Sukey bit back the sarcastic comment that almost escaped her. 'What about the art scam?' she said. 'You said you suspected he might be involved in that.'

'We put that to him in an attempt to put him off his guard by a sudden change of tack, but that didn't work either; all we got was a flat denial. In any case, we've got no firm evidence, only hearsay.'

'Have you questioned the other suspects? Could any of them be the killer?'

'You think we haven't thought of that? One's been in New York for the past week and the other is in hospital recovering from a hip replacement. You know something,' Jim went on in a flat, weary voice, 'I'm beginning to ask myself if we've missed something.'

It was on the tip of Sukey's tongue to mention that she had her doubts all along and had said so to Fergus the previous evening, but she merely remarked, 'It would be interesting to know what Anne-Marie found out. I don't suppose her handbag has turned up yet? She might have made some notes in her diary that could have helped.'

'I daresay that's what her killer – whoever he was – had in mind,' Jim said grimly.

'Probably.' Sukey glanced at her watch. 'Tell you what; it's time for a drink. Dinner will soon be ready and the wine should be nicely *chambré'd* by now. And I vote we think about something else for the rest of the evening.'

'Such as?' he asked with a sidelong glance at her.

She stood up, grabbed his hand, pulled him to his feet and gave him a fleeting kiss on the cheek. 'I'll tell you later,' she said in a throbbing contralto.

Despite some blissful moments with Jim the previous evening, Sukey's first thoughts when she awoke on Thursday morning were of Anne-Marie and her grieving family. She had not so far made any attempt to contact Miranda for fear of incurring Jim's disapproval and she resolved to have a word with him later to ask if he had any objection to her going to Muckleton to offer her sympathy.

In the meantime there was work to be done. Her first three assignments were in and around Gloucester city centre, but the next was to a break-in at the office of a firm of solicitors on Cheltenham's Imperial Square. As she reached the outskirts of the town she found herself thinking with compassion about Philip Montwell and what she had recently learned about the tragedy of his sister's death. She recalled Anne-Marie's description of his reaction when she had innocently enquired if the picture on his desk was of his wife or girlfriend. She suspected that his distant and at times arrogant manner was due, at any rate in part, to a need to avoid betraying his private feelings and she wondered how Anne-Marie's murder had affected him. It must surely have come as a shock to learn that someone who had worked for him, and whose talent he seemed to have been nurturing, had met with such a violent end.

The weather did nothing to lift her spirits. The day was dull and cheerless with a hint of autumn in the air. As she got out of her van a chill wind blew dust in her face and sent flurries of dead leaves from the chestnuts in the Promenade swirling above her head. By the time she had finished checking the crime scene and labelling her samples it was nearly one o'clock and she set off to find a quiet place to park her van and eat her sandwiches. Almost without realizing what she was doing she found herself driving past the Phimont Gallery. Spotting a notice in the window, she pulled up a short distance away and walked back to read it. It was short and to the point: 'Closing-Down Sale of Paintings and Objets d'Art. All reasonable offers considered'. Without thinking, she pushed open the door and stepped inside.

The walls in the showroom were crowded with canvases; even to Sukey's untutored eye they seemed to have been hung without any apparent attempt to classify them in terms of style or content. In the middle of the floor was a trestle table on which a few artefacts of metal, pottery and glass had been placed in a similar haphazard arrangement.

'Are you interested in buying or are you simply here to fill in some time?' Montwell had entered silently through the door in the far corner. Sukey jumped and turned round.

'I . . . well . . . neither, I suppose,' she said awkwardly. 'I happened to be passing and I saw the notice. I don't suppose you remember me, I—'

'I do, as it happens,' he interrupted. 'You're from the police, but you haven't come to tell me you've recovered the stolen painting.' His mouth twisted in a bitter smile. His features were as handsome as she remembered them, but the supercilious manner had gone and in its place was a kind of world-weariness. 'Anyway, now you're here, feel free to look round.' He went over to the table, picked up a pottery vase decorated in the Greek style and caressed it with his slender, artist's fingers. 'I picked this up in Thessalonika,' he said. 'It's modern, of course, but it's a nice piece.' He held it out to her and she felt obliged to take it.

'It's lovely,' she agreed, 'but I'm afraid I couldn't afford it.'

'There are more things in the back room,' he said. 'I don't charge for looking.'

Feeling vaguely uncomfortable, Sukey was tempted to make her excuses and leave, but he seemed almost pathetically anxious not to let her go so she went through the door he held open for her. The room was very much as she remembered it, except that the photograph on the desk was missing. There were a few pictures on the walls and a pile of expensive-looking art books on the table. Montwell picked one up and offered it to her.

'If you can't afford a picture, perhaps you could run to one of these?' he suggested.

'I really don't think—' she began, broke off and then stumbled on, 'I mean to say . . . that is, I didn't plan to come here today, but as I'm here I just want to say that the police are doing everything humanly possibly to find Anne-Marie's killer. I'm sure you must have been particularly upset when you—'

'Be quiet!' Sukey jumped at the harsh, almost despairing note in his voice. 'Don't say another word.'

'I'm sorry, I didn't mean to—'

She got no further before a voice behind her said, 'Philip, what are these doing stuffed at the back of your wardrobe? Oh, sorry, I didn't realize—'

Sukey turned round. Athena Letchworth, the woman she had last seen in the restaurant having lunch with Philip Montwell, had just entered through a door that appeared, from a glimpse it afforded of a staircase, to lead to the next floor of the building. In one bejewelled hand she held a pair of a man's brown leather loafers. Her voice trailed away as she looked first at Sukey and then at Montwell. Turning back, Sukey felt a cold sensation on seeing the expression on his face. His gaze was fixed on the shoes as if they were a snake about to strike; in that moment, the nagging doubt that had been troubling her for days, the vague but persistent feeling that something vital had been overlooked throughout the recent investigations, suddenly crystallized into a terrifying certainty.

Twenty-Eight

The realization caught Sukey unawares; she gave an involuntary gasp and put a hand to her mouth. 'Of course!' she breathed before she could stop herself. Too late, she knew that she had blundered; the sour taste of fear rose in the back of her throat and her one thought was to get away. The door leading to the outer showroom was still open. She glanced through it, hoping to see a passer-by who had dropped in while they were talking to look at the items on sale. The presence of such a person would have increased her chances of escape, but there was no one there. Praying that Montwell had not realized the significance of her startled reaction at the sight of the shoes, she murmured a conventional excuse and moved towards the door, but he was too quick for her. He grabbed her, clapped a hand over her mouth, dragged her to one side and shouted over his shoulder, 'The front door – lock it . . . now!'

Athena rushed to obey while Sukey tried desperately to free herself. She used every trick she could remember from her self-defence classes, but to her dismay he anticipated and countered them all. His strength was prodigious; he stifled her screams with one hand while his free arm pinioned her against his body so tightly she could hardly draw breath. When Athena returned he said tersely, 'Go and get some of your scarves – lots of them. We have to gag her and tie her up while we decide what to do with her. Don't argue!' he snarled as she appeared about to speak. 'You've caused enough trouble already, nosing around where you've no business to be.'

Athena scuttled upstairs and returned carrying an assortment of silk scarves, one of which she tied round Sukey's mouth before she and Montwell bound her wrists and ankles. They worked in silence; when they had finished he slung her

192

over his shoulder, carried her upstairs and dumped her on a couch in what was obviously his studio. Still breathing a little heavily from their exertions, her captors stood looking first at her and then at each other, as if in some doubt as to what their next move should be. After a moment Athena broke the silence by saying, 'Well, Philip, perhaps you'll tell me what this is about. What is it about those shoes that you know, and she appears to know, but I don't?'

Lying there staring up at them, Sukey saw his attitude change. His shoulders sagged; his initial anger seemed to have given way to despair. His eyes had a haunted, almost defeated expression and he passed one hand over his forehead. 'I should have got rid of them,' he said, half to himself. 'I was afraid they might somehow be traced – that's why I hid them instead of throwing them out.'

'You mean they're the ones you were wearing that day at Muckleton?' Athena's glittering black eyes narrowed. 'Now I understand. We were asked to hand over our shoes for examination because the police had found fresh evidence. You'd already left; you must have given them a different pair when they called to ask for yours.'

'I didn't have to give them anything, of course – they made that clear – but I thought it would look bad if I refused. I was pretty sure the fresh evidence they were talking about was broken glass.'

'From the one Una May broke when you . . . when she . . . ah, now I understand. And so, I think, does she.' Athena jabbed a scarlet fingernail in Sukey's direction. 'Who is she anyway?' She spoke with a trace of a foreign accent and her voice had a soft, sibilant quality that sent a shiver down Sukey's spine. 'Didn't I see her in the restaurant with Kirtling's housekeeper? They walked out when they recognized you.'

'That's right.' he replied. 'I don't know what she was doing there with Mrs Keene, but I do know she works for the police. I think she was probably the one who found the pieces of glass.'

'Indeed?' Athena's eyebrows lifted and a faintly mocking smile lifted the corners of her mouth. 'Don't tell me she came to arrest us!'

'Hardly. She came to offer her sympathy over the death

of—' Montwell's voice wavered and died. As before, reference to the death of his protégée appeared to cause him pain.

His partner had no such reservations. 'How touching!' she sneered. 'Well, Miss Police Lady,' she went on, gazing down at Sukey, 'like you, little Anne-Marie was too clever by half. You know what happened to her, so you know what to expect, don't you?'

'Oh, my God,' Montwell moaned. 'Do we have to? Hasn't there been enough killing already?'

'You want to spend the rest of your life in gaol while Kirtling goes free?'

'You know I don't, but—'

'Then stop arguing and let's decide when to do it.'

Sick with terror, Sukey turned away and closed her eyes. She was going to suffer the same fate as Anne-Marie and Sir Digby Kirtling would be tried, and probably convicted, for a murder that it now appeared Montwell had committed. Anything further that she might learn between now and what seemed her inevitable death could never be passed on to the police. All there was to hope for was that he and his accomplice would make some mistake, perhaps by leaving some forensic evidence, that would eventually lead to their arrest. It seemed a safe bet that they were involved in the art scam as well and that somehow they not only knew that Anne-Marie had uncovered incriminating evidence against them, but had also managed to spirit her away and silence her without anyone noticing. Whatever the final outcome, one thing seemed certain: she, Sukey Reynolds, would not live to see it.

Following these few moments of despair, her fighting spirit returned with a rush. She wasn't dead yet and she gathered from their muttered exchanges, of which she could make out only the odd word, that they were having a problem in deciding how to deal with her. While there was life, there was hope. She opened her eyes and glanced cautiously round the room. Against the wall, just a couple of feet from where she was lying, was a table on which tubes of paint, jars of brushes and other items of artist's equipment were spread out. Among them was a thin-bladed knife that looked wickedly sharp. In their haste, her captors had made the mistake of tying her

194

wrists in front of her. Even more obligingly, they had retreated into a corner with their backs towards her and their heads close together, absorbed for the moment in their deliberations.

As a result of regular workouts, Sukey's abdominal muscles were strong. With her stomach churning and her heart pounding madly against her ribs, she managed to sit upright without attracting attention. Inch by inch, she swung her bound legs over the side of the couch and stood up. There was still no indication that the conspirators, who were now behind her, were aware of her movements. She reached out for the knife; it was just beyond her reach and her feet and legs were tightly bound in several places with Athena's scarves, making it impossible for her to take a single step. There was only one thing to do, and that was to crawl. She sank to the floor, dragged herself on hands and knees to the table and struggled to her feet. The knife was within reach; she grasped it and turned towards her would-be killers.

They must have become aware of the movement. Now they were facing her across the couch and even in her desperate situation she noticed a difference in their expressions. Montwell's registered astonishment and alarm, but it was the look in Athena Letchworth's eyes that made her shiver. They seemed blacker than ever and there was a hatred akin to madness in them that reminded her of the actress who played the sorceress Medea in a performance of the Greek tragedy she had seen while still at school. It had given her nightmares at the time; now the horror had become a reality. Her situation appeared hopeless, yet she held the knife in front of her, pointed towards them, defiantly determined to do as much damage as possible to the one who reached her first.

The events of the next few seconds seemed to fuse into a blur. Later, when giving her account to the police, she remembered Athena saying, 'Oh, the hell with it! If we wait for you to make up your mind we'll wait for ever!' and seeing her reach into the pocket of her jacket. She heard Montwell's shout of, 'Not now, not here!' before she had instinctively thrown herself to the floor. She vaguely recalled sawing awkwardly with her bound hands at the scarves securing her legs and praying the argument would continue long enough to free them and give her a chance, however remote, of escape.

She heard sounds of a struggle, then a pistol shot, a woman's scream and a thud as if someone had fallen to the floor. There was a gasp from Montwell that was almost a sob. 'Athena,' he groaned, 'Oh my God, I've killed you!'

Sukey sat up and peered over the couch. Philip Montwell was crouching over Athena's recumbent body. Her eyes were closed and there was blood on her blouse; he was holding her deathly white face between his hands and repeating, 'I've killed you!' over and over again in a broken whisper. Knowing intuitively that she was no longer in danger, Sukey levered herself to her feet.

At that moment Athena stirred and gave a feeble moan. Montwell swung round and said, 'She's bleeding, but she's still alive. Oh, dear God, what am I to do?'

Sukey made an inarticulate sound and with her bound hands indicated the scarf round her mouth. He seemed bemused with shock; an eternity seemed to pass before he understood and untied it with trembling fingers.

'I've done first-aid training; if you want me to help you'll have to untie me . . . and be quick about it before she bleeds to death,' she gasped as the gag fell away. She was in the driving seat now; without a word he took the knife, cut her hands free and then did the same for her legs. 'Get me some clean towels,' she commanded, 'and give me back the knife. Now!' she insisted as he hesitated. 'I'll have to cut off her sleeve to get at the wound.'

It was only a matter of seconds before the bright red blood pumping from Athena's left arm told Sukey that the bullet had torn through an artery. 'We must get her to hospital,' she said. 'Call an ambulance.' Montwell, who had returned with an assortment of tea towels, appeared once again to hesitate and she guessed what was going through his mind. 'If you don't want her to die, call an ambulance – now!' she screamed as she snatched the towels from his hands. At last he responded; while she worked on the patient she heard him giving directions on his mobile. She did what she could by applying pressure, first to the wound itself using a towel as a dressing and then to the pressure point in the wrist. When that failed she gently raised the injured arm in a further attempt to check the flow of blood, but it was clear she was fighting a losing battle.

She had almost given up hope when they heard the sound of a siren. Montwell rushed downstairs to admit the paramedics and within a very short time they were carrying Athena downstairs to the waiting ambulance. Montwell followed, informing Sukey over his shoulder that he was going to the hospital and what she did from now on was up to her. Then she was alone with the heap of blood-soaked towels and the shredded remnants of Athena's scarves scattered on the floor at her feet.

It was several minutes before she was sufficiently recovered from her state of shock to call the station and inform CID of the events of the past half hour.

Twenty-Nine

'When you come to think of it, it's a pretty ironic result,' Jim remarked as he handed Sukey a glass of wine before settling down on the couch beside her.

It was Saturday evening and the first time since the dramatic events of Thursday afternoon that Sukey had felt able to relax. She leaned against his shoulder, took a long, slow mouthful from her glass and gave an appreciative nod. 'Mmm, that's good,' she said. She thought for a few moments while savouring the wine before adding, 'How d'you mean, ironic?'

'If Athena Letchworth hadn't shot Anne-Marie, Montwell might well have achieved his objective in killing Una May.'

'You mean by seeing Kirtling convicted of a crime he didn't commit?'

'Right.'

'But if Anne-Marie really had come up with evidence about the art scam that would have incriminated him and the rest of the gang, I suppose the pair of them felt they had no choice.'

'Ah, but another ironic twist to that part of the story is that Montwell has never been involved in the scam and had no idea Athena was part of it.'

'He didn't know she was behind the theft of his copy of the Matisse?'

'He didn't have a clue.'

'So the reason he was so upset about it was purely the financial loss?'

'No, it was because it had a sentimental attachment for him. In fact, it wasn't a commission, although that's what he led Anne-Marie to believe. He painted it in memory of his sister; the two of them saw the original together on a trip to St Petersburg some time ago and it was always one of their favourite pictures. He actually made an earlier copy of it and gave it to her, but she sold it for a pittance to buy the drugs that eventually killed her.'

'After Digby Kirtling dumped her, you mean?'

'That's right.'

'What a sad story. No wonder he was in such a state when the second one was nicked.'

'Yes, it's quite understandable,' Jim agreed. 'Going back to Athena and the art scam,' he went on, 'Montwell swears he knew nothing of her part in it until Anne-Marie started telling them about her discovery.'

'I've been wondering about that. Have you found out exactly what it was?'

'Oh yes, Montwell's told us the whole story. It seems she'd been doing some research on the Internet for her course when she stumbled across an article in an American magazine about an artist who specialized in faking copies of well-known paintings. One or two were so good they'd been sold at auction as original works. She went and looked up the *Gazette* reports about the art thefts in our area to see if there was any mention of copies being nicked, apart from Montwell's Matisse, but of course there wasn't. Just the same she thought she was on to something, especially as she remembered Montwell telling her that his copies had been known to fool the experts. In fact,' Jim added reflectively after breaking off to give some attention to his wine glass, 'I remember him boasting about it to me when I interviewed him over the Una May killing.'

'So she told young Picasso what she suspected and he panicked and nipped out of the Oasis to alert his father,' Sukey said sombrely.

'Right. He denied it at first, but admitted it when we told him he'd been picked up on one of the security cameras using his mobile. Andy Radcliffe has had his suspicions of Professor Dawden for quite a while, but he'd been covering his tracks so cleverly he couldn't get the evidence he needed to nail him.'

'They must have been in a real froth when they realized what would happen if Anne-Marie went to the police. I suppose they alerted Athena and suggested she try and intercept the girl when she left the night club?'

'No, that was just an appallingly unlucky coincidence. She

and Montwell had been out for the evening and they happened to be driving past the Oasis just at the time when Anne-Marie was hanging about waiting for her friend's car to be fixed. Their offer of a lift was perfectly genuine; it wasn't until she got into the car and started telling them about her discovery that Athena realized the whole scam was in danger of being blown out of the water. The girl was so excited, Montwell says, especially as she thought it might mean we'd get his precious Matisse back for him.'

'Poor kid.' Sukey brushed away an unexpected gush of tears. 'If only she'd gone straight to the police instead of blurting it all out to them—'

'If Montwell had been on his own he wouldn't have killed her, of course – as far as he was concerned there'd have been no need.'

'He would probably have told Athena,' Sukey said. 'They were pretty close; she knew he'd killed Una May.'

'That's true, but he swears he couldn't have been more shocked when she pulled the gun.'

'He was quick enough to grab me and tie me up when he realized I'd twigged the significance of the shoes,' Sukey pointed out. 'I wonder what made him change his mind about letting her kill me.'

'He probably knew the game was up. He admits he's sickened by Anne-Marie's death and Athena's betrayal, which is why he was closing down the gallery. Grabbing you was a panic reaction that he regretted almost immediately.'

Sukey gave an involuntary shudder at the thought of what might have happened. Jim put an arm round her and held her close. 'I keep picturing the scene outside the night club,' she whispered. 'Anne-Marie must have been over the moon when Montwell came by and offered her a lift. She hero-worshipped him; having the chance to tell him what she'd found out must have given her a terrific kick. Has he told you exactly what happened that night?'

'Oh yes, and to give him his due, it seems he was horrified at what Athena did, but it all happened so quickly and there was nothing he could do to stop it. He was driving and at one point – when presumably she saw that Anne-Marie was a threat – she told him to turn the car round and drive into

Muckleton Woods. He wanted to know why and she told him not to ask questions. Next thing, she pulled out a gun; the girl took fright and tried to jump out of the car, but she wasn't quick enough.'

'That woman seems to carry a gun with her like other women carry a lipstick,' Sukey remarked.

'It seems her grandfather was a crack shot with a pistol and joined the Greek resistance during the war. He taught all his children and grandchildren to shoot and filled their heads with horror stories about what happened under the occupation. Just before he died he gave each of them a gun and made them swear to carry it with them at all times.'

'He must have been a nutcase.'

'Disturbed, certainly. I suppose his experiences under the Nazis had something to do with it. Montwell seems to think Athena is the only one who kept the promise; she idolized her grandfather.'

'I'll bet he never intended his gift to be used that way.' Sukey covered her eyes at the thought of Anne-Marie's final moments of terror. 'That poor girl,' she whispered.

'It was touch and go for you as well, wasn't it, Sook?' said Jim. 'I know you've been having nightmares about it – and believe it or not, so have I.'

'It was a bit hairy,' she admitted. She took another deep draught of wine before saying, 'Montwell may be singing like the proverbial canary now, but he's hardly the gallant hero, is he? He helped his lover dispose of the body of an innocent girl after killing a woman he'd never seen before in his life with the sole intention of getting a man he hated convicted of murder. I assume that was a perverted form of revenge for what Kirtling had done to his sister?'

'Right. He'd harboured a grudge against the man ever since she OD'd after he dumped her.'

'The same sort of treatment he handed out to Una May?'

'More or less. When Montwell overheard him rowing with Una in the shrubbery that afternoon he realized that here was a situation where a man might be driven to murder a trouble-some mistress in a fit of rage. He knew Una's pregnancy would come out at a post-mortem; Kirtling would have to admit the child was his and with any luck – as he saw it – he'd be charged with killing her. All his pent-up hatred for the man simply boiled over and the minute Kirtling was out of the way he grabbed the poor woman from behind and strangled her. He's claiming he acted in a moment of uncontrollable rage and I imagine his counsel will plead temporary insanity.'

'D'you think he'll get away with it?'

Jim shrugged. 'Who can tell? To be honest, I think he's past caring.'

'That was my impression when he left me in the gallery to go to the hospital with Athena. What I don't understand,' Sukey went on after some further thought, 'is, if he hated Kirtling so much, why did he agree to copy *The Luncheon of the Boating Party* for him in the first place? He couldn't possibly have foreseen what was going to happen.'

'No, of course not, and he claims his initial reaction was to turn down the commission. Athena told him a refusal wouldn't do her business any good so in the end he agreed by way of a favour to her, but he says he never hated a job so much.'

'In a way that bears out something Miranda Keene told me.'

'What was that?'

'She says Montwell charged an extortionate fee for what she suspects is an inferior piece of work. She hasn't got a good word to say for him, by the way, because of the supercilious attitude he adopted towards her beloved Digby.'

'I wonder if she'll have Digby back, now all charges against him have been dropped?'

Sukey shook her head. 'After all the other revelations about him, I very much doubt it. If only I'd thought about the shoes earlier, when Anne-Marie told me the police had asked for them,' she went on sadly. 'It never entered my head at the time that Montwell might have handed over a different pair because everyone thought he was the one person who couldn't possibly have had a motive for killing Una May. I had a feeling for some time there was something I'd missed, but it just wouldn't come to me.'

'You mustn't blame yourself,' Jim said firmly. 'Even if it had occurred to you, I doubt if we'd have given it any serious consideration. As you say, Montwell was the one person we felt able to eliminate from the outset; we did follow up his claim never to have seen Una May before the party, of course, and it all checked out.' He held out a hand. 'Come on, love, let me give you a refill while you see how our dinner's getting on.'

'Right.' She surrendered her wine glass, stood up and led the way to the kitchen. 'You know something?' she said as she tested the potatoes. 'I'm still waiting for you and DCI Lord to give me a rocket for overstepping my function as a Crime Scene Investigator.'

'You know you deserve one, don't you?'

'On the contrary, I deserve a bouquet.'